M000234684

Negative Space

Negative Space

a novel

Donald Jordan

Deeds Publishing | Athens

Published by Deeds Publishing in Athens, GA
www.deedspublishing.com

Printed in The United States of America

Cover design by Mark Babcock. Text layout by Matt King.

ISBN 978-1-947309-81-4

Books are available in quantity for promotional or premium use. For information, email info@deedspublishing.com.

First Edition, 2019

10 9 8 7 6 5 4 3 2 1

In grateful memory of agent Alex Jackinson, who believed...

PROLOGUE

He has read, heard and schemed enough to determine that the success-
ful murder, the unsolved murder—he prefers to think of it as
expedient extermination—consists of three elements: circumstances, timing and disposal. You can have one, even two, but
without the third the execution is prone to fail. Like the stars,
the three must align, and the perpetrator must be prepared at a
moment's notice.

The execution must in turn follow a premeditated path.
There should be no struggle, no blood which crime technology
can reach beyond all perception of the human eye. There should
be no weapon, that is, no identifiable weapon anomalous to
the crime scene. Asphyxiation with the victim's pantyhose or a
twisted pillowcase would evidence nothing inconsistent with
her DNA. Gloves, a frayed coat, a face mask would circumvent
scratches and fingernail gouges by terrified, back-reaching hands.
Disposal should not be by burial. Graves take too long, and inevitably scavengers or cadaver dogs might dig up a limb or a bone.
Concrete blocks easily pilfered from any construction site and
tied to the body would leave no evidence in a swift-running deep
current. The entire rope itself would go, no cut and frayed ends to
be found in a garage or storage room.

Kelly would not have had to die had her demands not been so crippling. Sooner or later she was bound to hear about his affairs and she said she didn't want to be married to a man who didn't want to be married to her. But he had brought the boys into the world and he was going to support them until they were grown. He would be surprised at how much his unfaithfulness was going to increase the cost of their lifestyle. He knew she would try to take every cent he had and the court would no doubt sympathize with her.

He had never really been close to the boys, or to any of Kelly's family. She had seen this years ago and tried to invent things for them to do. Once she had found a remote campsite and insisted that they try camping out together. The weekend was not successful; the rented tent was too small, the campfire a nuisance, and there were arguments with the boys. Few people ever came here, fishermen from time to time in good weather, seldom when it was freezing as it is now, the approach to the odd metal bridge nearly washed out. At the time, he did not realize how useful the isolated site would someday be to him.

The sons he can take care of. They will do as he says, not interfere with what he does, where he goes. Kelly herself has provided him opportunity to qualify this. Every few months, perhaps under stress of their failing marriage, she announces that she has to get away for a couple of days. The boys somehow understand and accept this. She packs her easel, her paints, her paper and drives away, perhaps to the very remote camp she had discovered—which would work to his advantage should there happen to be any telltale car tracks. She returns refreshed for the boys, solemn for him. It's a ritual they have experienced the past few years.

Negative Space

The alignment of circumstances, timing and disposal occurs at last. Chase, 16, is spending the night with friends. Eleven-year-old Devin is asleep and Robert knows no less than a bomb will wake him. Kelly is sitting in the den, a book on art in her lap. It is late. She never goes to bed before one or two in the morning. And it is cold. She wears a light sweater even in the house. He approaches from behind, one of her scarves wound round each hand. There is no cry, not even a gasp. Her hands fly up to her throat, struggling, then over her shoulders to his hands. He is wearing gloves and a jacket. In a minute or less she collapses, the life suffocated out of her.

He drops the scarf beside her, breathes deeply, steadying himself. Soundlessly, he creeps back to Devin's room, cracks the door, confirms that he is asleep. Then the disposal: the limp body carried to her car. The rope, the two concrete blocks that had been secreted under a backyard tarp. The black night's drive out to the bridge. He is not unusually strong, but she isn't heavy. He lifts her up onto the bridge rail, then one by one sets the blocks beside her. The rope tied around her first, then looped through the first weight, the second, and secured with triple knots. He nudges everything together, careful that no fragment of clothing catches on the edge, the short rope trailing a few feet behind her. The splash. He runs to the other side, looks down. Not so much as a ripple.

He drives home, creeps into the driveway, lights out. In the house he steals to Devin's room and quietly opens the door. As expected, the eleven-year-old appears not to have stirred. Robert is free at last.

Even as clever as he believes he is, even in the alignment of the essential conditions there always exists the element of chance and of ignorance. Robert schemes the body will never be found in the deep black water beneath the remote bridge. He does not know that in a swift-running current, concrete weights can be tossed and rolled like twigs. He does not know that a mile or two downstream of the bridge the water runs wide and swift across rock-breaking rapids, or that even in cold weather fool-hearted fishermen brave the waters in their waders opting for cold water trout. He does not know the short trailing rope and blocks can snag in the clefts of a rock and hang there.

In less than two weeks Kelly's asphyxiated body will be discovered, but Robert does not know this. He walks into their bedroom, undresses, gets into bed and waits.

1

They are planning a trip to Venice, the honeymoon they were unable to take when they were young, poor, and in love. Perhaps the 25-year delay is better, shoring up a faltering romance. Why it is faltering, Paula cannot say. The children, Grant and Leslie, are grown and out of school, with good jobs in Atlanta. Mitchell's partnership in an investor advisor group provides more than enough money, especially now that the kids are on their own. With a smile of irony, Paula has always said that motherhood came upon her before she had a chance to be a young woman. But she has always been a good mother, she believes. She'd like to find a way to "express" herself.

They would have flown to Venice sooner but for the surprise, fluke heart surgery. Mitchell's heart had never been an issue, the clues few—a brief stabbing pain in his chest once on the golf course, a shortness of breath helping Leslie move into her new Atlanta apartment. Though her husband tried to ignore these, Paula had picked up on them. "You don't fool around with chest pain," she said.

The nuclear dye test, the catheterization, he endured pretty well, and it was finally concluded that some kind of viral infection had settled in his heart. "We don't know whether this is causative or coincidental," said the cardiologist. "But there's blockage in the main left quadrant which will require surgery." They were given a week to get ready, to put affairs in order, to ponder what would happen should he never wake up again. He did, the surgery was successful, but they had hardly reckoned on how much time recovery would require.

They want to go to Venice when the weather is right. Spring or fall is the best time, Paula is told. Choose a hotel on the main canal where you can watch gondolas and water taxis and even big passenger liners. She has been collecting brochures and reading history. The founding of Venice is intriguing, full of charm and pasta factories. She is excited in a reserved sort of way. Can one be married too long? But she knows Mitchell has clients who have celebrated their fiftieth anniversaries with apparently no less love than on their honeymoons.

Mitchell is diligent about compelling himself to rise from his lounge chair to do the requisite walking. They stand together looking out into the backyard where there are azaleas, holly and nandinas. A brown thrasher, the Georgia state bird, is busy about the branches. In the descending winter sunset, its russet feathers appear iridescent. All these things, the house, the yard, even the old elm Mitchell has worked hard to save from Dutch Elm disease, have become precious to them since they have been given a new lease on life.

Until the shocking threat with the heart neither had thought about death that much. Life is precious, they know. Death is real. "I wonder," Mitchell says to Paula, "just what my forty-nine years have meant. What've I done to make the world a better place? What have I accomplished? What do I believe? How will I be remembered?

Paula is patient. "How would you like to be remembered?"

"As one who has made a difference."

"Then think about our lovely children. Bringing them into the world makes a difference."

Mitchell is a slightly built man with ash brown hair flecking to gray, blue eyes, a right knee which sometimes rebels. His mouth is sensitive, his feet rather flat, his ankles bony, his complexion clear and dark. Since the heart surgery his movements have been more deliberate, his awareness more self-conscious. They are learning to treasure little mundane things.

He is in his chair, which Paula has made comfortable for him with pillows and blankets, when she receives the first phone call. After hesitating she walks into the den, her expression perplexed. "Your nephew Devin called. He says his mother is missing."

Mitchell is not alarmed. "Another one of those odd disappearances. Wonder why my sister does that."

"I guess sometimes she just has to get away for a day or two. I would too if I were married to that jerk Robert."

"He's always seemed weird, all right."

"The strange thing is Devin said she left without her things. No art supplies and no coat. Even her car is in the garage."

Mitchell sits up straight. "What does Robert think?"

"The only thing he can figure is she left with somebody."

"Never. Kelly might walk out on that sorry husband, but never those boys. How long has she been gone?"

"Couple of days. They've been looking for her, calling her friends, her art buddies."

"Have they notified the police?"

"They have."

"I'd better get up there," Mitchell says.

3

"No. You can't do a long drive like that. Not now."

"What am I supposed to do?" His voice is grim. They know his sister Kelly is a free spirit, but nothing makes sense about this.

"All we can do right now is wait and hope she shows up." Paula realizes something is unnatural about Kelly's disappearance with no sign of transportation and nothing they can identify missing. Mitchell practically raised his young sister. Their mother died of cervical cancer when he was eleven, exactly his nephew Devin's age now. Their father pretty much closed up and Mitchell had instinctively taken it upon himself to be the protective older brother. He'd taught Kelly how to ride a bicycle and how to skate. He'd helped her through college and walked her down the aisle when she married Robert, and drove up to Raleigh when she had Chase and then Devin.

For two days they hear nothing. "I'm going up there," Mitchell says. "The least I can do is be with the boys."

"No, you're not. You don't need any stress."

"Kelly would never walk out on them. Maybe somebody forced her to go with them."

"Right now you must just think about yourself," Paula insists. "I spoke to the Raleigh police. There was no sign of a break-in, or a struggle."

"I can't believe that damn husband knows nothing about where his wife is."

"He says she must have slipped out sometime during the night. She was there when Devin went to bed. Chase was spending the night with a friend."

She pushes Mitchell to concentrate daily on his heart therapy, knows that it is painfully slow for a man who has always been physically active. One night the phone rings. Paula answers, gives a muffled cry. She stands frozen, finally puts the receiver down, walks into the den and stands rigid before him.

"Mitchell, I'm sorry." Her voice is a whisper. "Your sister's dead. She was murdered."

"What? How do you know?"

"Some fishermen found her body. She had been thrown off a bridge."

His shoulders and hands begin to shake.

"I'm so sorry, but it's even worse. The police suspect Robert."

"No! Why? How?"

"Something Devin told them. I don't know what it was. Concrete blocks were used to weigh her down, and I think they found residue of blocks in their yard." Paula drops down beside the chair and puts her arm around him. "I'm sorry. Kelly was such a dear, sweet person. We all loved her. But please don't let this break you. We've got to get you well."

He begins to cry. "She was my only sibling. I practically raised her."

"I know. But we still have life to live. You. I."

She thinks, despairingly, together or separately. But, no, it hasn't come that far, she will not think of separation now. She thinks only of Kelly and her boys, Chase and Devin. Without a mother. Without a father. For them all ballast gone. Helplessly drifting. Her heart breaks to see the emotion cave in on her husband. She puts her cheek down against his, trying to still his trembling. "We'll get through this," she whispers. "We'll get through it."

* * *

Mitchell wants to leave at once, but Paula insists that the drive from Columbus to Raleigh is too long. "Remember, you are prohibited from driving for four to six weeks and you must protect your chest at all costs." He has been instructed to lift no more than eight or ten pounds. If he has to be a passenger in a vehicle he should ride in back, hold a pillow against his chest when he coughs, use a walker until he gets his legs back. She knows this discipline is hard on him. Weeks ago he was physically active, playing tennis, jogging. The fluke infection, the blockage, the opened chest has been too sudden, a monkey wrench in all their hopeful plans.

"Where are the boys now?" Mitchell asks.

"I think they're a charge of the court. In foster care."

She insists that she will make calls to the Raleigh police and feed him information in nibbles, trying to shield him from as much stress as possible.

She sees Mitchell sit staring for hours, thinking about his sister, their young lives together. "I taught Kelly to swim," he says. "She trusted me completely and would jump to me when no one else could coax her."

"She had such a winning smile," says Paula, "such a winning personality. And was so spontaneous—serendipity in body."

He nods solemnly. "From the time she was a little girl she carried sketchbooks, with page after page of figures, flowers, vines growing around rusty pipes, the shadows of patio chairs. 'Look at things in a mirror,' she told me, 'it gives you a different perspective.'"

It pains Paula to watch him struggling so hard against the tears. "It's such an irony," he mumbles. "Heart surgery has given me another shot at life; Kelly will never see her sons grow up.

How can I be so full of hatred yet realize the smallest treasures matter?"

She tries to help, to be the sponge absorbing his confusion and sorrow, his rage and regret. His moods have been unpredictable; sometimes he can hardly eat, sometimes he feels starved.

"I'm better now," he says. "At least I could speak to Chase and Devin."

Paula makes the calls, runs down the nephews in a ranch for homeless children. When she finally gets Chase on the phone she hands an extension to Mitchell. "Chase? It's Uncle Mitchell." His voice is near breaking. "How are you?"

The response is all but inaudible, then detached, almost cool. "Okay, I guess," Chase says.

"Are you really? Are they taking good care of you?"

"We're making it."

Over and over she hears Mitchell ask, "How are you? Do you need anything?" and a faint response, "Okay…no…all right…" The conversation is not reassuring. She wonders if his nephews have forgotten him—or think he has forgotten them.

Almost every day she sees her husband mailing the boys little gifts, sometimes no more than packets of chewing gum with a card, a C.D., a few dollars. Most times he receives no response and if any, only a cursory note. "Thanks…we don't really need anything."

One morning when Mitchell returns from walking he tells her about something which brings Kelly to him in sparkling memory. A neighbor's golden lab had run along the street, frolicked around him a moment, and raced away. When they were children, Mitchell says, there was a similar neighborhood dog that was people shy. Even its owners had difficulty petting and bathing him. But when Kelly was out jogging, the untouchable golden lab ran to her, moiling and scampering about her feet. The neighborhood was amazed. It was much the same with people. Perfect strangers gravitated to Kelly. When she entered a room, men and women approached her. It was not what she said that attracted them. He really did not know what it was. Warmth, perhaps, vulnerability, an openness. She trusted everyone. This was why no one could ever understand how in the world she married a man like Robert. Why did she? He was deviously charming. A man who was always going to make a great splash but never could quite pull anything off. His greed, his self-centeredness, must have been hidden during the early days of their romance.

"I wonder," Mitchell says, "if Kelly ever saw anything in Robert that warned her of his violence."

The police are releasing no details. How did Kelly die? he asks. Did she suffer? Was there pain? Was she alive when she was thrown into the water? Was there a struggle? Paula shakes her head as Mitchell questions. Did the grieving boys know exactly what happened? What evidence is there that Robert killed her?

Some nights Paula tries to make her husband comfortable, get him to read or watch television, then slips out into their yard, her eyes adjusting to the light. The evening sky is clear, there is a multitude of stars, an eyebrow moon. From some teenager's radio she hears faint music. Beneath her feet the grass is resilient, a good thick layer of Emerald Zoysia. In a garden cart are cuttings from some of her plants, ready to bag and take out for pickup. She inhales the sweet scent of drying green, of truncated petals. She takes a deep breath, experiences the origin of life. Are they going to make it, she wonders. Is this tragedy going to bring them together or widen the distance between them?

Negative Space

* * *

Finally Mitchell is strong enough to make the all-day trip to Raleigh. Paula drives. They stop for lunch, for rest, giving him a few minutes to walk. They are both apprehensive about the visit and talk little. Paula says, "I wonder if the boys are more like their mother or their father?"

"You know they're like Kelly. It's their only hope of survival."

The children's home is not an unfriendly looking place—two story brick with wide front porch, white columns, one wing for girls, one for boys, a white picket fence around the perimeter. New Beginnings, it is called. Paula is shocked to find how many homeless kids there are. Chase and Devin are waiting in one of the guest parlors. The meeting has been pre-arranged. They hug tentatively, shake hands. There is a momentary struggle of recognition—it has been several years since they have seen one another.

Paula says, "We wanted to come sooner. Your uncle has been recovering from heart surgery."

"That's okay," says Chase.

He is tall, fair-complexioned, with a strong jaw, a high fore-head revealing the strain of sadness, an expressive, almost pretty mouth, good looking despite his stony stare. Something about him is cold, but Paula can't say what. Something about the mouth and eyes, or maybe it is his gestures. Still, his very flesh exudes youth, there are boyish signals in his shyness, his rigidly respectful manners and motions. Devin stands slightly behind his older brother as though waiting to venture out. In some re-spects he looks more serious, more disoriented. His jaw is hard, his glance wary, as though he expects to receive a blow. He, too, is nice looking. It pains Paula to think how their childhood has been snatched from them, what exuberant vital young men they should be, and she sees the pain in Mitchell's eyes too. She places her hand on Devin's shoulder and he responds gratefully, it is a light blinking on, he presses his face a moment to her side. So needful, so lost.

"How are things here?" Mitchell asks.

"Not too bad," says Chase.

"I hate it!" Devin turns grim, his young mouth screwed up bitterly. "I want to go home!"

"Never mind, Devin." Chase turns a harsh stare on him. "We don't have a home."

There is an electric wall of silence. Paula asks quietly, "Where is your father?"

"We don't know where he is," Chase answers. "Some fuc--" He catches himself. "Some lawyer called a week ago. He said Daddy's sorry for the fight."

"The fight? You mean with your mother?"

"No. With me."

"He knocked Chase around," Devin says vengefully. "We never want to see him again!"

Chase turns toward Mitchell but seems to look right through him. "He did it," he said tersely.

"How can you be so sure?"

"It'll come out. He did it!"

The incontrovertible certainty of it is condemning. If the boys are so convinced their father could take their mother's life, Paula wonders, as Mitchell had, if there had been a time when Kelly sensed this, too.

The reunion does not go well. They had hoped the brothers

10

would open up. Instead the air is charged with tension, with resentment and confusion. She feels them reaching out, feels their desperation, yet they are throwing a cautious barrier between them. They do not want to be hurt again. They do not want to expose nerves stripped raw from pain. It is as though their very skin breathes withdrawal, defense—you've done your duty, now if there is no more you can offer, leave us alone.

Mitchell says, "Kelly was my only sister. I'm sorry we didn't live closer, couldn't get together more often."

Paula suspects he is thinking of something drastic—getting them out of here. She catches herself resisting.

Chase murmurs, "She talked about you a lot, how you took care of her after your mother died. About your children, Grant and Leslie, too."

"She was fun," Devin says. "She did fun things. We never knew what to expect." He holds himself so tightly his face flushes. He seems determined not to cry.

They talk for an hour, then the parting is no less uncomfortable than the greeting. Paula says, "We should go, Mitchell. I think you should rest."

"Yeah, sure," says Chase, "you were nice to come."

It is not bitter, only pathetic, there is a stinging sadness in the air.

* * *

They have a light dinner, spend the night in a motel, and drive back to Columbus. Not until they are on the way does Mitchell say, "We have to do something, Paula. They're my sister's kids."

"What do you have in mind?"

11

"That the boys might come to live with us."

She looks straight ahead, her hands tight on the wheel. "Do you know what you're saying? Our children are grown, do we want to begin again? What about all the things we planned to do? Travel. Bum around. Sleep late."

"What choice do we have?"

"I don't think I'm prepared to start over."

"It wouldn't be starting over."

"Wouldn't it? Devin's eleven. It'll be at least ten years before he finishes school. Ten years." Grimly, she says, "My heart is broken for those boys. I just…don't know that I can be their mother."

She wonders if he understands how hard this would be for her. Two strangers in the house, someone underfoot. Since Grant and Leslie moved out, she can be sloppy if she wants to, sleep late, not worry about dressing, about appointments for kids, about transportation. They had planned to do things they'd never had the opportunity to do. Be together, trying to fill the gaps that have developed between them. She believes he wants this, too—the resurrection of their youth, their togetherness, their romance. All her expectations for a life of liberty would come to earth with a shock. It would be another decade until their renewed liberation, until she could express herself like she has yearned for.

At home she is distressed to see how hard Mitchell tries to put on a good face. She loves him, decides that they can't, mustn't, live like this. With cool resolve she finally says, "If we are going to do this, we have to clear Grant's and Leslie's rooms."

She sees uncertainty and relief quake through his jangled nerves. "Maybe not. Maybe we could just rearrange things."

"No. I cannot half do this. We can't let them think they're temporary guests."

* * *

Moving the boys to Georgia is not a simple process. Everything progresses slowly. Papers, documents, phone calls initiated at both ends. They cannot say the brothers are wildly excited about trying to start life over again. How could they be? They must pull all roots, leave the school, friends and town they have always known. Phone calls are laced with apprehension, fear, but also with a gestating sense of wonderment.

Reluctant, uncertain, terrified, Paula says, "What kind of boys are they? We hardly know them. What are they like? What has this thing done to them?"

"I'm hoping counseling has helped," Mitchell says.

She is troubled. "I wonder what Leslie and Grant will think?"

"That we've done the right thing."

"You may be surprised."

She knows Mitchell suffers fears of his own. What if they bring the brothers here and despite her best intentions she cannot adjust and not even pretend to cherish and nourish them — and feels somehow that she is the intruder?

Finally arrangements are made. This time she tells him, "You go without me. It'll allow more room for the boys to bring some of their stuff."

She waits at home as he makes the long trip, meets, talks, loads their things in the car — pitifully little, he tells her on the phone. Most of their possessions have been stored somewhere in Raleigh. She can only imagine how broken their hearts are as she feels how troubled her own heart is. This starting over, this entering into a dark unknown. All they can hope is that it turns out to be an invigorating rebirth.

But then she reroutes the dark thoughts and gets to work. She will put all she has into this. She goes out and collects red and gold and green crepe paper, glittering stars, and balloons. She devotes the better part of a day to this. When they pull into the driveway, the first thing the brothers will see is the brightly decorated side door and a big poster that says, "Welcome Home, Chase and Devin."

2

When Chase first sees her there is a sharp plunging quake in the pit of his stomach. She is in Gayfer's cosmetic department. She is neither especially pretty, nor is she young. He judges her to be about forty, a slender dark haired woman wearing pants and a fitted shirt. Her arms are bare and she carries a big shaggy purse with shoulder straps. He cannot distinguish her features, but her gestures and motions are familiar. As she moves deliberately down an aisle, she turns her torso slightly to pass oncoming shoppers and it is a motion which stabs his heart. He does not follow her.

Half an hour later he sees her again in Parisian's men's department. It is a shock, this second encounter in a shopping mall jammed with people. There must be a reason, some connection as yet unclear. She is working her way through a stack of shirts, perhaps for her son or husband. This time he is close enough to register her features. Dark, arched brows, delicate cheekbones, a pensive mouth, tiny radial creases about her eyes. He is not ten feet away, but she does not notice him. As she looks through cellophane-wrapped shirts her hands are tentative, careful—small wrists and long narrow fingers, a painter's fingers. Giving up on the shirts, she disappears behind a rack, reappears, disappears again. His heart racing, he searches for her, finds her leaving the store. This time he follows.

At the Mole Hole, she selects a five by seven pewter picture frame. At Liz Claiborne she deliberates over cosmetics, sweeping from one glistening display to another. At the corner cookie shop she asks the clerk something, smiles and nods, then points with her finger. It looks as if she has chosen oatmeal and raisins, the kind he likes. As she opens her purse, he can tell it is a repository of many things, but she does not have to rummage to find what she wants. She goes straight to the inner pocket which holds her wallet. From the cookie store she continues down the mall, pausing fractionally to examine shoes in one window, jewelry in another.

He maintains a safe distance, yet there is no reason she should suspect he is following. There are people all through the mall, sweeping as hard in one direction as in the opposite. If she happens to turn, he averts his glance, saunters over to a bench or gazes into a window. Sketchily, painfully, he contrives her background. At home she has children, perhaps one in college, a husband who values her, maybe a dog, an aquarium. From the mall she'll head to the grocer's, choosing food and snacks they like best, planning meals for a regular family dinner. They'll watch TV together, play a board game, drift to bed, secure and safe. It is a stupid thing, he realizes, these foolish inventions, but he is unable to restrain himself. He glances at his watch. In twenty minutes he must meet his Uncle Mitchell in the food court.

Outside Playtree she pauses before a window displaying children's clothes, books, kites, a tiny cordless radio. He props his foot on a bench, forces himself to look away. Two or three twittering girls exit Victoria's Secret, a man in an electric wheelchair controls his direction with the touch of his fingertips. A dozen school age children clamor from the Dollar Store bearing sacks of minute treasures. A young couple walk by sharing a huge cinnamon-covered pretzel, breaking off chunks and licking their fingers. When he turns slowly back to her, she is staring directly at him. Blood rushes to his face, he stands and strides over to a kiosk selling leather goods, belts and bags. Through pyramids of hanging purses and totes he sees that she has turned again, not looking toward him at all. With her hips she traps one of her packages against the glass, freeing her right arm—another of those little gestures painfully familiar to him. He feels his shoulders sag, his knees turning liquid. She fetches out a cell phone, makes calls, walks toward the food court. Good enough, it is where he must meet Mitchell anyway.

On either side of the court are the usual Burger King, Taco Bell, Arby's. Out in the middle are tables and chairs, a carousel, more kiosks selling personalized T-shirts, sea shell sculptures, porcelain and fabric dolls. She slows her pace as if trying to decide. Just as she turns into Chick-fil-A, a voice behind him says, "Just a minute there, son."

He spins around, startled. His heart sinks, then hammers violently. It is a security guard, a thin, wiry man with suspicious eyes.

"Whatcha doing here?"

He searches for something plausible, then shrugs. "Shopping."

"Yeah? For what?"

He does not answer.

The guard nods toward the woman who has suddenly emerged from the restaurant and stands watching them.

"Lady says you been following her."

"Why should I follow her?"

"You tell me."

He looks her way again, trying to keep his voice calm. "I've never seen that woman before."

"I been behind you a while. You never took your eyes off her."

"So what?"

"You know we got laws against stalking."

He tries an indifferent laugh. "You're out of your mind."

The guard does not back off. His eyes are narrow, penetrating—retired military perhaps, or moonlighting policeman. His name tag says Williamson.

"How old are you?"

"Sixteen. Whose business is it?"

"Don't get smart with me, son. I'll run you out of here."

He starts to tell him to go to hell, instead clamps his mouth shut. He must guard against any sort of expression, any emotion, which would expose the slightest hint of himself. Still, he can't restrain the stab of anxiety when he sees his Uncle Mitchell walking toward them.

"I gotta go," he says.

"Yeah, you do that. I'll be keeping an eye on you."

He cannot refrain from saying, "Sounds like something out of a movie."

The guard fixes him with a cutting stare, as though embedding his face into memory. "Smart ass kid. They get worse every day." He turns, walks toward the woman who is still watching from the food court.

Mitchell reaches him a second later, probably has heard the guard's parting shot. "What was that all about?"

He shrugs again. "Nothing."

"That was security, wasn't it?"

"I guess so."

His uncle's glance is perplexed, concerned. "You get into any kind of trouble, Chase?"

"Yeah, I was shoplifting. Look at all my loot." He opens his arms wide like an angel. Then helplessly he says, "He thought I was following that woman."

Already he notices that Mitchell's gaze has tracked the guard, who stands talking to the dark-haired lady.

"Why, Chase?"

He sets his jaw, rams his hands into his pockets.

Mitchell examines the woman again, then shifts back to him. "Is it because she looks like your mother?"

The words cut through, falling cold and dreadful upon his chest.

"That's why, isn't it? She looks like your mother."

He drops his chin, murmurs. "Shit!"

His uncle doesn't flinch. He holds him steady in his gaze, not condemning, sad perhaps. Finally Mitchell says, "Well, let's go see if we can find you some shirts. In those baggy pants you do look a little suspicious."

Chase manages a smile, finally, pulling his hands from his pockets. "It's the style."

As they walk out of the food court he refrains from looking back. Probably he'll never see the woman again. He's tried, God knows he's tried to keep up his guard. But seeing her was such a shock. For a moment it tore down his defense. He can't let that happen. And now he must go through this pretense with Mitchell. He owes him that much, he concedes. He only wishes he could give a damn about new clothes.

Donald Jordan

* * *

At home—he calls it home for lack of a better term—they pull into the driveway, get out. It is a pretty house, very nice. Cape Cod, with attic dormers, two story, plenty of shrubbery, grass. Three bedrooms, three baths, a spacious den with bookcases. The window shutters are blue-gray. He should know it all by now, should be comfortable with it, but a little cord of resistance twists through him. They have been here three months, enrolled in school. He wonders if he'll ever stop feeling the half-welcome visitor here.

As he and Mitchell walk in, his arms full of packages, Aunt Paula says, "Well, let's see your choices."

He opens the packages, displays the shirts.

"Hey, nice. Very stylish."

He laughs. "Yeah, I guess."

"You like?"

"Sure. Thanks."

Dutifully he collects the wrappings, gathers up the clothes. He goes up to his room, closes the door, then stands rigid, letting the great depth of heaviness drop away at last—the insufferable loneliness which is a twisting cord in his gut. The room feels alien, ill-fitting. There is tension everywhere. It had been his cousin's room. Grant, out of college now, working in Atlanta but returning to Columbus on periodic weekends. He knows it was with reluctance that Grant had heard they had to move most of his things out of the room. Chase and Devin have been allowed to bring a few personal items down from Raleigh. Framed photos, pictures, baseball paraphernalia, posters and model cars and stuff to personalize their new surroundings. He suspects Aunt Paula

20

is sorry to see her children's rooms disassembled. That was three months ago, but seems longer.

On the dresser is a photo of his mother, small gold frame. He picks it up, examines it with renewed intensity. The lady at the shopping mall could have been her sister. Maybe not, though. His mother's hair was shorter, denser, brushed back on her forehead. Her cheeks fuller, her chin squarer. Still, the resemblance is startling. He knows what he did was stupid, hopes he didn't frighten the woman, hopes she has a long and happy life.

He tosses the packages aside, walks down the hall to Devin's room. From his computer, Devin looks up, eyes hopeful yet defensive, too. His childlike features have tensed to something remote, Chase realizes, like the china dolls in the kiosk. He's lost weight, too, the pudginess has disappeared. His light caramel-colored hair and fine nose, his dark long lashes cage troubled hazel eyes. He looks more like their father—their father, rotting, they assume, in his own personal prison of hell.

"How's it going?"

"Okay," says Devin. "You know what I'm researching? The mysterious homicides."

"That isn't funny, Devin."

"It's true. That was one of our choices. English essay."

"And you chose that."

"There haven't been that many, not recorded at least. One woman crushed a man's head with a frozen ham, then cooked it. Another an icicle to the jugular." Devin is talking fast, too fast. His eyes are blazing.

Chase said, "Forget it, Devin. Find something else to report on."

His young brother sits back, draws a deep breath. "I could do a Family History."

"Sure. Why don't you do that?" Irritated, he turns to leave.

Devin reaches out. "Sorry, Chase. But … I'm scared, you know?"

He pauses, turns back. "I know."

"Even this room scares me."

He glances around. It was Leslie's room, all frilly and female. When Leslie comes home now, never for more than one night, they must shift everything around. The real problem will come when brother and sister come to visit at the same time. The room has been painted, redecorated, the scalloped curtains, the womanly touch retrofitted for an eleven year old. This must have been hard on Aunt Paula, seeing her little girl's room translated into boy's stuff, baseball mitts, military boots.

He says, "I know what you mean, Devin. But it's okay. Just a matter of getting used to it."

"I don't think I'll ever get used to it." Tears spring into Devin's eyes so suddenly it surprises them both. "I want my old room back."

Chase tries to check himself, but it's no use; he says crossly, "Well, you can't have it. That's past history."

"Don't be mean to me, Chase!"

"Then don't talk about things that are never going to happen." He sees the hurt in his brother's face, tries to ease his tone. "This is your home now, Devin. Mitchell and Paula try to make us feel welcome here."

"I don't think they really want us, though. Not Aunt Paula anyway."

"Look, it's not great for them either. They've had to give up a lot to bring us here."

"I don't know why we couldn't have stayed in our own house."

"You do know, Devin. How were we going to pay the mortgage and upkeep? Let's try to make the best of it here." He knows his voice sounds hollow, but it is all he can do—always trying to keep up a front, especially before his kid brother.

Defensively, Devin turns back to the computer. His shoulders are tense, all his body seems to have closed into a tight knot. The room isn't bad, really, Chase thinks. They've allowed Devin to hang his own posters and banners on the walls, plaster pictures on the mirrors. He has a bathroom of his own, a large closet, a few of Leslie's summer clothes still hanging in one end. "What happened to my *clothes!*" Leslie cried the first time she came home after the cousins moved in. Paula's response was inflectionless, resolved. "Everything will be here when you need it."

The double window with upholstered blue valance looks out onto a pretty yard, trees, grass, patio with wrought iron table, lounge chairs. Mitchell is meticulous about everything. The walls of Leslie's room are dark blue, white trim, the carpet blue with gold highlights.

What is scary about this room? Chase wonders. An anxious aura of unreality. A concept transposed from another place, another atmosphere. Grant and Leslie grew up here, got through college, moved to Atlanta. It is impossible not to realize that he and Devin have displaced the original inhabitants. He wonders if his young brother will ever sleep peacefully again.

He returns to his own room, closes the door, stretches out on the bed. He never used to lie down in the early evening. Too much to do, too many challenges, too many activities to waste time loafing. The bed is a reprieve now; he yearns for it. Still, it's an enemy, too, allowing thought. A moment to get away, to pretend sleep, to shut himself away from the concerned watchfulness of others—but an insurgent in disguise.

* * *

Their mother had been more or less both parents. Robert was always too busy, trying to hit it rich, to make a big number of himself. When the boys were little he engaged in a few things with them, but it seemed these were to keep up a front, to play the dutiful role. The more mature and independent they became, the less he had to do with them.

Chase once came across the fragments of a letter which had blown out of their burn barrel and he was able to make out enough to determine that it was from a woman. There were other little clues telling him his father was probably having affairs. He tried hard not to believe it, but he finally realized his mother had caught on, too. Was this why men offed their wives, so they could be free, live the wild life, avoid the expense of divorce? Or for the money, the insurance?

What his father was doing now, where he was Chase didn't know and he didn't give a damn. Yet, Robert had brought them into the world; they must have some of his makeup, some of his looks, his nuances. Deep down was the faintest, faintest glimmer of hope that he was not guilty; yet when Chase told Uncle Mitchell he knew his dad did it, he had no doubt it was true. Was there strong evidence against him? When would they know without doubt? When would the trial be? It seemed to take forever to prepare a case, especially a capital murder case.

Chase scrunches down into his pillow, forcing thoughts of his father aside, evoking thoughts of his mother. Kelly had been talented with pen and ink. In the park, when he was 10, Devin five, she would sit on a bench sketching. Kids on seesaws, the eyebrow bridges over ponds, ducks and herons. "You have to get the perspective right. Keep your verticals vertical. Take advantage of your negative space."

"What's negative space?" asked Devin.

"Those areas of white you leave untouched."

"Negative space," grinned Chase, "is all the empty thoughts in your head."

Some of her sketches looked sad to him. A girl sitting alone in the grass, head tilted. A playhouse with porch, balcony, stairs but no children. Kelly liked to walk, taking them with her. All the way around the lake, three, four miles. Stopping to investigate—wildflowers, weird mushrooms, carvings in a tree. "Take time to notice little things. The iridescent backs of beetles, the way leaves curl to send water down to the roots. Try to make small discoveries. Big ones don't come very often." She wore jeans, fitted overshirts like a girl, her sweater tied about her waist. Sometimes she made sandwiches, peanut butter and jelly, banana. On rare occasions their father joined them. They all rode bikes together. Chase thought they were happy.

He closes his eyes, drowses, jerks awake. Darkness is pressing against the window. Up and down the block street lights are flickering on. In another half hour, it'll be night. His mother used to say dusk is the loneliest time. He didn't understand then, but does now. When she was alive he counted on her to prompt him to his day's requirements, school functions, homework, dental appointments. Now it's dusk, the hardest time for him. Day dying. Questions of success. "Every day you get through is a victory. Live for that." Famous words of the foster home therapist. He rolls over, drives his fist into the sheets, not angrily, resolutely. Rolls onto his back again.

His mother was unstructured, careless, even sloppy sometimes.

Looking into his room she'd remark, "Did a tornado whip through here? You like living in squalor?" Still, she was messy herself, to a degree. Books, sketch pads, recipes everywhere. She encouraged looseness. "Be yourself, but remember others. Self-expression doesn't violate the rights of cohabitants." His room could be a restless breeze, but not cyclonic destruction. She was glad to see him create, this place where he *lived*. Now in this room, Grant's room, he merely abides. He doesn't want to touch anything.

"Why don't you hang a few pictures?" Only two or three times has Aunt Paula come into his bedroom to see him. Is this to allow him space or because she can't get over the disassembling? "We could have left some of Grant's, but thought you'd like your own."

"Maybe I will when I decide."

"It's up to you, you know. Paint one of your own. Your mother—"

Paula catches herself, breaks off. "I remember in grade school you were quite the artist."

Feigning pride he does not feel, he says, "Yeah, I even won a couple of ribbons."

"Whenever you're ready, we'll get you some materials."

Lying on his back he turns toward each wall, wondering what he would like. Nothing personal, no pithy little aphorisms. *He who travels light travels fast.* Meaning—dump the emotional garbage, grab every fleeting morsel. *Grief is a species of idleness.* Old Samuel Johnson may have known what he was talking about, but tell that to a twelve-year-old. Or a sixteen-year-old. Back in Raleigh he had been a rising star. He liked to draw, paint. Day by day he learned from his mother, who'd never had formal art lessons, taught herself with books and inspiration. His creative talent took second space to sports, especially baseball. His fast ball suggested championship possibilities. He had brought none of this with him, not even pictures of his team. He'd decided he could not pick and choose. Bring everything or leave everything. The happy moments did not come close to mitigating the horrendous. Yet, he yearned to get back into baseball again.

His room here is grander than anything he had at home, newly painted walls, the color of trees, earth, harvested hay. He has his own bath, thick towels, marble topped dressing table, shower large enough for two. He should be grateful. Why does he not want to touch anything, to spoil anything? What if he should get sick here? Soil the carpet. *All that mess! With the bowl ten feet away!* His stomach churns. He swallows. Calm yourself, Solomon. Breathe deeply.

He knows that Mitchell is trying to stimulate his interest in something—anything. "Come on, let's catch a game. Or go hit a few golf balls."

"Thanks, no. Just let me rest…"

Occasionally he finds himself coldly combative. "If any of the kids in school bully you, Devin, just let me know."

"What would you do?"

"Shut them up."

It scares him, these murmurs of aggressiveness. He doesn't know who he is, wants to be like his mother, is terrified of having even one little gene of his father's. Mitchell and Paula must think about this, too, must wonder what is under his stoic surface. He gives them credit for trying, especially his uncle, who has done his best to make them feel wanted.

During their months in the ranch for displaced children Mitchell sent them gifts. Clothes, CD's, variety packs of snacks. Things that could be bought, handed over as little tokens. Their uncle did not understand, how could he? He wanted to say, "We don't *need* this shit! Keep your money, Uncle Mitchell! Give it to charity!" Then remembering that their mother was Mitchell's loving sister, he thought, "You mean well, I guess. You knew Mom before we did."

He goes to the bath, splashes water onto his face, straightens the bed, lays out the new clothes, shirts, pants. Things. Probably he'll look okay in the shirts. Just over six feet and growing, a hundred seventy pounds, strong shoulders — a pitcher's shoulders. At school in Raleigh the coach pressed them into workouts — push-ups, body squats, chin-ups. He has tried to watch his diet, for the most part avoids junk food. His hair is burnt umber, his eyes a little lighter. His tastes vary — art, music of any kind, he has fiddled a little with the guitar. He likes video games, stays away from booze. And girls. He felt lost without a girlfriend.

He remembers his mother laying out his clothes when he was Devin's age, younger. He wonders if she had realized, just in the last instant, that she was about to die. He slumps to his knees, presses his face into the bedcovers. Not now, he thinks, not now! But the thoughts, the horrible images come ...

He was spending the night at a friend's house. Devin called him early, frightened, panicky. "We can't find Mom!"

"What?"

"We don't know where Mom is!"

"Oh, God, she must have taken one of her little getaways."

"She's never done that without telling us. And her car's still here."

"I'm not even up yet —"

"Come home, please! Hurry!"

He dressed quickly, mumbled to his sleepy friend, "Something's come up. I gotta go."

He got home, found Devin sitting on the steps, fearful, waiting. "Where is she, Chase? All her stuff's still here. She'd never just walk out!"

They searched every inch of the house, closets, pantry, nothing was out of place. Her car, car keys, shoes, clothes—everything was there. They decided that in one of her zany moods she must have taken off on an early hike. He jumped onto his bicycle and rode urgently through the park, around the lake. "Kelly! Kelly Solomon!" Devin ran down the street, around blocks crying, "Mama! Mama!" At home, their father made phone calls to anybody they could think of—friends, art supply houses, the beautician who trimmed her hair.

"Aw, she'll be back," he said. "You know how crazy she gets sometimes."

"Not like this, though. Not without telling us."

Finally the police were contacted. They arrived, looked around, asked questions. What was your mother doing the last time you saw her? Did she seem depressed, angry? Did your mother and father quarrel? Has she ever gone away like this before?

"Just find her, dammit!" Chase cried. "Find her!"

The investigators took things from the house, brought them back, took other things. They called in a medical examiner to examine each of them—arms, fingernails, neck, stripped to the underwear.

He and Devin grabbed pictures of their mother, her clear eyes and winning smile, and ran up and down streets knocking on doors. "Have you seen this lady?" He stopped a postman a mile, two miles from home. "Sir, will you look at this? Have you seen her?"

The postman squinted. "That's Miz Solomon. I deliver her

mail sometimes." He looked up, slowly handed back the picture. "I heard about her. Son, if I had any idea ..."

Their father, standing before volunteer searchers who met at one of the parks, tears in his eyes, pleaded, "Thank you for helping us. We want Kelly back. To anybody out there who might hear this, please, please let us have Kelly back!" The volunteers fanned out, walked through parks, through wooded areas, behind shopping centers, dumps.

One horrendous day dragged into another as the detectives returned again and again, questioning, questioning. What was your mother wearing when you last saw her? Was she dressed? Ready for bed? What time was this? Did she seem worried? Did your parents have a fight?

They took her hairbrush, wallet, and they took sofa cushions. If they failed to make contact for a day or two, Chase ran to the phone. "Why haven't you called us? It's just hell not knowing anything!"

His father yanked the receiver away. "Leave them alone, Chase! They're doing all they can."

"Why can't they find her!"

"I'll do the talking to the police. You leave them alone!"

Devin murmured, "She wouldn't do this. She wouldn't leave us. Somebody's got her." He slipped into Chase's room late at night. "Chase, I can't sleep."

"I know. "Neither can I."

Their father made desperate appeals; while at home he fell across the sofa, snoring heavily, exhausted, they thought, drained. He ordered an over-abundance of flyers with Kelly's picture, phone numbers, an urgent message. Some of these they handed out or tacked to power poles; most remained in the trunk of his car.

Chase asked, "What about Uncle Mitchell? Maybe she went to see them."

"No," his father answered tersely, "Mitchell just had heart surgery."

"Why, that's why she would go then!"

"No, she didn't. I already talked to them." They suspected he was lying.

"Why don't I call them anyway just to be sure."

"Kelly's not there, and we don't need them coming here breathing down my neck!" Chase called them anyway, not telling his father.

There was no evidence of foul play, the investigators insisted. Everything was where Kelly left it—house keys, purse, money still in her wallet. This was not a good sign. If she left of her own free will, she would have had to have money, clothes; somebody would have seen her. They examined windows, doors, carpets. There was no sign of forced entry. Was there an assailant? Did she know him? Let him in? Go with him?

"You think your mom might have had a special friend?" a detective asked.

"You mean lover? Hell, no!" Chase cried. "She would never do that!"

"It isn't that rare. Mothers with children have been known to run off…"

Then after the initial shock Devin remembered something. Once he went to bed he rarely got up before morning. But the night Kelly disappeared he developed a headache, rose, went first to his parents' bedroom and then to the den trying to find his mother. He found neither parent but was too sleepy to think much of it. It was not unusual for them to go out onto the patio or even sit in the car to have long private talks. He took a Tylenol and returned to bed.

When Devin told the police about this, their investigation appeared to change direction. The boys sensed that their father was furious, but with the investigators he calmly insisted Devin must have been dreaming, Kelly was reading a book on art when he himself went to bed.

One or two nights after this, Devin stole into Chase's room and in a husky voice whispered, "You think Dad might know something?"

It reinforced Chase's own doubts. "He better not!"

What was it they had picked up on? In public, their father's anguish was pathetic, but at home some of his actions were peculiar. He stayed away all day, leaving them alone to monitor phone calls. He grilled himself a steak while the brothers could hardly stand the thought of food. He made midnight phone calls behind his closed bedroom door.

Desperately, accusingly, one night Chase yelled at him, "Where *is* she?"

"How the hell should I know! Don't be a dumb ass!"

Still, when the investigators intimated their own suspicions, he thought, *don't let it be him! Dear God, don't let it be him!*

The only horror Chase remembers that comes close to the day his mother's body was found was the night his father was arrested, handcuffed and taken away. He thought he would die, thought he could not stand it. Son of a bitch!

When an autopsy revealed that death was by asphyxiation Chase cried, No! Only a monster would do such a thing! Dear God, please don't let her have suffered! Don't let her have died slowly in helpless terror! He hates himself for imagining something too horrendous to articulate.

Caseworkers came to move them to foster care.

"You'll be fine there. There are boys and girls your ages."

"We're not leaving here!" Chase said.

"I know this is hard—"

He stood firm, his muscles dangerously tense, his fists clenched. "Hell no! We're not going anywhere!"

"You're underage," she said. "You can't be allowed to live here alone. You have no way of supporting yourselves."

"We're not going! Get the hell out!"

They retreated to gather reinforcements, to regroup maybe. Through some fluke, perhaps oversight, the brothers were left alone, were in the house when their father, released on bond, came rioting in. With a violent explosion of rage and bitterness, Chase flew at him, fists flailing, face distorted, eyes tear blurred. His father dealt him such a vicious blow to the head he actually saw stars. Devin ran to the phone, called 911. Then the police came again, and Family and Children's Services forced them to leave the house, "For your own safety." With gut-wrenching incredulity, he and Devin walked out of the only home they'd ever known.

As Chase presses his mouth to the bedcovers, memory stabs on, piercing flashes all at once, gut-blows of betrayal. He lifts his head and finds the spread wet with his tears. He wonders if somehow, somewhere, his mother feels their pain. He wonders if his father senses their hatred.

He hears Mitchell tap on Devin's door, then his own. "Dinner in five minutes." He knows he must straighten up, put on a civil face. He has made it through another day—almost.

3

*Paula is putting dishes on the table when Mitchell comes back down-*stairs. "You called them?" she asks.

"Yes, they're coming."

"Don't you think they should make some moves on their own?"

He tightens his lips. "I don't know that we should expect too much of them just yet. We need to make them feel wanted."

She looks at him, perplexed. "We have to feel wanted, too. It would help to know this is where they want to be."

"I think right now they're terrified of feeling anything for any-body, ever again. I guess it starts with us."

"We brought them into our home," she reminds him.

"And I know they must believe we wanted to."

She thinks he must realize this has been hard on her. All her hopes and plans—the incursion of two young boys into their home has played havoc with them. She likes everything spelled out, admits she has difficulty with compromise. Her opinions are sometimes caustic, sword-sharp. Mitchell has never minded her definiteness, says it has been a stabilizing force with his own id-iosyncrasies. She thinks it is her sense of rightness about herself, about her needs, which first attracted him to her. Still, she knows he wants to breathe, too.

The nephews come in, Chase wearing one of the new shirts, jeans, and flip-flops. The washed faces, the brushed hair and fresh shirts all imply respect, Paula thinks. Devin starts to drop down, hesitates, waits for Paula. She has begun teaching them gently, sculpturing their refinement. As they all sit down together, she says, "I hope you boys like this chicken casserole." Trying to please them, "It's a new recipe."

"We used to have stuffed bell peppers," Devin volunteers.

"I can do that." She passes the dishes to them first. Manners. "I do like that shirt, Chase. Whose choice, yours or Mitchell's?"

He manages a grin, "Mine, I guess. Thanks."

"What else did you do? At the shopping center?"

"Walked around. Looked through Barnes and Noble."

"Anything special? You use CliffsNotes now?"

"No, not much. Mostly we resource the Internet."

"We used CliffsNotes," says Mitchell, "but they were never a shortcut. The teachers know how to head them off."

"We read the classics." Paula spoons food onto her plate, conservative, measured. "*Silas Marner*, *Wuthering Heights*. I guess a lot of those aren't required now."

"I read *Pride and Prejudice*," says Chase.

"You like?"

"I just read it for fun." Self-consciously, he remarks, "You can't always read the easy stuff."

"My mother read a lot." Devin is eating slowly, unenthusiastically. "She didn't watch television. Too much violence."

He speaks without inflection, but Paula notices that Chase shoots him a swift glance. They have known violence and it is not entertaining.

The conversation is polite, courteous, guarded. She remembers the spastic energy of their own children, the animation, the music, the hectic friendships. She feels the nephews' stifled energy, the constrained fervor to be wild, spontaneous, gobbling up life. She knows they subconsciously reach out for love, perhaps even for forgiveness in a weird way. Does having something so precious and basic torn away make them terrified of their own faults?

She asks, "Chase, when you were at the mall did you happen to go to the Mole Hole?"

She sees something defensive and withdrawn sweep over him. His lips draw tight, his arms and shoulders stiffen. "No. Why?"

"I was just wondering about their summer stuff, if it's coming in yet!" She looks up, watchful. "It doesn't matter, I'll stop by in a day or two." She is silent until the meal is over, the table is cleared, and the boys return to their rooms upstairs. Do they make themselves scarce because they are not comfortable with the adults or because they try not to disrupt otherwise placid lives?

Until now she and her husband have always felt they were a regular family, a typical American household. But when a sister is murdered and her husband is the number one suspect, all the ordinariness is cast asunder. Surrounding lives—in this case hers, Mitchell's, the children's—are thrown into complexities and turmoils, a cataclysmic crash. Crashes leave scars, but healing and rejuvenation are all one can reach for.

As the boys bound upstairs Paula asks, "What happened at the shopping center?"

She thinks he is trying to dodge a bullet. "Nothing much." But as she fixes him with a cool stare he answers quietly. "Chase saw a woman who looked like his mother."

"And?"

"He followed her. No contact, no words. Just wanted to see what she would do, where she'd go."

"How do you know this? He tell you?"

He hesitates. "Evidently the woman realized she was being followed and contacted security. A guard stopped him and told him to lay off. He would never have done this, I don't think, had he any idea she'd notice him."

"Why exactly *did* he follow her?"

"You can figure as well as I, Paula. She looked like his mother and he was just absorbed, I guess."

"Did you see her?"

"Yes. There was a remarkable resemblance."

She stands motionless. "Are you certain these boys are going to be okay, Mitchell?"

"What d'you mean?"

"Who knows what's going on in their heads?"

"They're my sister's kids."

"Yes, but their father is a murderer. They got some of his genes, too."

He demands, "Can't you cut them some slack? Children this age shouldn't have nightmares, but they do. What do you think will ever heal them?"

"That's what I'm asking you."

"They lost both parents in one horrible night. I think all they want is to live normal lives. To believe someone wants them and will love them. Maybe this won't work, maybe we don't have the courage. I just know they're my family."

"Mine, too," she says. "Please don't make that distinction."

"I think Chase followed that woman because she looked like

a moment to remember, a breath of fresh air. I'm sorry he felt he had to do that."

She feels a stab of pain. "You think I'm failing them, don't you?"

"I didn't say that."

"You as much as said it. Chase is looking for reassurance because I don't give it."

He walks over, puts his arms around her. "I want to help those boys, but I'd never do anything to hurt you. You come first."

She leans back, looks into his face. "I'm not asking you to make a choice. But we have to know it can be just us sometimes."

* * *

It is a clear fall afternoon—layered blue skies and the October red glory are leafing out. The air is pleasantly cool with the promise of a hard chill to come. Mitchell, Chase and Devin are bicycling the Riverwalk. The cardiologist has given his okay for short rides. Paula has decided to refrain—to give the men time together or to claim some space of her own? Mitchell leads them below the Dillingham Street Bridge, and then south toward Fort Benning. Other cyclists breeze by, joggers, walkers. They cross a long wood and steel bridge and turn up a hill to a gazebo, a lookout with memorial markers all around.

With a sweep of his arms, Mitchell says, "This is our river, the Chattahoochee. Columbus was founded as a river trading town."

The boys nod attentively, realizing he is trying to make them feel part of everything.

"River boats used to come up and down the Chattahoochee from Florida. It was quite fashionable."

They circulate around the gazebo looking at markers.

"There are mills all up and down the river. Textiles was the big industry. They're mostly closed now. Imports have taken over."

Mitchell has encouraged them to dig out the old three-speeds and tune them up. It is Devin who is good at this. He is mechanically inclined. Mitchell has made it a point to do special things with them, let them know they are worthy of special care. He has insisted that they walk with him, too. Sometimes he rouses them from bed at 6 a.m. before work and school. Devin cries, "Why are you punishing me, Uncle Mitchell!"

"You want to get strong and healthy, don't you? You should be excited to walk with me."

"If you ask me, it sucks!"

They complain, yet have a natural desire to be under the authority of someone they respect. Whenever one of them gripes too much, Mitchell uses the same trick he'd employed with Leslie and Grant. He goes to a closet and digs out an old Halloween mask, a grotesquely ugly rubber face with warted nose and pop eyes and veiny distorted features. He calls it the whiney monster, revived when one of the brothers grumbles. The first time he sprang out, Devin cried, "You scared the pi— you scared the life out of me!"

"This is the whiney monster," said Mitchell. "When he comes after you, remember what brought him out of hiding."

Some mornings Mitchell gets up early, rushes over to Krispy Kreme or Panera's for doughnuts or Danishes, has them warm on the table when the boys come in to breakfast. "Hey, thanks, Uncle Mitchell, Aunt Paula. We know this is extra trouble." Sometimes they can eat, sometimes they can't.

On their walks and rides Chase usually brings along a sketchpad, pencils. This he's inherited from his mother. He makes quick, spontaneous sketches of weeping willow trees, wrought iron benches, iron lamps, gazebos. He'd never given drawing much thought, but now it has become a reprieve to him, a creative distraction—something like playing the piano.

They turn and head back north along the Riverwalk. Long pink and orange reflections of the sun ripple on the current. River rocks are lit with little sparkles of fire. They reach the van, extract their water bottles from the holders. As they load the bikes, Mitchell asks, "Well, how did you like the ride?"

"It was hard," says Devin.

Mitchell is surprised. The Riverwalk is not difficult, but in a way he understands, Devin is carrying an invisible weight that makes him plant his feet heavily.

Chase says, "I like the river. That steep hill at Rigdon Park, though—I don't know if you should pull that, Uncle Mitchell. It'd be different if we had twenty-one speeds."

"What! You don't like my old cruisers?"

"Actually, I do like them. They make your legs work." Chase grins. "When were they made? Eighteen hundreds?"

Mitchell laughs. "I'll make you a deal. Show me you'll stick with it, and I'll get us some 21-speeds."

"We could bring our bikes down from Raleigh," Devin says. "But I don't think they're any better than these."

On the way home, they stop for a snack. Mitchell is always trying to push food on them. He looks over Chase's drawings. Not bad. The one of the river, though, is too busy, too cluttered. His sister Kelly used to say, "Remember your negative space." Mitchell thinks, Funny how the absence of anything enhances the presence of something.

* * *

Sunday morning. When Mitchell calls them early to breakfast, Devin groans, and Chase mumbles, "Okay!" They aren't quite ready for the night to end. Not that they're dead to the world, exactly. Sleep eludes them, he knows, then drugs them too close to morning. "Don't forget it's Sunday," Mitchell says. "We're going to church." Chase doesn't respond, Devin grumbles, "How can I forget?"

A couple of weeks after they arrived Mitchell had called them three times, and when Devin still refused to get up he playfully threw back the covers and pulled Devin's feet to the floor.

"Don't do that!" Devin was furious, irrational. "I don't have to do what you say!"

Mitchell was startled, but answered evenly, "You do as long as you choose to live here."

"I don't choose anything! I *never* get to choose!"

"Maybe you can't change things, Devin. But you can choose your attitude."

"You're making me go to church! You're *making* me! Fat lot of good that does!"

"You have a point." Mitchell's tone was steady but determined. "But we don't know, do we? Maybe it will do some good. It can't hurt."

"It's just a big lie anyway."

"*What's* a big lie?"

"God and everything! It's just a big lie!"

"You know you don't believe that," Mitchell said.

"If there's a God, why does he hate us? I didn't do anything to him!"

"He doesn't hate you. We can't blame God for the cruel things people do."

"Oh, that makes sense." Devin's tone was sarcastic. "We give him credit for good things but can't blame him for hell!"

"Bad things happen to good people, Devin. We have no assurance against that. It's not only this world we live for."

"I don't know why I'm supposed to love somebody who doesn't love me!" Devin held fast, adamant, repeating himself. "Mother went to church and look what it got her!"

Mitchell said without anger, "I hope you relearn some things your mother taught you."

It seems longer than three months ago that this battle occurred, but hopefully there is no reason to fear history will repeat itself, Mitchell thinks. The groaning still takes place, the muffled complaints, but more out of habit than heartfelt objection.

Paula has returned to preparing her traditional Big Sunday Breakfast, something she'd pretty much abandoned when Grant and Leslie left. Cheese eggs, bacon or sausage, grits, fruit, hash browns. This morning as they walk into the breakfast room she exclaims, "Look, surprise! Egg and sausage quiche. I made it yesterday."

"Hey, thanks, Aunt Paula," says Chase. "Sure looks good."

"It looks great!" Devin plops down, too eager to wait. "We haven't had quiche since Mama—" He breaks off. "Where we lived for a while the food wasn't that great. You're a good cook, Aunt Paula."

They finish breakfast, manage to leave on time. Mitchell knows their mother took them to church, and Robert seldom attended. He thinks her beliefs rubbed off on them, but for now they are suffocated by fear and doubt. She allowed them latitude, encouraged a free spirit, taught them to assume a broad perspective and weigh viewpoints not their own. But how can they not distrust it all? He realizes in a way her death has invalidated God, prayer, everything.

And it makes Mitchell wonder, All this about living forever—just how far will people take their desire to be immortal? Their mother believed this, too, and she was an intelligent woman. So where is she now? His thoughts are troubled, yet he knows he must teach the brothers that down beneath the cynicism is a work of hope. He has seen enough pain, enough life without humor, to know how important it is to find light in darkness. Mitchell wants to believe his life has meaning, too. He remembers one of his favorite poems by Elizabeth Barrett Browning. "Earth's crammed with heaven, and every common bush afire with God; but only he who sees takes off his shoes—the rest sit around it and pluck blackberries." This is one poet's point of view, he knows, and he wonders what good it did Kelly in her last breath. And what does it take to "see" anyway? Something beyond consciousness, beyond the volitive grasp of thought. He realizes the brothers feel church is one of the rituals they must endure.

They park between a Villager and a Chrysler town car as big as a van. As they walk in, the music is playing, up on the screen flash brief power point messages. The choir files in, the music director, the minister. Mitchell leans across Devin. "See that dark-haired girl in the choir, Chase? Second row, third from the end. Think she's pretty?

"Yes, I guess," he says.

"She *is* pretty. We know her family. We could introduce you."

"Thanks. Maybe later."

"There are some nice kids here, too. You should get to know them."

"I will, just give me time."

Mitchell thinks that pushing 17 a regular guy couldn't stay away from a girl like this.

The sermon is about patience, gentleness, kindness…Too idealistic for the real world? Mitchell wonders. We can't change what happens, the pastor says, only the way we respond to what happens. Belief and doubts are bedfellows.

Driving home he asks, "How do you boys like Pastor Hagen?"

For a moment neither answer. Finally Devin says, "He's okay."

"Yeah, sure," says Chase.

"What do you think about talking to him?"

"You mean therapy?"

"Talk to him."

"We've had therapy, Uncle Mitchell."

"I know, but Dr. Hagen may have a different approach. Why don't you think about it? It can't hurt."

"Right," Chase answers. "We will."

God knows I've tried, Mitchell thinks. But how does he help heal young boys who have lost everything—their mother, their father, home, school, friends. Their counselor at the children's ranch had told them, "You have a life. Your mother would be disappointed if you throw that away, too." Maybe Pastor Hagen could add little to this.

Mitchell turns to Paula. "Why don't we drive up to Atlanta, see what Leslie and Grant are up to?"

"Oh, you know we can't," she says. "Not without arranging it with them first. They have a thousand things to do."

"Okay, you're right. Maybe we'll take the boys down to Little Grand Canyon then. They haven't seen that yet."

"What is it?" asks Devin.

"Our own deep canyon. Pretty spectacular."

"Can you hike?"

"Yes. And see all kinds of formations."

"You're sure you're up to that?" asks Paula.

"I think so."

"All right, then."

They make plans. A little of the heaviness lifts. The long Sunday afternoon seems less forbidding.

* * *

Leslie and Grant drive down from Atlanta, the second time in three months. Grant is twenty-three, two inches taller than Mitchell, perfect white teeth, dark trimmed hair, inquisitive glance. Leslie is twenty-five, looks and talks much like her mother. She has a degree in finance and says someday when her dad retires she'll step into his shoes. "I think we can find a place for you," Mitchell tells her.

"No, no, I want to get some experience first. When I come I intend to bring something to the table."

They all sit down to dinner. Mitchell knows the boys are nervous, ill at ease, that they feel like intruders. Leslie asks, "What do you think of Columbus, Chase?"

He hesitates, as though he doesn't want to say the wrong thing. "I don't know. I guess all towns are about the same."

"Not the people, though." Devin forces himself to join in. "They're different...at least until you get to know them..."

"North Carolina is beautiful in the fall," Leslie says.

"Just don't drive through Atlanta on an October Sunday," laughs Grant. "People go crazy heading to the mountains."

Everybody tries to be nice. Mitchell perceives that the cousins haven't decided how they feel about one another. He wants them to bond, to act like family. It's significantly different for the children to come home, he knows, deprived of their old beds, their pillows, most of their stuff put away in boxes. He sometimes thinks Paula is so structured they have grown up in a molded childhood. Chase's and Devin's mother would do crazy things, things that surprised even her—sweep them into the car and rush them off for some unexpected event, grab one of their father's rods and take them fishing. She enrolled them one summer in Huntsville, Alabama's Space Camp. Nonconventional was Kelly's mode of operation. During their grade school days she'd slip into their classrooms to draw happy pictures on the chalkboards. The kids loved her art, the teachers didn't mind but couldn't grasp her zany moods. Mitchell is poignantly conscious of the differences in their childhood.

Leslie and Grant do not spend the night. After dinner they both say, "We've got to get back."

"But we see you so seldom," protests Paula.

"We'll stay longer during the holidays."

Everyone hugs, then they take off for Atlanta.

The boys as usual run upstairs to their rooms. Mitchell draws a deep breath. He had not realized how strung his nerves were.

* * *

He goes back to work full time. Their offices are located in north Columbus, a settlement of buildings perched atop a wooded hillside. On a brick and stone pedestal at the entrance, his name is etched in bronze letters: Mitchell Ingram, Financial Advisor.

Since his surgery it strikes him as ironic that while his profession is advising clients on managing wealth, he is harshly reminded that the most precious things are not material. This makes him both curiously detached and poignantly aware of things going on around him. The nation's humble healing after 9-11 is spotty, quickly obscured by a kind of national self-interest. Still, when a tsunami wipes out half an island, the outpouring of compassion is overwhelming.

He arrives at the office a little later than he used to, leaves a little earlier. One whole wall of his office is glass. It affords him a pretty view of trees and shrubs, but also invites staring and reflecting—something he has been more and more inclined to do since he first faced life-threatening surgery. Sometimes he wonders what he and Paula were thinking when they married just out of college. They had crammed and fought their way through school, studied, worked, laughed, played, cried, gone to games. Leslie was born a year later. They had a baby to pay for, loans to pay off, his young sister Kelly to help support. What happened to the ecstatic freedom between college and family? They'd missed it.

The first dozen years were hard, Mitchell reflected, but they had made it at last, were now pretty well set. He had no apologies for what he'd been able to give his wife and children, knows of nothing they have missed. Still, in recent years he wonders what legacy he will leave beyond family and worldly success. What might he tell the nephews which will be significant? Focus on what you want to be and do, based upon your values and principles, not what the world tells you. Maybe this is enough.

When his own mother died, he was just the age Devin is now. The sense of loss, the lack of direction were staggering. He appealed to his father for closeness, but got little. His father was lost, too, had no heart to reach out. And little Kelly, just six, so desperately wanting her mother, could only turn to him, Mitchell, who loved and protected her as much as he knew how. They cried and prayed together, sometimes they laughed together. Mostly what they had to fall back on was the faith their mother had taught them. How, he wonders, is a believer's response to grief different from any other? Hope versus hopelessness, perhaps. Sooner or later, one must conclude that life either is no more than accidental evolution or that it has purpose beyond gut-wrenching circumstances. He is a manager of wealth who has come to the conclusion that money, power, ego are about as lasting as the dew on the grass.

He swivels in his chair, leans back, puts his feet up on the credenza. It's good for the circulation, he believes, stimulates his heart with an extra pump.

He and Paula had married, had already brought a child into the world, when Kelly announced her engagement. She was a pretty bride, Robert handsome in his dark blue tux. It was not an elaborate wedding. Their father, who came down with pneumonia just prior to the ceremony—Mitchell walked his sister down the aisle—could not afford much. Mitchell dug deep to help pay for everything.

Robert was so unlike Kelly they all wondered what she saw in him. He was attractive and had a certain iconoclastic charm. At times he was loud and boisterous, at others meek as a lost child. Probably it was his charm that was contagious, Mitchell thought, especially to young women. Robert's goal in life was to make it big. When he had some sort of deal going, he was a happy back slapper. When something crashed, he accused everybody of being against him. Mitchell doubted if his brother-in-law ever provided his family much ballast, much focus. It was Kelly who'd shaped the boys, helped them decide how they would view life. He remembers that early on Robert had been decent to them, playing the father role. But he wonders if Chase and Devin ever felt paternal love, ever heard him express it, ever picked up on his propensity for accusing others of his failures.

Mitchell thinks of their first trip to Raleigh to see the boys, when they made a point to talk to the detective investigating the Solomon case. His name was McLendon, a stout man wearing blue jeans, a casual shirt, sneakers. He was willing to speak with them but reluctant to provide details. "We're still building this case," McLendon said. "There's not a lot I can divulge at this time."

This was difficult, Mitchell wanted answers, wanted to understand. "Can you tell me where you found her?"

"A fisherman found her body hung up on some rocks. Her assailant evidently thought the weights he used would hold her forever."

"She died of drowning?"

"No. Asphyxiation."

Paula gasped. A terrifying death—perhaps looking her murderer in the eyes…

"Sorry I can't tell you more," said McLendon.

Mitchell muttered, "You're pretty certain it was the husband?"

"I'm sure the charges against him will hold up."

Leaving the office Mitchell drives to his afternoon appointment with Dr. Simmons, his cardiologist. As they talk, Simmons moves his stethoscope around. "You still walking, exercising, watching your diet?"

"All of the above," Mitchell says. "I think I'm getting stronger."

"I'd say your recovery from coronary surgery has been exemplary." The examination is brief, everything is normal. Simmons asks, "How are your new charges doing?" They all live in the same neighborhood.

"I guess the boys are adjusting. We're trying to get them to resume therapy. What do you think?"

"I think it's a good idea." Simmons smiles wryly. "I'd say you have not only a strong heart but a brave one. Just try to avoid undue pressure."

Mitchell establishes his next appointment, starts back to the office, then decides instead to go home, see what the nephews are up to …

4

The mornings are cool. Still in her nightgown, Paula walks out onto the porch to test the weather. Fall leaves are collecting on top of azaleas, sasanquas, splotchy brown blemishes on shades of green. The air is rarified, the sun warming fast, turning limbs into elfin rivulets. Golden light flashes through houses, trees. Today is her regular Tuesday tennis day. Her friend Marge called to remind her. "No copping out! Wear your hat!"

Mitchell is off to work, the boys at school. This is not her week to carpool, so she takes her time to dress, first to see if the regular four are going to play, second to decide what to wear. She prefers tennis shorts and skirts to long pants. Mostly their valley weather is mild.

Inside, she makes up her mind, it will be warm enough for a short skirt. She chooses one of Grant's baseball caps, wide-brimmed, tight-fitting, white with green triangles. It accents her hair which frames her face, making it fuller, more vital. When she was younger, she could wear her hair any way. It was thick, vivid, honey colored. Just in recent years has she given up length, which she decided made her appear trying to look younger than she is. Only the tearful withdrawal from bikinis had been more dreadful. She is just under fifty, a good age overall, she thinks, yet scary, too.

After Leslie and Grant finished college, got jobs, moved out, Mitchell encouraged her to sleep late, meet no deadlines. She tried this for about a week, saw it wouldn't work. "I just can't let you go off without kissing me goodbye." As much as possible, she strives to be there when he comes home, too — trying to hold things together, not to fall into the humdrum dissatisfaction of so many couples their age. She is inclined toward routine, specifics, regrets she can't be more spontaneous, can't enjoy surprises more. One surprise she did used to enjoy was when they made love on the spur of the moment. Some little thing, some incident, some word or occasion, would trigger Mitchell's ardor and next thing she knew they were crumbled onto sofa or bed in a frenzy of passion. Their lovemaking now is sporadic, and she misses it — not just the sex but the closeness, feeling desired and desirable. She'd thought after the children left their long-awaited time together would rekindle romance. Expressing love, receiving love — with her husband!

She slips on her skirt, top. Mitchell used to say she had gorgeous legs. Well, they are still there, more or less functioning as they always have. Perhaps he still notices, just doesn't say so much. She adjusts the cap, pulls her hair out through the band. After two children and twenty-seven years of marriage, she's decided she hasn't too much to apologize for. Delicate, faintly curved nose, high cheekbones, thin nostrils, dark long lashes, lots of energy. There is a small crescent scar like the print of a thumbnail across the bridge of her nose — the result of a skating accident when she was a teenager. She remembers to stuff her pocket with Kleenexes.

She goes upstairs to check the boys' rooms. On the stairway wall is an Ingram picture gallery. There is another on the garage wall. Her mother and father, Leslie, Grant, various school and occasion settings. There is one of her and Mitchell in the mountains, standing before a waterfall. She is smiling, young, pretty, Mitchell handsome in his dark blue windbreaker, tousled hair, masculine features, and protective glance. Already she was pregnant, but didn't know it; perhaps this was what gave her face an inner glow. They had little money, but it didn't seem to matter. She sighs, takes a few more steps, glances at photos of her mother and father when they were younger. She feels a little stitch in her breast. Paula was thirteen when they split, she remembers the crushing blow. She blamed herself, her own unpredictable hormones. "If you love me, how can you leave me!" She knows what it is to lose a parent, understands a little of what Chase and Devin are going through. When her father decided to come back a couple of weeks later, there was a great relief of sadness, yet it was hard to forget all the unhappiness. To her knowledge, her parents have enjoyed their past thirty or so years together.

In Leslie's room, now Devin's, and in Grant's room, now Chase's, she remembers how terrified she was when the doctors first informed them of Mitchell's heart blockage, the expedience of a swift and serious operation. She made every effort to keep up an optimistic front, hide her fears from Mitchell. She brought in cruise brochures, land tours—Ireland, the Panama Canal, Paris. "Look! When you're all well again, we'll travel at last." She picked up magazines on home décor. "Let's redo our living and dining rooms. I've been wanting to a long time. Then we can do more entertaining." She did everything she could think of to convince them both there was still life in their togetherness.

The boys' rooms look pretty good. They are relatively neat. Their mother's training, then the requirements for order in the children's ranch. In preparing for their arrival, she'd boxed up pictures, cleared walls, closets. Leslie had cried, "What happened to my room! I've been thrown out!" And Grant, looking through old mementos, "I guess these have nowhere to live now. Might as well dump them." She felt a moment of panic, sheer terror of starting over. Still, she wants to make the boys feel loved, knows that to survive anywhere near whole will demand every ounce of their courage.

Almost every day she tries to think what their mother would do. Kelly was nobody's fool, Paula knows. She had changed the beneficiaries on her small life insurance policy to her sons, one of the few details the Raleigh police have divulged to them. Robert had mortgaged the house to the hilt, there is little money expected for the boys' support. He is now out on bail, the D.A. preparing the case. The trial could be months, even years away. Robert has made no contact with his sons. One little word of confession, of remorse, even of denial would mean much, yet she knows in another respect they never want to see or speak to him again.

Downstairs, she fetches a racquet, a couple of cans of balls, shoes. She locks up and runs out to the car. Starting the engine, she sits a moment to let it warm up. Her car is neat, free of clutter, just as she tries to keep her house, her life. She wishes Mitchell were a little less focused on the nephews, that he'd make them a little less a personal mission; yet she knows such thoughts are petty, knows she is a curious combination of two dyes, one flowing into his, the other inevitably separating. She is pragmatic, loyal, devoted. She believes in her husband, trusts him, yet defends her own space. As she drives to the courts, her thoughts are distracted. She hardly notices when two parallel air hoses, traffic counters, thump under her wheels, or when a loose top flips off a can and three balls roll round on her neat, clean floor.

* * *

Paula picks Devin up from school. It's her week in a four-way carpool she alternates with three other families. Not since Leslie and Grant began to drive had she carpooled. She's not excited about a fixed obligation five afternoons at a stretch, but is often intrigued by the dialogue from the backseat.

The boys pile into the car from both sides, Devin in front, the others in back. They do the talking, Devin mostly listens. She's hoping he'll loosen up, join in. Her efforts to encourage him — "How was *your* day, Devin?" "How did the report go?" — merely embarrass him. She remembers that as a small child he was outgoing, inquisitive, responsive. It is a pity that he has so dramatically pulled back, much like his brother.

From the backseat she hears, "…my third time to see Lord of the Rings."

"Lisa claims she's been ten times. I doubt it, though."

"It may take that many for Lisa to get it."

Giggles all around.

"Why does she get all that special attention? She teacher's pet?"

"She's on Adderall."

Adderall, thinks Paula. How many kids are on Adderall?

"It must make her mean sometimes."

"Yeah. She's too bossy."

"Not always. Sometimes she's okay."

"Somebody stole a bunch of money from Lisa. Right out of her purse. It was on the floor beside her desk."

"Who? Did they catch them?"

"No. Mr. Franklin threatened to strip search."

"Strip search! Ho, ho! Strip search!"

"Nobody's gonna strip search me!"

She lets two of the boys out at their homes. Scarcely is there a farewell. She stops, a door opens, slams, a voice is missing. With just one left on the backseat, Devin in front, conversation dries up. She feels a pang of pity, knows he wants to talk, wants to be included, but just can't bring himself to join in. The others have been friends most of their lives, a little clique not sensitive to his aloneness. Except for Will, who doesn't ride with them, he has been unable to form close allies.

As they drop off the last boy she asks, "What about it, Devin? Need anything? Want to stop for a snack?"

"No, thanks, I have to do my homework."

He is good about attacking his assignments the minute he arrives home, something Leslie and Grant never did. She's sorry Devin carries the weight of the world, at times feels strong maternal instincts toward him. She remembers once when Grant got lost. They were in Paris, she, Mitchell, Leslie and Grant, browsing some crowded artist's corner looking for oils and watercolors. First Grant was there, then he wasn't. As they began frantically looking and calling, she had never felt such helplessness, such fear. It was no more than five minutes before they found him doing exactly as he had been instructed; not trying to make his way back to them, but standing calmly where they'd become separated, waiting for them to come for him. Grant was, she thought, more heroic than she. She herself as a child had been lost once, and it was an experience of utter fear she hoped never to suffer again.

As they pull into the driveway, she steals a glance at Devin and sees that he looks sad. It clutches her heart. Tentatively, she says, "Devin, are you all right?"

"Yes, ma'am." Hardly more than a whisper.

"I was just thinking about one time Grant got lost. It's so scary. Do you feel a little that way?"

She sees his lips tremble. He nods, can't answer.

"Life can be so confusing. And sometimes we feel alone even when there are people around. Your uncle and I want to help. It's just that...sometimes we don't know how."

"It's okay," he mumbles.

"Why don't we ask some of your classmates over? Maybe have a spend-the-night party. Would you like that?"

"I don't know. Maybe."

"Well, you think about it. We want to help," she says again.

"Okay. Thanks."

He scampers from the car, hastens into the house. Even discussions like this are painful to him. She follows him in, perplexed. She knows Mitchell is committed to these boys. Once she asked him, "Is this love? Compassion? Or simply an absolute bent toward responsibility?"

"I guess some of all," he said. "Is that wrong?"

"No, not wrong. I've always trusted your judgment. Somehow I'm just afraid we're missing out." She hates the way she is torn between sympathy and isolation.

They enter the house and Devin continues on to his room. She wishes she could see things as they are now as new life and challenge; instead she sees something slipping away.

Suddenly on impulse she picks up the phone and calls Mitchell at the office. "How would you like to take your wife to dinner?"

He is surprised. "You mean tonight?"

"Why not?"

"Well, sure. What's the occasion?"

"The occasion is we will go out and have a nice quiet dinner together. We can order pizza in for the boys."

"Okay, fine. They'll like that. I'll leave early."

She walks down the hall, her step quickened, wondering what she will wear that'll be pretty and sexy.

*　*　*

And she does have that, at least — the desire to be pretty and sexy. She hopes she can sustain this.

In her walk-on closet, she decides — a slinky black thing with a deep neckline and skirt just above her knees. Mitchell likes her to show her legs. In the full length door mirror, she checks herself, front, side, back, decides she'll do. Vanity, vanity — does one ever live through it? She's nearly ready when Mitchell comes in, finds her applying the finishing touches.

He kisses her, sniffs. "What's this?"

"Transgressions."

"Aha! A new perfume."

She laughs. "I remember when you were crazy about Indiscretions."

"Mmmm. I wouldn't discount those possibilities either."

She looks at him coyly. "I wouldn't discount the possibilities of anything." He gets it, smiles, but they both know the time is not quite yet.

While he showers, she finds her little black purse, puts in a few tissues, a lipstick. He emerges freshly shaved, wearing the black blazer she'd given him his last birthday, a pretty silk tie. "My, how handsome you are," she says.

"So as not to look shabby for a beautiful lady."

He goes upstairs to check on the boys, then leaves money on the table for the pizza. They drive to Michelle's, a favorite restaurant they couldn't have afforded to stick their noses in thirty years ago. Paula slips her arm through his. "Remember when we first ate here? It was our anniversary," she laughs. "At least now we don't have to pay as much attention to the prices."

An eel-like girl in a sleek mint green cocktail dress seats them.

As she looks over the menu, Paula says, "They serve such large portions here. Why don't we share a meal?"

"Good enough." When their server comes he orders—crab cakes, prime rib, asparagus, a special fruit salad made of lettuce and apples, cranberries and pecans.

"When the time comes this would be a nice place for your Christmas party," suggests Paula.

"We're thinking this year we'll combine the office party with open house for clients. There's plenty of room and the secretaries are enthusiastic about decorating."

"All right, but keep this in mind just in case. Summer will be gone and Christmas here before you know it. Leslie and Grant will come home, I'm hoping for at least two or three days. And I've asked my parents this year. That okay with you?"

"You know it is. Will we need to get a motel room?"

"I think so. With the children and the nephews, we won't have a place for everybody to sleep. They'd rather be in a motel anyway."

They have a salad, with moist, freshly baked sourdough bread. The main dish arrives on two plates, divided by the chef. Paula says, "I wish we could go ahead and get our living and dining rooms redecorated."

"Why don't we do it?"

"It's just that we have so much to think about right now." Paula has an unexpected pang of nostalgia. What is she—a devoted wife and mother or a fish out of water? Can one be restless, misplaced and committed too?

"You remember Marge, my tennis partner," she says. "She's having medical problems. It's funny that Adam is a doctor, but all he can do is try to get her into the right hands."

"He's a gynecologist, not an internist."

"Still, I think sometimes Marge feels he isn't paying much attention."

It is a small, intimate restaurant with walls decorated with the works of local artists. Beside each painting is a card with a price—the art can be purchased. The lights are low, candles on the tables. The servers move smoothly, silently. Water glasses are never allowed to become empty. It's nice, but perhaps a little too close. She feels that if she dares put down her fork her plate will be whisked away...

Mitchell says, "I was thinking of taking some sort of trip with the boys. Hiking maybe, up in the mountains."

"Just the three of you?"

"You, too, if you'd want to. During the holidays."

She feels a slight tensing in her fingers. "I guess it wouldn't occur to you that *we* might have a little holiday. Just the two of us, while they aren't needing transportation."

"You think they'd be okay by themselves?"

"It never occurred to me that everything we do would have to revolve around them."

She sees that he, too, has tensed a little.

"No, of course it doesn't."

"I just don't want us to ... to lose out, Mitchell. We haven't that much time left."

"Nobody knows how much time they have." He appears to struggle, then says, "Let's give it a couple more months and see how things go. I promise it'll all work out."

"I just want you to remember I have needs, too."

"I know you do. I've always told you, you come first."

She's sorry for this slight fissure. It is a night for love and she knows she must hang onto this. By the time they finish dinner with a shared dessert, a sinful concoction of chocolate brownie and ice cream and whipped cream, they are talking freely again. Mitchell signals for the check and they leave the restaurant in good spirits. At home, he goes upstairs to check on Chase and Devin. She walks into the kitchen to prepare the table for breakfast. It is part of her nightly ritual. Everything is organized, so much of the typical morning hassle is eliminated. She knows exactly where everything is, exactly what time it will need to be on the table.

In her dressing area, she hangs up her clothes, removes makeup, washes her face. She slips into a thin gossamer gown, reanoints herself with Transgressions, sweetens her mouth with Scope. When Mitchell comes to bed fifteen minutes later, she is waiting.

"You do smell good," he says.

As they lie side by side, there is a little small talk. He reaches for her and she slides into his arms. His hands are familiar along her hips, her legs and breasts. She wants to be kissed and she is, her mouth, her neck, and all the pulsing parts of her. Passion has an instinct of its own and when she is ready she gives a little signal she is hardly aware of—a faint pressure on his flank, a slight rotation of her hips. He lifts himself over her and for the next few seconds there is no time, no world, no complication. She grows intense, releases a climatic, helpless breath. He drops down beside her, motionless. When he stirs to move, she holds fast with her encircling arm. "Stay close to me," she whispers.

He does, drawing her tighter into his arms. He goes to sleep first, breathing deeply with his face in her hair. In the soft glow of nightlight, she watches patterns on the ceiling and walls. Several convoluting shadows form shapes like a string harp. And then she sleeps, too.

5

Chase is in his room, faintly adrift, surrounded by the inevitable mu-
sic. Something has made him think about how different his
mother and Aunt Paula are. Kelly was spontaneous, blowing with
the wind, Paula maintains a relatively steady course, skirting surprises. It is Paula, actually, that he thinks he needs now. Or rather
her set sails. Structure. Routine. Organization that he's lacking,
some sort of daily centering. What time to get up. What shirts,
shoes to wear. When to shower, morning or evening. He needs a
job, too, though the Ingrams have pushed an allowance on them,
insist he should concentrate on school, extracurricular activities.

He glances over his report on *Macbeth*. Strange, poetic violence. He feels no panic, likes *Macbeth*, knows his report is okay.
He likes algebra, too. Algebraic equations, solutions to life's rid-
dles.

At school there is a girl who suffers from deep down depression. Exactly why, no one can figure. Not bipolar, they say. Her
name is Kimberly Compass. He first saw her leaving the library
one day after school. Books in arms, face set purposefully, motions
fluid and rhythmic. He was jolted, much as he was when he saw
his mother's lookalike in the shopping mall. She is pretty, damn

pretty, he thinks, though he is never confident of his judgment. Her hair is thick and blonde. She has a knock-out figure, blue eyes, a slightly lopsided smile. Her family is well off. She makes top grades, has been on the cheerleading squad but dropped out.

His friend Bryan Upchurch — really the only friend he's developed so far — tells him, "Kimberly's a nice girl. A little spastic sometimes. Not always the warmest with her friends."

"What makes her spastic?"

"A few years ago, she suffered a concussion in an accident. Maybe that has something to do with it. I don't know. Her mother's a neat lady." Bryan gives a little shrug. "One day she's joyous, the next, life is in the pits. You can tell by just looking at her."

Once Chase saw Kimberly out under the trees where some of the kids park. Around her, boys and girls were cavorting, glad school was over, but she had distanced herself, sitting on the hood of her car. Something was strange. He saw her arms go up, back, sweep forward, up again. He asked a boy walking toward him, "What's she doing?"

"Ha! Braiding her hair."

"Why would she braid her hair in the middle of a parking lot?"

"God only knows."

What is it exactly that throws her into one mood or the other? he wonders. Why does he care? Chase Solomon, who has withdrawn from almost every emotional contact, resisted getting close to anyone ever again. What is it he would like to ask this pretty girl? How do you cope? How do you fight? What gives you joy? Pleasure? He and Kimberly do not share class schedules, but when he glimpses her in the halls, he notices. Strange how one can yearn so longingly for a smile, a gesture, some small intimacy, yet resist every suggestion of warmth, of sympathy.

Communication is expressive, reveals personality, emotion, opens one to risks—all of which he has to avoid.

Routine. This is what he needs most. Ritual. Poultice for deadly distraction. He should be happy with Aunt Paula. ("Call me Paula. Forget the aunt.") She is methodical, and if there's such a thing as functional objectivity, he needs all he can muster. Try to sleep. Rise at seven. Eat—he has to get his appetite back before he dries up. Arrive for homeroom no later than eight-fifteen. Act on instinct, on blind habit. Think less of purpose than of simply living. Better still, not think at all. He envies Leslie's and Grant's stenciled childhood.

He sits on the bed, takes a folder from the nightstand and writes out a schedule. Think about spring baseball training. The coaches have no idea he can play, outpitch anything they've seen. Help more with the yard, house, win some points. Think about Kimberly, about other girls. Stupid, he knows, but he must remind himself he is not as old as he feels. At school the halls are electrified with laughter, yells, sexual energy. Only he is isolated in his own pitiful void of loneliness. He doesn't like what he's become, hates the shield he throws up at a kind word, a casual touch.

During those months as involuntary wards of the state he would have fled had it not been for Devin. The fear, the confusion, the sense of abandonment were worse for his younger brother, he knew. "We will not be here forever," he tried to reassure Devin. "Details must be worked out. Everybody wants what's best for us."

"What's *best* for us." Devin was bewildered, afraid. "But not *us*."

"You can't expect them just to throw away their own lives. It's a big decision."

"Why did he do it, Chase? *Why?*"

"I don't know. Probably he'll plead insanity."

"Did we make him insane?"

"No, it wasn't our fault. It wasn't our fault! Never think that. We haven't been bad kids!"

He remembers times they slipped out onto the grounds somewhere, behind an outbuilding or a clump of trees, sat down and talked and talked. It was so hard to sort it all out, to believe what had happened.

"I wish I could see Mom one more time," said Devin. "Just one more time."

"I know. So do I."

"What would you say to her?"

"I don't know. That she's a good mom. That I'm sorry for the bad things I said and did. That I love her."

"She knows we love her! She knows!"

"Yes. That'll never die no matter what."

Devin began to cry softly. "You won't leave me, will you, Chase? You won't go away and leave me."

"What? No. No, of course I won't leave you."

"If you did, I think...I think I'd die, too."

They grieved and wept together.

The memories are haunting. Always he tries to force them from his mind, but they have a way of pushing themselves in.

He goes into the bathroom, examines his face in the mirror. Is the news good? Bad? Would a girl want to kiss him? Have his features hardened or are they more defenseless? He must force himself to care about clothes, review *Macbeth*, think about Mitchell's wanting them to resume therapy. Another load.

Routine. Organization. Not like his mother, rather like Aunt

Paula, more or less. A formula for survival. Replacement of thought with action. Thought is sometimes the heaviest load...

* * *

His aunt carpools the younger kids, but Mitchell usually drops him off at school on the way to work. It is a nippy, brilliant morning, a residue of frost melting from the hood of the car in pretzel-shaped patterns. The exhaust of jets five miles up draws a warped tic-tac-toe, the upper clash of heat and subfreezing air. As they turn into the school's long driveway, crawling in a line of cars expelling students, Chase catches the scents of the cafeteria, something sweet, cinnamon rolls maybe, or one of those spaghetti sauces using raisins. It stimulates vague and poignant memories of one of his mother's recipes, pot roast with raisin and tomato gravy. His appetite is urgently aroused, then almost immediately turns sour.

Mitchell says, "You know, we can get you a car, then you can drive yourself, Devin, too."

He knows his uncle is not ducking responsibility, likes these traveling moments together. Why he is not excited about driving, he can't say. Insecurity, maybe, fear of another portentous change. "Insurance is high for kids," he says. "We don't want to cause problems."

"What kind of problems?"

"Money. Room. We shouldn't be your responsibility."

"I wish you wouldn't think like that," Mitchell says.

"We just don't want to screw up another family." He knows he sounds bitter and doesn't mean to.

"You didn't screw up the first one. Is that what this is all about?

You're scared to venture out, prefer to remain in your own little hole?"

The words pepper him like bullets. Coming from Mitchell they are particularly biting. "I can start driving," he says, "if it's important to you."

"I want it to be important to you," his uncle says. "I want something to be."

He feels sorry for Mitchell, blames himself for these feelings of displacement. What does he expect? The Ingrams have offered them everything they gave their own children. Why can't he believe it's more than mere responsibility? He's lost trust in everything, in the good of people, in their sincerity. He forces himself to relax, manages a smile. "I once told Devin he has too much negative space in his head. Maybe that's my problem."

"Negative space?"

"Mom said in art it's the space left untouched, sometimes the focal point. In my head, well, you figure."

"I get it," Mitchell says. "So what do you do?"

"Change the focal point, I guess. With something exciting."

"And colorful?"

"Yeah. And colorful." They both grin.

As they reach school, he is relieved, opens the door quickly. "Thanks. I can get a ride home."

"Somebody bringing you?"

"Bryan, I think. I'll be okay." Dismissal? Maybe. Avoiding more talk? How can he want to dodge contact and intimacy while at the same time be desperate to shock himself conscious again?

Just before he jumps out of the car Mitchell says, "Hey, listen, Chase. I really think we should set up some time with Dr. Hagen. Just so you can talk."

He feels pressure sweep over him, prospects for more pointless words. "Okay, if you want to."

"I think it's a good idea."

"Okay."

He slams the door, turns, runs into Bryan Upchurch.

"I saw you coming," says Bryan. "What was that all about?"

"What?"

"Something was going on in that car."

"What makes you think so?"

"Man, the tension was purple."

He feigns a laugh. "Right. My uncle wants to know when I'm going to let him get me a car." He avoids the issue of therapy.

"Well, when are you?"

"I don't know. Why does he care?"

"Because it ain't natural for *you* not to care."

"Yeah, that's the gist of it, I think."

They enter bedlam through the double doors on the south end of the school. It is noisy—laughter, catcalls, the shuffle of feet. There are kids all up and down the hall in small cliques strung out like loose ribbons. A chemistry teacher, a man named Bernard, nudges a passage through, headed toward his homeroom. Bernard is wearing a long-sleeved shirt with sleeves turned up. He has hairy wrists and stubby fingers—the fingers of a man with no fear of volatile chemicals. Chase hasn't had him yet but looks forward to his class, perhaps next year.

Three or four boys are huddled close together, leaning slightly in toward one another—a sort of secretive circle. He wonders if they are doing drugs, has decided for himself it is a stupid false escape. A good-looking redhead brushes by him, shoulders touching—does she do this deliberately? Why? Looks up at him and smiles. Despite the hundreds of faces, the pitch of voices, he cannot dismiss the sense of incongruity. The surging throngs in the halls provide him both anonymity and a desire to belong—another contradiction. The hairstyles are wild—purple hair, tomato red hair, multi braids, Mohawks, frizzed out hair you could hide a dagger in. He wishes he could make such a personality statement, wonders if these kids aren't seeking identity just like everybody else. He wishes he could get all wrapped up in sports, music, boobs, anything. My God, he's still a kid! But something inside him is dead—well, not dead exactly, quivering and struggling for survival. He wants to yell, laugh, jostle just like they do; wants to be like Bryan without a doubt for a sparkling and exciting future. He feels so much older than he is. His grades so far average 4.0, not because he is brilliant, but because it is easier to pound his brain with facts than to expose himself to slack time.

He says, "What about Jessica? You meeting her this morning?" Jessica is Bryan's girlfriend.

"Naw. She came in early to make up a test."

"I just don't want to be the third party if she's looking for you."

"Jessica likes you, Chase."

"We hardly know each other."

"But I've told her what a neat guy you are."

"Yeah? Well, thanks."

As they weave their way through animated bodies, a boy hands Upchurch a black binder. "Here's your notebook, man. Thanks."

A girl appeals to him with her startled grey eyes. "Bryan, you're my lab partner today. Will you *please* not make me dissect that frog?"

Bryan is liked by everybody, has many friends, even teachers favor him. He and Chase are about the same build, around six feet, Bryan a bit heavier, perhaps one ninety. He keeps his hair short, combed forward, slightly impish, the color of maple syrup. His attitude is even-keeled, always friendly, he smiles a lot and even in serious discussion seldom raises his voice. Why he has chosen to befriend Chase Solomon, Chase doesn't know.

"I gotta split," says Bryan. "Teacher conference. You need a ride home?"

"You going my way?"

"One condition. We get something to eat first."

"You always make eating a condition to everything."

"Hey, man, we got to put some weight on you. Besides, I'm paying."

He watches Bryan move up the hall, deliberately bumping a few, squeezing the arms of a couple of girls. Then Chase walks to his locker where he discards the books he won't need the first two classes. Inside his locker are no pictures, no spicy magazines, nothing of a personal nature. On the interior of the door someone has scratched a crude skull and bones, but it has nothing to do with him, has been there forever. Boys drift by him, some grunt and speak. Overhead a hot water pipe thumps and rattles, a three minute bell rings. Perfect timing. He has the routine down.

* * *

As he emerges from the locker room he is surprised to see the pretty blonde who snagged his attention the first week he was here. He's never encountered Kimberly Compass in this hall before, assumes her first class is in another wing. She is standing against the wall, her arms cradling a stack of books, a sheet of paper on top. As she glances down, her hair falls over her shoulders smooth as velvet. She looks up, apparently checking room numbers, then frowns over the paper again. Her lips move faintly, forming some perplexing question. He is halted in mid step, people crash into him, step around. She is pretty enough, but it's something else that attracts him — a demeanor, or maybe merely what he has heard about her. The corridors are clearing quickly, latecomers rushing to their classes; still he cannot bring himself to move. She seems oblivious to everything. Indifferent? He wonders. Confused? In aloof control.

She says, without ever raising her eyes, "Why are you staring at me?"

It startles him. He was certain she hadn't been remotely aware of him. "I was hoping —" He gropes for an explanation, thinks of something clever but stumbles over it. "I was hoping for a compass to show me the way."

"Yeah, sure."

"You've heard that before?"

"Only about a million times."

"Sorry, I didn't mean to stare."

She raises her eyes finally, regards him coolly. "Where would it take you? This compass."

Again he doesn't expect this, blunders, "I don't know. Out of a dark forest."

This appears to interest her. She releases the book with one arm, pushes back her hair. It is thick and luxuriant, dancing with the overhead lights. "Sometimes a forest is safer."

"That has occurred to me. Still, it's not good to feel lost."

"No. Until you realize everybody else is lost, too." The bell rings, they are the only two left. Probably will be sent to the office together. Perfect. "You're new," she says.

"First year."

"I was born here, I think."

He laughs. "In this town? In this school?"

"School. It's a forest, too." She thinks a moment, evidently resolves to drop this line. "I was asked to bring some work to Mr. Bernard's room. 217. Mr. Bernard is not in 217 first period."

"Some screw up. Isn't that the way?"

"I'll find him."

"Won't matter if you're late, then. Ready-made excuse."

"Not you, though. I hate going to the office."

"Today it's worth it."

She parts her lips. Even white teeth. A smile or merely casual inquisitiveness? "My name's Kimberly. I guess you know. Kimberly Compass. How do you know?"

He feels awkward suddenly, embarrassed. "I asked about you."

"And they told you I am unpredictable, fickle and moody?"

Something has closed on him, some reminder that he can't do this, can't let himself go, charm and all. "All of the above. I said thank God she isn't normal."

She doesn't laugh exactly, just cocks her head. "So you decided to find out yourself."

"It's just that I didn't ... I've never seen you down here —"

"Oh, never mind." She suddenly thrusts the stack of books at him. "Find Mr. Bernard and give these to him, will you, Chase? You're late anyway."

As she turns to hurry away he asks, "But how did you know my name?"

Over her shoulder she says, "Because I asked about you."

73

He stares unmoving until she's halfway up the hall. He wonders if he has blown a perfect opportunity, tripped over his own feet. Not bothering to check by home room, he finds Mr. Bernard, gives him the books, and heads to the office. It'll be his second late slip so far. One more and he'll have to take some paper home to be signed. This'll delight Mitchell and Paula, he's certain. Then he feels a sudden unexpected elation. He'd give ten late slips to have this conversation with Kimberly Compass again. It's a feeling he hasn't experienced for a long time. It's nice, truly nice, even for five fleeting minutes.

* * *

As they order sandwiches, drinks, Upchurch says, "So you talked to her."

"Not talked exactly. We met."

"I'd say that's progress."

"Why? She's that hard to communicate with?"

"Like I told you, Kimberly's weird. Anyway. When's your date?"

He feels a moment of panic. "You don't understand. We met. Maybe we'll talk some time."

Bryan narrows his eyes. "Why don't you ask her out? Take a walk in the park. Bring her here for a sandwich. Good reason to get your own car."

They are sitting in Chick-fil-A, an afternoon hangout for teens. A modernistic building, half a dozen serving lines, patio tables and children's playground, wrought iron fences. The place is filling up fast. At the table next to them, four or five giggling girls pass a cell phone around, taking turns to giggle with the party on the other end. Bryan has insisted on buying their two sandwiches, fries, Coke. Chase eats slowly as though at any moment his stomach might rebel. He forces it down, trying to please Bryan.

"Next time's on me," he mumbles.

Bryan takes a hearty bite. "You know what a teacher once told me? We were in social studies, I think. She said there is danger in growing up too young. Then when you're older you tend to want to go back. And you can never go back."

"Why'd she tell you that?"

"I think I must have looked pretty morbid on a personality test. Anyway, it taught me something. Don't be in such a hurry to grow up."

"Yes, well, youth has its delusions," Chase says.

"Hey, don't forget in two years I could be a billionaire. How old do you think these computer whizzes are? Babies."

"And why are you"—Chase turns serious, too serious—"wasting time with me?"

"Who says I'm wasting time?"

"Some assume I'm from a rotten barrel."

"Nobody thinks that, Chase. You got a bum rap, man."

It is a stab in his chest. He swallows hard, thinks the lump won't go down. A few other boys like Bryan Upchurch have made an effort toward friendliness; most have shied away. When he first came here from Raleigh, he was determined to keep up a good front, pick up a new life, one of optimism. He'd been in school only a couple of weeks when there was a big field day which most of the high schools attended. He was standing alone and watching when he saw three or four boys from another school looking and then walking toward him. Instinctively he knew something was up and he stiffened, closed in upon himself as though preparing for a blow.

"Hey, dude," one of them said, "is it true your old man offed your mother?"

He held stunned, almost anesthetized. Then a furious rage whipped through him. Only by the sheer forces of will did he refrain from leaping forward, tearing the boy's eyes out. All his senses, his very nerves wanted to lash forward. Then just as suddenly the fury gave way to pathetic despair. Tears sprang into his eyes. It was as if those very tissues of outrage wanted to cry, "Please don't hurt me..."

He turned, walked away. Nothing like this has happened again, but the impression is indelible. He is the weird kid orphaned by a murderous father, a biological specimen to be studied at a sterile distance. He is afraid of his own violence, the outrage boiling close to the surface.

To Bryan Upchurch he says suddenly, "I had a good mother. Always glad to do things for people. She encouraged us to open our minds to ideas, experiences. I really don't know how the two of them—the man who used to be my father—ever came together. Maybe at first he was a challenge or something."

They have both stopped eating now. Bryan says, "Why do you think he did it?"

Chase looks down, looks up. "I've asked myself that a million times. All I can think is he wanted to be free and he didn't want it to cost him anything." He presses forward against the table. "It's hard, you know? I have his genes. I know people think that. Hate doesn't change anything. He fathered me."

"So what? You're a victim just like your Mom was. I know he's part of you, sure. Biology 101. Just because he's a loser doesn't mean you are. Plenty of great minds have risen from ashes deeper than yours."

"I guess so."

"At least you're talking now. *That's* progress for sure."

Some classmates pass their table like a platoon, yell, "Bryan! Yo!" and head for the counter. He throws up his arm. "Want more Coke?"

"No, thanks," says Chase.

"Think I'll replenish my wineskin." He goes over, stands talking to the group as they order.

Bryan is vice-president of the class, a fair ballplayer. Chase hasn't met any of his family, but figures they're pretty solid. A solid loving ordinary family. So what is he supposed to feel? Envy? Jealousy? Reassurance? Glad that Bryan has offered this friendship.

But he's terrified that Bryan will ask him home, expose him to the sweet domestic scene. Still, why is he negating his *own* home, the one Mitchell and Paula are trying to make for them? He suddenly recalibrates the scales, measures two good things — Bryan's friendship, a home environment light years ahead of half the world. A peculiar affirmation sweeps over him, a mystic source of energy. A moment of joy. The second in one day. "I asked about you," Kimberly had said. The unexpected precious sense of being floods through him like hot blood, a brief glimpse of elation, an almost forgotten friend.

At the end of the serving counter is a plumpish older woman doing paperwork. Manager, maybe, or owner. He hesitates, then with resolve goes over and stands where she has to notice him. She is checking receipts or inventory, computer readouts. Her expression is pleasant enough as she looks up. He has no reason to fear her, yet finds that he almost stutters.

"Yes, may I help you?"

"I was just wondering…are you by chance hiring?"

"We take applications, yes."

"It would have to be after school. Nights or weekends."

"We aren't open on Sundays, you know."

"Right, I forgot."

"I can give you an application if you like." She goes away a moment, comes back with a single form. "Here you are. Good luck."

"Thanks." He takes the application and walks back to the table. A job is what he needs. His own money. Taking some of the pressure off Mitchell and Paula.

Bryan returns with his Coke, they sit another ten minutes, then Bryan says, "I guess I better get going."

They wave to everybody, leave. As they pull up to the Ingrams' home, Bryan offers, "I can pick you up any morning, Chase."

"Thanks. I think Uncle Mitchell likes to bring me."

"A male bonding time, huh?"

"Something like that. See you tomorrow." He grabs his books, coat, heads into the house.

* * *

Devin and Paula are in the kitchen. Devin is making himself a snack of cheese toast, Paula is neatly arranging serving dishes on the counter. His mother used to not plan a thing, then throw something together at the last minute. He would be surprised if Paula has not known for days what the meal would be tonight. He wonders if he and Devin have changed everything from the way she had been cooking for Mitchell. If so, a good or bad thing? A breath of new life, of opportunity, or just another unexpected load? He wonders sometimes if she has decided how she feels about them. His inclination is to head straight for his room but instead he pauses in the kitchen, tells Devin, "When you're finished there be sure and clean up."

"I always do."

Not always, Chase knows. Some of the biggest fights parents and kids have involve kids leaving stuff around — clothes, empty cans, empty cups, food. He asks, "Anything I can do?"

"Not here," says Paula, "but may I ask you something? It would be helpful if you two could coordinate your use of the phone and the computer. It pretty much ties up both lines all evening."

"What's the chance of getting another line?"

"We could do that, I suppose, but isn't three lines a bit extravagant?"

"I think maybe I could pay for it," says Chase. "I'm trying to get a job."

She turns to look at him. "Why don't you just share a line and leave one for us? We didn't even have computers when we were in school."

Something tightens in his chest, some ingrained, hateful alienation. "I'm sorry to be such a nuisance."

"Did I say that, Chase? This is a question of consideration, nothing more."

He nods, turns to his brother. "We need to work on that, Devin. Consideration."

There is a moment of silence. Then coolly, Paula says, "I see no need for sarcasm."

"Neither do I. I wouldn't presume that right."

In his room he flings his books furiously onto the bed. They bounce off and scatter across the floor. *Shithead!* Why is he so angry? What Paula asks is reasonable. How can a good day, one of the best he's had, turn so unpleasant? Because he has become the all-time screw-up. Throwing up barriers, tearing down relations. If he so dislikes himself how can anyone else like him? That's the point. If they seem to, he suspects hidden agendas, wonders what he will be expected to give up.

He paces the floor, balls his fists and pounds the air as though punching his own head. Finally he sees how stupid this is, drops down at his bedroom desk. He pulls out sketchbook, pencils, begins furiously to draw Kimberly Compass as he first saw her today, head bowed, hair dropping down across her cheeks, lips pursed. Then deciding this is looking pretty good, he slows down, is more attentive to the lines, the shadows. He really doesn't know why drawing, perpetuating impressions, getting a little of himself on paper, is such a reprieve. Other kids resort to video games, skateboarding, baseball statistics. But no, he has to fall back upon something solitary, an isolated interest. Still, he thanks God for this little thing to keep him going, keep him absorbed. And somehow it brings him back to his mother and her passion, too. Maybe what he should do is get back into baseball; he remembers his old team in Raleigh where he was star pitcher...

He does not leave his room until it's time to eat. He hears Mitchell, goes in, speaks, then in the kitchen offers, "I'll set the table, Paula."

"Good." She reveals no evidence of irritation. "We'll need two hot pads."

Not much of an apology, he realizes. But a start.

6

Devin says, "He'll probably send a note to my Uncle Mitchell."

"Y'think so? Why?" his friend Will asks.

"I talked back."

"What'd you say?"

"I told him I didn't give a shit about my grades."

They are in Will's den. Will's mother, Mrs. Lasiter, has picked them up from school, invited him to come home to dinner. She is a large, outgoing woman who has encouraged this friendship. They are in sixth grade together. Will is tall, big-boned like Mrs. Lasiter. He makes straight A's, reads a lot, is interested in science. He wants someday to be an anthropologist or maybe a brain surgeon. So far Wills' is the only family that has reached out to him.

"I hate gym," Devin says. "I'm no good at sports."

"You don't have to be good. Just go through the motions."

"That two-mile run sucks."

"Maybe you have something wrong," says Will. "An iron deficiency, maybe."

"Crossbones thinks I'm not motivated." Devin has learned all the nicknames for the teachers. They call Mr. Zachery Crossbones because he can make his thumbs, elbows, and knees bend backward. "He says I don't cooperate."

"Maybe he's trying to help, Dev."

"Everything just feels so heavy. My uncle already worries about us without some stupid gym teacher complaining."

More than anything, Devin wants the big hole, the sickening emptiness in his stomach to go away. Whenever he runs out on the field or onto the gym floor, the weight is so pressing he can hardly breathe. It is strange how there can be such a painful vacuum, at the same time a burning, staggering weight. "You aren't trying, Devin," says Mr. Zackery.

"I am, too!"

"Don't you ever want to win?"

"Who cares?"

At the foster ranch they had been required to exercise daily. The older boys, those who never expected to leave until they were grown, called themselves the b-wops. Boys without parents. A half-baked stab at irony. Some were glad to be there, liberated from threatening homes, from cruel live-in boyfriends. Some prayed every day to be taken away. He shared a room with two other boys, each with a single bed, a small chest to keep a few things. He fought bitterly to be with Chase, but they would not allow eleven and sixteen-year-olds to room together. Nights were the worst times. He couldn't sleep, struggled to muffle his tears in the pillow. Seeing his brother in the morning and through the day became his only connection with sanity, with reality.

"Why are we here, Chase?" he'd asked over and over. "Why can't we go home?"

"They won't let us live by ourselves."

"Who won't? We can do it anyway. Just us. We can get jobs."

"The house will be sold, if it hasn't already. We won't be here forever, Dev, I promise you."

"Doesn't anybody want us?"

"I don't know. They can't just yank us out. Maybe there's a law against taking kids out of state."

He knew Chase was making up excuses.

Will says, "Mr. Zachery's okay, I guess. Maybe he's just trying to get you going."

"He doesn't know what it's like," Devin says.

"No, probably nobody does."

They are sitting on Will's den floor, close by a library of video games. There aren't many Devin really likes to play. They are so aggressive, some terribly violent. He and his mother used to play video games. Usually he would win, but not always. Her hands were clever and swift. She put a lot of body English into it, moving her torso as if to nudge the figure or chip over.

The last night he saw his mother, Chase was spending the night with a friend, his father working on some deal. He and his mother brought out the Rummikub. "It's more fun with four," he'd said. They played two sets, he taking one, she the other. He grew sleepy, hugged her goodnight, crawled into bed and fell into a dead sleep. During the night he developed a headache, got up, looked for his mother. Finding neither parent in the house, he assumed they'd gone out onto the patio or somewhere to talk. He took some medicine, went back to bed, too achy to think much of it. The next thing he knew his father was shaking him. "Have you seen your mother? She say anything about going out early?" It took him a moment to register. Then he was on his feet, hurrying through the house, the bedrooms, bathroom, the kitchen, the den. He ran out into the yard. His mother loved plants, gardening.

She was not there. Not until a couple of hours later did he begin to feel near panic, and telephoned Chase at his friend's house. "We can't find Mom!"

Chase came home. Nothing was missing, her car, clothes. The first thing the two of them did was look for her favorite pair of hiking shoes. They were where she always kept them.

"Where can she be!" Devin cried.

"You know how crazy she gets sometimes," his father said. "Maybe off in one of her moods."

"Not without letting us know." He ran and rode through the neighborhood yelling her name as loud as he could. At home again, he insisted, "Call the police, Daddy!"

"I can't yet. They don't even consider a person missing until she's been gone twenty-four hours."

How did his father know this?

That first night was a torment, the black days that followed a nightmare. Every day they searched frantically, stopped people on the streets, knocked on doors to show their mother's photograph. The police began their investigation, the days endless, unbearably empty. "Where is she?" Devin pleaded. "Somebody must have her!"

"Maybe." His father was dry-eyed, stoic. "We just don't know yet."

Robert seemed remote and tense, but when he spoke to the police or appealed tearfully to the public, he choked up. Once when he didn't come back all day, Chase demanded, "Where were you! Did you find her?"

"I had things to take care of."

At night Devin crept into Chase's room and hoarse with sobs, whispered, "Do you think Daddy knows where Mom is?"

"He better not!"

Then one horrible night the police rang the doorbell, told his father they wanted to speak to him alone. In his own room Devin sank to the floor, frozen with fear. A moment later, he heard Chase give a cry, followed by snatches of information...the body found...a remote deep creek...weighted down with concrete blocks...

When Chase walked into his room like a man drugged, he did not move, only drew himself into a tight ball. "They've found Mom, Devin. She's dead."

"No! No!"

Devin can hardly remember the funeral service that followed, attended by a few friends, church members, sympathetic strangers. He and Chase sat in drained silence, in a daze. They were too tormented to console one another. "Why would anyone want to hurt Mom!" Only days after the investigators began putting their case together did he remember getting up during the night, finding neither his mother or father.

Devin is struck by a pain in his leg, realizes his body is rigid as iron. On Will's floor, he pushes his legs out, stretches his toes, trying to relieve the pressure.

Will asks quietly, "What about your father? When did you find out—"

"After about a week," says Devin. "They came and told us..."

It was early evening when the doorbell rang. Both he and Chase, desperate for a reprieve, hoping it was someone bringing good news, ran to the door. "We would like to speak with your father." Devin ran to get him and saw a dark scowl on his father's face. Then he stood in shocked silence as they read the charges. "...arrest for the murder of Kelly Solomon..."

"What!" His father was outraged. "You're fucking crazy!"

"You have the right to remain silent..."

They put him in handcuffs, led him out to the car. At the last minute, one of the officers said quietly, "Sorry, fellows. Someone will come talk to you."

Pounding his forehead with his fists, Chase cried, "Damn it to hell! Damn it to hell!" Devin had seldom heard his brother curse like that.

Following these tragic days, Devin has never ceased to claw into his memory to reconstruct all that happened. That night, the last night he saw his mother, did he hear her cry out, "Don't! Don't!" Or now in torment did he just imagine it? He could not distinguish nightmare from reality. Was he there, at home, when it happened? Could he have stopped it?...

Two caseworkers from the Department of Family and Children's Services came to take them to some temporary home or shelter. Chase stopped them at the door. "We're not going any-where!" He was furious, the veins in his neck bulging, his fists tightly clenched.

"Chase, let us help you. The two of you can't remain here alone."

"We don't need your help!"

The caseworkers finally gave up, perhaps not wanting to remove them by force. As they left, Devin whispered, "Chase, what's going to happen to us?"

"They can't make us leave!"

"Will we ever see Daddy again?"

"I don't know. If we do, I'll—" He closed up, his expression hard.

Somehow, they were left alone; maybe because of some screw-up, maybe because no one cared. A day or so later their father was released on bail, and Chase flew at him, fists flailing. "Son of a bitch!" They fought savagely, Robert brutal to his son. Terrified, Devin ran to the phone, called the police. That night is utter confusion. The caseworkers coming back, yanking them out of the only home they'd ever known, insisting they'd be better off in another place, with other boys ... foster care ... their own safety ...

Unlike so many who shy away, Will says quietly, "Maybe your father didn't do it, Devin. Maybe it's all a mistake."

"He never told us he didn't do it."

"But he thinks you hate him, the fight and everything ..."

"He doesn't even try to talk to us."

"Do you want to talk to him?"

"No."

"Where is he now?"

"I don't know," Devin says. "Some lawyer called, said Daddy was sorry about hitting Chase. Said we'd be better off there, where someone could take care of us."

"Oh, sure. Strangers."

"He doesn't want to see us. Why should he? We don't mean anything to him."

"You can't know that," says Will. "Something might have just gone wrong. Maybe he went crazy ... How did it happen?"

A jolt quivers through Devin. He imagines he hears his mother cry again. "Don't! Don't!" He doesn't know if it's embedded in his memory or if it's his mind's tricky vision of what might have happened. He told the police he heard nothing, no cry, no car leaving ...

Stonily he answers, "Suffocation, they think. By the time they found her ..."

"How long?"

"Almost two weeks."

It crashes wildly through his head. Struggling to breathe. Thinking, this is the end! My boys! My boys! His father coming into his room next morning pretending to look for her. The uncertainty, the desperation. The lies.

He says, "I didn't even get to tell her—"

"What?"

He starts crying suddenly. Unexpectedly. Dammit! "That I love her…"

His chest heaves with sobs. Will doesn't move, doesn't touch him. After all this time he still can't confront it calmly. Always he breaks down, embarrasses himself. He turns away, scrubs his face on his sleeve.

Will hands him a handkerchief, asks, "What about the place you lived. Was it awful?"

He blows his nose, looks down at his hands.

"The staff was okay as long as you acted right. There were a few troublemakers. They gave us duties to keep us occupied."

"What kind of duties?"

"Mopping floors. Kitchen sometimes. Yard work. I guess it helped. It's better to stay busy."

"I'd hate it," says Will.

"What sucks is not having your own room, your own bed. And being anywhere you don't belong." He draws a deep breath, tries to control the trembling. "I guess it was okay for us to be there to have someone to talk to. Then they had to sort out where we should live." His voice throbs with confusion. After his mother was found, his father arrested, after the crushing grief, came the bitter rage, the disbelief, the unfathomable aloneness when he could not understand why someone didn't come for them. Did what his father had done make them ugly, unacceptable? He hated the excuses, the unending delays. The alibis were all the same. "Right now they can help you here better than anywhere else. Then we'll decide where you should live, work out the legal arrangements..." *Bullshit! Nobody wants us!*

He wonders if he'll ever truly belong again, if Mitchell and Paula will really want to keep them. He wonders if the terror and guilt will go away, if he'll ever grow up to be on his own. He says finally, "My aunt and uncle are okay. Especially Mitchell. They brought us here because they had to, I guess."

"Your uncle seems all right to me," says Will. "Trying."

"Yeah, I guess."

"At least you and your brother are together."

Another jolt. He thinks about this all the time. Chase could leave. He's driving now, can get his wings. Maybe he's tired of his little brother. They used to squabble, natural sibling rivalry. Now his greatest fear is not seeing Chase every day, missing this last tie to family, to some semblance of security. In foster care Chase, losing patience, exhausted, had cried, "All right, so nobody wants us! What the hell? We don't need them!"

"Don't be mad, Chase!"

"But I don't have the answers! Don't keep looking to me for answers! It's a fucked up world!"

Will says, "Thanks for telling me, Devin." He grins. "Mom says you're a nice kid." He winks. "She likes you."

For a moment the weight lifts. "You think she does?"

"I wouldn't shit you, man."

They laugh, start rummaging through the video games to see what they would like to play.

* * *

He is sitting on the bed in Chase's room. He says, "You remember that summer we went to Myrtle Beach? We rode bikes. You got stung by a man-of-war."

"I remember," says Chase.

"Dad took us out at night with big flashlights. Sometimes the sand looked—what is it called?—iridescent. Like tiny blue lights. What caused that?"

"I don't know. Someone told us but I don't remember."

"Did Dad love us then?"

"God, I don't know, Devin. I thought we were okay."

"I hardly remember Mom and Dad fighting."

"Well, they probably did."

"We went to a place where there was a guard. A gated community, I guess. Dad made up a name of some doctor we were supposed to see. He didn't know the guard had a list of all the owners. We were all laughing when we drove away."

"I'm surprised you remember. How old were you? About five, I think."

"Oh, I remember things when I was younger. Two, I guess. Or one, even." From the bed the spread has been removed, folded obediently and laid across a chair. "Mom was sick nearly every morning. She wasn't pregnant, was she?"

"No. They finally decided it was some kind of intestinal parasite or something. Took her months to get over it."

"Why didn't they have another child? Didn't they want one?"

"I don't know. Why do you ask me? I've told you I don't have the answers."

Devin knows there is a limit to the tolerance of an older

brother. He sits silent as Chase sketches something from a biology text, identifying parts and organs. He is good at it, has an eye for measurement and symmetry, makes top grades. Devin remembers his mother sketching scenes on their holidays just as Chase does now—Myrtle Beach with its grey sand and duned beaches, sea oats, sandpipers, shrimp boats with their tall rigging masts.

"Do they catch shrimp every day?" he'd asked his father.

"They go out several days at a time."

"What's it like sleeping on a boat?"

"It's hard work, I guess."

"I bet they eat lots of shrimp."

"Probably can't stand them."

His father answered dutifully, but almost always with a faraway look in his eyes as though he never found himself quite in the right place. On these holidays he dressed sloppily, baggy shorts, shirt out, sandals without socks. Once he couldn't get cell calls to go through and was about to throw the phone into the ocean. "Piece of shit! "

Kelly stopped him, the phone falling into the sand. "Now, now, Robert, remember we're on a holiday. Be sweet."

It was one of the rare times Devin was frightened by his father's rage.

He remembers lying on beach towels, digging his toes into the rough sand, the sun golden caresses on his back. His mother sat in a low, legless beach chair, her nails painted, sun visor shading her eyes, big, white-rimmed sunglasses. Chase and his father walked out waist-deep into the surf, casting, expecting to catch no fish. He tries to remember his feelings then. An ordinary family on holiday, excited about every new place to eat, about sweeping through gift shops looking for affordable treasures. His parents instructed Chase to keep an eye on him as they went up to the condo. He was too young to realize it then but he supposes now they must have gone to make love. Music came from beach chairs close by. Then later, in the last embers of day, they had a foot race when his father swept him into his arms and rushed him along, sometimes running backward, laughing, his mother and Chase speeding ahead in a dead heat.

A harsh spear of anguish pierces his chest. He wishes his brother would stop drawing and take him into his arms. What was different about them then? He reaches back, trying to find a clue, trying to understand where the spirit of carefree love went, trying to see if somehow he himself had torn his family apart. He tries not to think of his mother now. When he does he strains to remember only those good times, when he thought they were happy, when there was no hate and ugliness in their lives.

He sees that Chase's expression has changed, realizes he has aroused dreaded memories. All their lives, or at least until their mother died, his older brother had badgered him, tormented him, yet never let anybody else bully him. He hopes now that Chase won't be angry with him, wonders why he so often pushes him away. Why, he wonders, can't he be a regular eleven-year-old, hooked into computer games and Walkmans and fast food? He's tried, but everything is so heavy.

He rises suddenly and heads for his room. He has just reached the door when behind him Chase says, "Hey, wait a minute."

He pauses, does not turn, blinks hard.

"What d'you think of this?" It is his sketch, shaded, labeled, professional. Chase reaching out.

"Looks just like the one in the book," Devin says. "Why do you have to do that?"

"I don't know. I guess they think if you draw and label it'll help you remember."

"You think you'll be an artist, Chase?"

"An artist? Oh, sure. I'll paint nudes." He grins.

Devin laughs. "I'll come and watch." He feels some of the weight lift a little. Not much, some. He's grateful for this, though. Every little bit helps.

* * *

The gym class is supposed to run two miles in no more than twenty minutes. It is a measured course around the track, out onto the street, through the residential section, and back to the school grounds. Two abreast, watch the cars, keep a disciplined pace. Devin starts out in a determined burst. The scenes cruise by as in a slow-moving movie; the great oak trees, the black Lab who always stands in a yard barking, the tennis courts and pool of a condo complex, the small city park where there are picnic tables. Less than halfway, he begins to fall back. Everybody passes him, even girls forty pounds overweight. "Get the lead out, Solomon." Someone slaps him on the shoulder. He tries to resume the pace, but his legs rebel. He slows to a jog, finally drops to a walk. People swing around him, griping that he's holding up the show. "Let's get through this frigging run!" Everybody has to report back before class is dismissed.

He summons courage, runs frantically, overcomes a trailing few. Then it falls again like mercury or molten lead, seeping down into his thighs, calves, the unbearable weight that he has carried for months now. When he and Chase used to jog with their mother, he felt weightless, neutrally buoyant. Now his muscles are tight cords, a fabric of knots and bunched bruises. What has set this off? He knows well enough. Ten minutes ago in the locker room he'd overheard a conversation not intended for him. Someone is planning a big party. Everybody is invited but him and a couple of creeps. He and his weird personality. Well, what the hell does he care? He tried to force it aside, took the initial fast walk and warm-up around the track, then burst out onto the street. Will caught up, fell into stride beside him. "Got any plans this weekend, Devin?"

The first rush of draining pain fell upon him. "Yeah, sure."

"Doing what?"

"I don't know. Depends on Chase."

"You have to check with your brother, I guess."

Unexpected, unreasonable anger rushed to his face. "I don't have to check with anybody!"

"I mean, he's sorta the dad in your family now. No disrespect to your aunt and uncle."

He clamped his jaw shut, tried to draw ahead. Will stayed with him, refusing to fall behind. "I won't go either."

"What're you talking about?"

"The stupid party. Sorry about that, Devin."

"It's none of my business."

"Look, you have to understand," said Will. "This bunch has been in school together for years."

"Yeah, and I'm an outsider. Who cares?" He spoke with indifference but his chest was burning. "You'd be stupid not to go. Your friends."

"Okay, Dev, it's your call." Will ran ahead, apparently irritated. As Devin treads on he tries to fix his thoughts on his surroundings, the kind of things his mother loved. A shower of leaves rush skittering across the street. In a big wooded yard a man is raking pine straw. An ornamental iron fountain is gurgling monotonously. His mother could have sketched these; so could Chase. He attempts to put on the steam, but the full burden of loneliness crumbles down from his shoulders into his crying legs. Maybe it's this way everywhere, he thinks. The town is full of cliques, of impenetrable circles. Well, the parties are all dumb anyway.

In minutes he has fallen so far behind he can't see the others. As he turns the last corner and heads to the school he picks it up a little, jogging, hoping to keep Crossbones off his case. No chance, though, the instructor is standing at the door, arms folded, frowning. "You sick, Devin? What's the problem now?"

"I didn't feel like running."

Zachery looks at him, his voice not so cutting as expected. "Okay, we'll talk about it after class tomorrow."

Everybody has already cleared the showers. He enters the locker room, ignores one or two stragglers, strips and steps under the spray. He lets the noise and heat blast him until he's certain the last two have left. Then he towels down and dresses. Paula is picking him up, probably aggravated to see everybody leaving while he drags behind. He is putting on his shoes when he hears a couple of boys outside passing under the high window. "How the hell long is he going to use this thing with his mother to screw everybody?"

"Yeah, get over it, man, don't drag me into your hole."

"And what's with Will? What the hell he sees ..." They move on, he cannot distinguish their trailing voices.

Furiously he slams his locker shut, opens it, slams it again. The pricks! Damnit to hell forever! Crossbones, too! Who needs them! Who needs anybody? All that weight dragging you down, the load on your chest — nobody's going to help you, fuck it, nobody! Not even your brother! He yanks on his jacket, picks up his books, bag. As he steps out into the afternoon he sees that everybody is gone.

Out in the drive Paula's is the only car left. He has a moment of repentance, knowing he has kept her waiting. Common courtesy demands he make things as easy for her as possible. As he opens the door and drops in she is reading, holding the book open across the steering wheel. He expects reprimand, stony silence at best. Instead she says, "I was getting worried. Aren't you late?"

He nods. "Couldn't get a shower. Everybody took their time." It is a poor lie but how the hell is he going to admit the bitter words that run through his mind, the furiously profane.

"Your face is so red," she says. "The water must have been steaming."

Good. Let her believe it's the frigging shower, dodge the torture seething beneath the surface. He glances at her briefly, sees something in her expression that is cool, uncertain, yet struggling, trying to reach out. Mothers don't have to struggle, he thinks, only strangers, aunts. No, this isn't true. Something in him pities her burden of responsibility, something else hates it. What do they expect from him? Still, Mitchell and Paula have rescued them from foster care. Why can't he be grateful? It is like trying to resurrect his mother's face. Sometimes it is merely a blur, other times his picture of her is as crisp as the morning. His inability to feel as he wants to feel, to experience the relief of gratitude and of kindness is just another weight dragging him down, locking him in the prison of his own unhappiness. Why should anybody invite him to a party? He doesn't blame them.

As they pull into the driveway, Paula says, "We're bringing in dinner tonight. You'll be excited."

It fails to give him a lift. He mumbles, "Okay."

She glances over at him. "Okay."

He follows her in, heads straight upstairs. In his room he drops down at the small desk he uses to study, read. It is Leslie's desk, old, an antique, probably sanded and varnished and restored by Mitchell—iron legs, inkwell, pencil slot. He opens a book, circles it with his arms, leans over, shadowing the light. He sees nothing, no words, no cohesive sentences. Even the white of the pages is an unfocused blur. He looks through everything into nothing, only the pangs of emptiness. Why did his mother have to die? Why must he and Chase live in this home that is not theirs, that doesn't feel warm and familiar? When he hears Paula over the intercom say, "Come set the table for me, will you, Devin?" an unexpected resentment sweeps over him, hammers him harder into the desk.

As a small child he had hidden by tightening himself, legs, arms, neck, fists, into a small ball. Still as a monolith. Sometimes it worked, people actually seemed not to notice him. An inanimate, molten sculpture. He does this now, certain everyone will understand they must leave him be.

"Devin?"

He blurts, "Why can't Chase do it?

"Chase isn't here. They're on the way."

He jerks himself up from the desk, stalks down into the kitchen. He opens and closes cabinet doors with emphasis, an exclamation of denial. Wordlessly he arranges the table as Paula moves briskly behind him. It is a small enough contribution, he knows, yet his nerves are strung tight, his emotions jerky. He hates the feelings that come over him.

Paula says, "You all right, Devin? You're awfully quiet."

"I'm okay."

"How was school? Anything earth shattering happen?"

"Nothing happened. The same dumb stuff."

She laughs. "Well, enjoy it while you can. It'll be over all too soon."

Mitchell and Chase arrive, discussing current issues—the tsunami devastation in Asia, the war on terrorism, the incomprehensible national debt, financial issues Mitchell deals with every day. Devin sees that Chase's interest is more courteous than intrigued. As Mitchell gives Paula a kiss, Devin turns away, knowing this display of affection is at least in part supposed to communicate something to their nephews, something which at this moment strikes him as exaggerated and false.

"Hey, look, Dev," says Mitchell, "filets from Outback. What do you think?"

"Okay."

"Okay? I thought you'd be excited."

"Yes, so did I," says Paula.

"Well, *I'm* excited," gulps Chase.

He is uncertain about this good humor from his uncle. Is it forced, contrived—natural? He feels he is supposed to respond in some way. Paula says, "We'll serve our plates here. Buffet style." She arranges the dishes on the island, removes the steaks from the Styrofoam containers and heats them briefly in the microwave.

"We'll divide these," she says.

"Why can't I have one of my own," says Devin.

"Because we're sharing. None of us ever eats a whole steak."

"I can."

"You think you can," says Mitchell gently. "But I'm pretty sure half of one of these will be plenty."

"I don't think so."

"Now don't be so negative, Devin," says Paula. "Remember last time you didn't even eat half."

"This isn't last time."

"Devin," says Chase, "don't talk to your aunt like that."

"How am I supposed to talk to her?"

"You must have had a bad day," says Mitchell.

"Yeah, a frigging bad day."

"Devin," Chase says.

"Oh, leave me alone!"

They all fall silent, this soggy blanket dampening everything.

Morosely, he spoons food onto his plate, potato casserole, hot rolls, passing on the steamed broccoli. Paula says, "Have some broccoli, too, please, Devin."

"I don't like it."

"You'll learn to like it."

"Why should I learn to like something I don't like?"

"Because it's good for you."

"You eat it then."

She turns to him, her expression cold. "I don't know what's wrong with you, Devin. You've had this mood all afternoon. But no matter how bad you feel I insist you remain civil."

"Paula," says Mitchell.

"No, I'm right in this. We all have horrid days. That doesn't give us the right to take it out on those we live with."

"I'm not taking anything out on anybody!" Devin spits.

"Oh, but you are. We thought this would be a nice treat for us all but you just can't be pleased tonight."

"Did I ask you to please me?" He tries to control his voice but it quivers, rises. "Is this what I'm here for? To show you how much you please me?"

"You're a spoiled smart aleck, Devin!" says Chase.

"Oh, what's it to you! You're not the boss of me!"

"I think everybody's said enough." Mitchell sets down his fork, trying to take control. "Eat what you want, Devin. Forget the broccoli."

"I don't want anything!"

"Don't eat, then," says Chase. "You don't deserve it anyway!"

He slams the plate down on the counter. It shatters, steak and potatoes splattering onto the floor. He suffers an instant of horrid regret, then jumps up and runs from the room. Up the stairs, into his bedroom, smashing the door shut. Behind him is startled, black silence. He flings himself onto the bed, the tears he has fought all afternoon blinding, uncontrollable. He buries his face in the covers, determined that they won't hear, won't pity him, won't know how miserable he is. There is a complex twisting in his breast. He wants them to stay the hell away, he wants someone to touch him. He turns to his side, draws his knees up to his chest, scrunches his head down. Defensive, hidden. Pitifully guarded. He is almost twelve years old. Why is he crying like a child?

The door opens. Chase says, "What the hell's wrong with you, Devin?"

"Nothing! Leave me alone!"

"I guess you want to get us thrown out of here."

"Not you. Me! You never say anything wrong! "

"Yeah, sure. You get nowhere acting like a jerk."

"You don't know anything, Chase! Go away!"

"Okay. I hope you have a good night's sleep."

Chase's sarcasm stings bitterly as the door slams shut. Devin pulls his body tighter, making himself a bunched knot. The house is soundless. There are no voices, no rattles from the kitchen. The room is dark, illuminated only by a weak nightlight under the desk. He remembers battles he'd had with his mother at age five, seven, passionate confrontations over small issues. Always she let him suffer a while, then came and put her arms around him. No one comes now. There is no one to come. The house is distant and silent. No one to dry his tears.

* * *

Paula and Mitchell are finishing the cleanup when he says, "He's just miserable."

"I know."

"He didn't mean any of this."

"I know that, too," says Paula. "Overall, though, I think things are getting better."

"Do you?"

"Yes. We're having a few good days."

Long ago, with their own children, they had learned that a space of silence is advisable. An outburst, a fit of anger, the heartbreak of a lost friend all require a moment of self-healing. She has heard Chase enter Devin's room, waits until the door opens, closes again. She says, "I'll see what I can do."

She leaves Mitchell, goes up to Devin's room, taps on the door and enters. He is on the bed, curled up, his eyes closed. "Devin?"

He starts, jumps up and stands. "Yes, ma'am?"

She is touched by how soft and defenseless the simple words are. It tugs her heart. He feels so scathed, she knows, so unbearable. "Devin, I don't want you to worry about tonight."

"I broke your dishes," he murmurs.

"It doesn't matter at all. I did that once."

"You did?"

"I was so upset I threw a vase. It broke and shattered all over the carpet."

"What made you do it?"

"A fight with my parents. I don't remember what it was about. What I do remember is they made me spend an hour picking the pieces out of the carpet."

"I didn't know you'd ever do anything like that, Aunt Paula."

"Oh, yes. Sometimes I still want to throw things."

"You do?"

"What you have to try to figure out, is why you feel that way. And maybe try to replace those bad thoughts with good ones. It's hard work but it's the only solution I can think of."

"Even having bad thoughts doesn't excuse doing bad things," he says. "Like breaking your dishes."

"Probably not, but this is something we must work on. You. Me. Actually, I think it's sometimes better to throw things than keep them buried inside."

"You do?"

"As long as you're careful with your aim."

He smiles faintly. "Like a wall, not a head."

"Something like that. Sometimes life's hard, I would never tell you it isn't. But I guess it makes more sense to do the best we can with it than to hate it."

His voice becomes husky, as though he is about to tear up again. "I don't want to be a problem for you. I don't want to be here because I have to."

She feels the struggle in her own breast. She doesn't wish

to lie to him. It would be a lie to deny that she's terrified of this starting over, of trying to bring along someone else's children, of growing old without realizing some of her heart's precious passions. Resolutely, she says, "You're here because we want you here, Devin. We brought you here."

"You didn't have to"

"No, we didn't."

So in a way she does lie. It is the only way she can remain loyal to her husband. She says, "What's done is done. We'll all try to forget it. I don't want you grieving over this."

He does not speak for a moment. She sees the muscles in his neck tense. "I don't want to get mad. I never want to get mad. I'm afraid it'll make me do bad things."

She knows he is thinking of his father. This occurs to her, too, and it frightens her. Robert's genes. His violence. "I think it's a good idea to control one's temper," she says. "But stop worrying so much, Devin."

"You aren't mad at me then?"

"No. Let's forget it, okay?"

"Will you tell Chase that you're okay with me?"

"I do believe Chase knows already."

She reaches, squeezes his hand, then walks back down to the den where Mitchell is waiting. She says, "If Robert killed Kelly no punishment will ever justify what he did to those boys. Do you think it's possible he didn't do it?"

"I don't think so. Neither do the boys."

"I guess if he didn't, if he cared for Kelly or his sons, he would never have let them go like this. What do you think happened, Mitchell?"

"Maybe Robert and Kelly had a big fight. That's unlikely.

Devin would have heard. Maybe Kelly told him she was leaving him after all these years. It could have been another woman, money...That's the one thing I'd like from Robert. Why."

"I just cannot imagine a more terrifying, painful death," she murmurs. "To have your breath choked off...maybe to look into your killer's eyes, or know he is a man you loved. I just hope it wasn't that way. I hope he came from behind, she blacked out before she realized..."

"Yes, maybe it was something like that. Kelly would have fought, there would've been bruises, scratches. The police didn't find anything. Or if they did, they aren't revealing it yet. I just hope we can spare Chase and Devin the trial..."

"So do I." She leans back, looks into his eyes. "We mustn't forget one thing, Mitchell. We can't live in the past. To survive, we have to put this behind. Somehow we must show them how to look ahead."

"We're products of our past, though," he says. "Only emotional rebirth is going to help them, if they let it."

"Maybe they will. Kids have been through worse things, witnessed worse things, and grown into decent young men and women." She presses her forehead against his arm. "Devin will be all right, I think."

"Good. What about you?" he says.

She sighs deeply, rubs her forehead. "I just wish we'd had a year or two before this, Mitchell. Just a year or two to work things out."

"Work what out?"

"Our future. You. Me. Us. I want us to enjoy our late life together."

He stands, puts his arms around her. "Me, too. I'm sorry."

"But I know that's wrong. We should be glad we're here for them. What if we weren't?"

"I don't know. God takes care of the blind bird, I guess."

She draws away, stands with her head bowed. "Tonight happens to be a moment of courage, Mitchell. But I cannot promise you I'll have it tomorrow or the next day, or the next." She sees the frown forming between his eyes, yet he merely nods. "I just hope nothing worse than tonight happens."

7

In his own room Chase drives himself down onto his bed like a pis-
ton—not sitting, not lying, rigidly planted. Stupid kid, he thinks,
but he knows this is wrong. Devin is neither stupid nor is he normally confrontational. So what had gone wrong? The so-called
nice domestic evening, grilled steaks, the four of them together, a
family affair. All engineered, arranged. Then suddenly everything
twisted. Paula disgusted, Mitchell disappointed, pulled in ten di-
rections. Devin bitter and miserable. What happens, exactly to
cause such explosions? A tiny fuse, burning brighter as it travels
along the wire of unhappiness, of depression, anxiety, then an
emotion-rattling blast. The fuse this time is Devin, lashing out in
his grief, reacting to some black moment with anger.

No, he is not stupid, Chase knows. He is really a pretty sharp
kid, older than his years but still reaching back to being a child
again. Why does God invent kid brothers for the older to take
care of? Who know not how to care for themselves? At home
he had from time to time snatched Devin from the jaws of danger—just before he poured gas into a lawnmower five feet away
from an open fire, just before he started to ride his bike down
an impossible rocky incline. His kid brother who was almost

recklessly adventurous like their mother. But he, Chase, was not equipped for parenting, for the cultivation of hope, of attitude. Exactly what is demanded of him? He did not bring Devin into this world. He feels tired, dragged out.

He turns on the television, surfs the channels looking for something arresting. He realizes how little of this crap relates to real life. He wonders if there is anybody in entertainment who gives a damn about people caring for one another.

He clicks off the set and goes to the window. There is plenty he should do but he can't settle down. He feels cold air pressing on the panes, puffs of cold seeping in around the window. He wishes it would snow, but this is unlikely in the Chattahoochee Valley. Why is he drifting like this? He feels an urgent need to press forward, to get his life organized, yet one little slip, one ordinary evening gone wrong reminds him just how little one can guard against chance.

Once in Raleigh when it snowed, their mother grabbed TV trays and rushed them down to the school where there was a steep hill. They sledded for hours, spinning, tumbling. Devin got hurt, his nose bled, making bright crimson streaks in the snow. Chase felt sorry for him, trying so hard to be brave, trying not to spoil the afternoon. Little Dev who needed his mother so much. A father. A brother.

With a sudden stab of pity, he jumps up and walks down the hall, taps on Devin's door. His brother is lying on the bed, knees drawn up, the fetal position. Return to the womb. It seems wrong, a boy this age dodging the blows, abandoned, mixed up. Quietly he says, "Devin." There is a confused stirring. He sees the wetness of the bed covers beneath his cheek. "You awake, Dev?"

"What? No."

"Come on, you have to get your homework. Shower, get ready for bed."

"No. Just let me sleep." Nevertheless he sits up, swings his legs to the floor.

"Need any help? Homework?"

"I can do it," Devin says.

"Well, look." Chase sits down beside him. "Sorry about tonight. What was the matter?"

"Nothing. Something happened at school."

"Want to tell me about it?"

"No."

"Okay."

"They don't like me, that's all. They think I'm a weirdo or something."

"I know how that feels, Devin. There's not much you can do except be yourself."

"It's not as if I bother them or anything."

"I know. But Will's your friend. I think you're lucky if you have one friend in the world."

They sit silent a moment, then Chase says, "I'll try to do better by you, Dev. It's all such a damn struggle, you know? I guess I get wrapped up in myself."

"Everybody does. You're not supposed to take care of me."

"Who says?"

"I just make it harder on you. Mitchell and Paula, too."

"Remember, though, they brought us here. We should never belittle that."

Devin looks down at his feet. "I'm sorry I've been a jerk, Chase. Tell Paula for me, will you?"

"Why don't you tell her?"

"She won't understand."

"Why shouldn't she? They've raised two kids, you know."

"Maybe theirs were perfect."

He laughs. "I doubt that seriously."

"Besides, I don't want all this stuff they give to make us happy."

"What do you want?"

Devin holds still a long moment. Then he begins to tremble. He presses his chin down into his chest and begins to cry. "I want...I want my mom to hold me."

Chase does not move. Tears begin to flow down his own cheeks. Soundlessly, burning his eyes, his lips. Quietly he slips over and puts his arms around his little brother. Devin drops his head onto his shoulder. He smells his hair, his bones feel fragile, pitifully vulnerable. They sit huddled together, their tears becoming one. Only when he is back in his own room and hears Paula going in to see Devin is he reassured they are not alone.

* * *

Chase has been through counseling before. Maybe it helps a little, but overall talk is cheap. Waiting for Mitchell, he spends half an hour out on the practice field watching the track team practice. They look okay, were a pretty good relay team; he considers himself no judge. His game is baseball, but so far hasn't convinced himself to go out for spring training. On the edge of the field is a clot of girls half watching, mostly chatting. Girlfriends of the runners, he imagines. He wishes he had the audacity to walk right up to them. 'Hey, look, notice me.' Ridiculous. Who does he think of? Cool Dude Chase. Yeah.

He sees his uncle coming, walks out to the driveway, gets into the car. They talk en route. Mostly questions, answers. Mitchell drops him off, says, "I'll see you in about an hour."

"Right. Okay. Five o'clock or so."

Chase gets out, heads up the walkway. The building is multi-winged, with a tapered spire, round stained glass windows, and lawns and shrubbery. He enters, crosses a large reception area and approaches the information desk. A dark-haired young lady looks up, smiles. "May I help you?"

He introduces himself. "I have an appointment with Dr. Hagen."

"Oh, sure. I'll let Marsha know you're here."

As she speaks on an intercom phone, he drops down into a chair. Why he is here, he doesn't know—to appease Uncle Mitchell who evidently believes another counselor might have a different slant. He's skeptical, has been through all this months ago. In a few minutes a door opens and a smiling young woman standing very erect asks him into her office. "I'm Marsha, Dr. Hagen's administrative assistant. He'll be right out. Would you like something to drink? Coke? Coffee?"

"No, thanks."

"Have a seat. He's off the phone now." She pushes a button, speaks, and the pastor opens the door between the two offices. Chase knows him, has heard him speak most Sundays for the past several months, but he looks different. No coat, open collared shirt of an electric green color, tan trousers, tan loafers. His hair is bushy on the sides, his cheeks clean-shaven, fingernails clean and bluntly cut. He looks like a man who would be just as comfortable with a fishing rod as with lecturing a thousand congregants.

"Hello, Chase, George Hagen. Come on in."

They shake hands, Chase follows him into his office and

Hagen closes the door. It is a long room with desk and credenza at one end, sofa, coffee table and chairs at the other. The walls are warm mauve, the paintings bright and colorful, bursting with life. Chase suddenly remembers once when his mother submitted a watercolor painting for consideration for a hospital's new cancer ward. It was a peaceful scene of a marsh, dawn breaking, leafless swamp trees. The decorator turned it down flat. "Never," he said, "would you place paintings of dead trees in a cancer unit."

His mother was not rebuffed, took it good naturedly. "Live and learn. I see his point. Everything should be quiet and peaceful."

Chase thinks, something that works all through life, when the nonverbal says everything. He notices a trophy on a shelf in the bookcase, a baseball glove and ball cast in bronze.

Dr. Hagen says, "Our team won that last year. They presented it to me."

"Nice."

"You a baseball fan? What do you think of our Atlanta Braves?"

"They've got some good pitchers."

"That what you do? Pitch?"

"It's been a while."

Hagen motions him to a chair. "Why don't you sit here, Chase? So how are things going?"

Chase slips into the chair but does not lean back, does not feel caged exactly, pushed, maybe. "My uncle wanted me to come. He means well, but I don't see the point in it."

"Maybe he'd just like us to get to know one another."

"Busy as you are, I doubt that you need another client."

Hagen laughs. "Don't worry about that. I think Mitchell just hopes you can open up a little."

"I've been to therapy before. Not with preachers, though."

"Forget that I'm a pastor. I counsel with people who don't believe in God at all."

"And they end up converted?" Chase makes a stab at irony.

"Not necessarily. Your world view is yours, Chase, not mine. How long were you in the home?"

"Four or five months. I don't care to talk about myself."

"Okay, why don't you tell me about your brother, then? How do you two get along?"

"Okay. Devin's a kid."

"I guess you sort of have to carry his load, too."

His chest tightens, his throat goes dry. "He leans on me for answers. I don't know how to help him."

"What is it he asks of you?"

"He wants to know why our father offed our mother. How this could have happened to us. If we are to blame."

"Do you think you're to blame?"

"I don't know. Not in the sense that we were bad kids."

"In what sense, then?"

"Maybe just being there. Consuming space. Demanding time. Getting in the way."

Hagen stretches out his legs, looks at him obliquely. "How exactly have you reached this conclusion?"

"I don't say it's a conclusion. Devin wants answers I can't give him. I don't think he'll ever have them."

"Perhaps you're right. Sometimes people do things that cannot be explained."

"I'm tired of feeling responsible for him."

"Maybe all you really need is to be there."

"Forever?"

"No, not forever, Chase. Two years can make a big difference to a boy that age." Dr. Hagen relaxes in his chair, big hands folded loosely. "Tell me, what is your general view of life?"

"Huh? What kind of question is that?"

"By now you've developed a world view, whether you think of it that way or not. How do you see your relations with others?"

"I don't know. I had a few friends back in Raleigh. I don't have any here."

"Not even one?"

"Yeah, one maybe. I don't know why he bothers."

"Because you're a rotten failure?"

"Because I'm the kid whose mother was strangled to death by his father—the weirdo everyone stares at."

"Why do you think they're staring?"

"Maybe they're wondering what kind of kid it is whose father is a murderer. Am I like him? Am I dangerous?"

"Are you dangerous?"

"I'm not sure. Sometimes the anger ..."

"The anger is so intense you want to lash out. Why don't you? Lash out?"

"Because the last thing I want is to be like him. I'm *not* like him. But part of me is, maybe the part—"

Hagen looks at him with patient eyes. "I don't think you can ever use background or environment to justify brutal behavior. That's a cop out. You make that choice. You. Nobody else."

"Yeah, I get that. Tell it to the kids at school."

"The ones staring at you? Do you think you imagine that? Do you think it's because you're a good-looking, cool guy?"

"God, I don't know. What are friends for anyway, except to ditch you when things get rough?"

"Is that what they did in Raleigh? Ditched you?"

"Not a single one visited or called the ranch we were in."

"Maybe they didn't know what to say. Think about it, Chase. What if that had happened to one of your friends? What would *you* have said?"

"I don't know. Something."

"Sometimes people want to reach out but don't know how. Your uncle's your friend, isn't he? Your aunt?"

"I guess. Mostly they feel responsible for us."

"Oh, I see. It's not that they like you very much, they just had to invite you to come live with them."

Chase shakes his head, looks at his hands, looks at his feet. "Mitchell and Paula are good people. Too good for us, I guess."

"What does that mean? Too good for you?"

"They've got it all together, you know? A nice loving couple. No major traumas."

"That is, as far as you can tell."

"They're religious. I'm not sure we believe that stuff."

"What do you believe?"

He feels pressed suddenly, faintly badgered. "I'll think about that and write it down."

Hagen is not rebuffed. His eyes are bright, optimistic. "You know, that may be a very good idea. Write down just what you do believe. Meanwhile, take a shot at giving me your overall view."

Chase shifts nervously in his chair again. It's not the pastor, though. The guy seems okay. How can he explain that everything he thought he believed in has been torn out by the roots?

"Some days I want to like people, I want them to like me. Other days this life doesn't mean sh—this life doesn't mean any-thing. Everything we see and hear is a big lie."

"A lot of what you see and hear *is* a big lie. One of our inherent gifts is to choose what we believe. What we believe in."

"What if we choose wrong?"

"Well, then you try to right your course. I don't think it's ever too late."

"Yeah, but that takes caring. It takes energy."

"How much energy do you think is required to hold in all those black feelings?"

The question catches him by surprise. "God, I don't know. Some things you can't help."

"I notice you refer to God quite a bit. Does that mean you realize there *is* a God?"

He ducks his head down. "It's a habit, I guess. Not a very good one."

"I see. Well, tell me how you feel about your uncle and aunt."

Another stab of suspicion. A cute way to bait someone. He says, "Mitchell's okay. He worries about us."

"What about Paula? Doesn't she worry about you?"

"I think maybe she's a little jealous."

"You mean of Mitchell. The time he devotes to you."

"Something like that. I don't blame her. We pretty much interrupted their lives."

"And she's making a Big Sacrifice, is that it?"

"I think there are a lot of things she doesn't like. For example..."

"What?"

"Him spending the money on me coming to see you."

"I don't charge for counseling, Chase."

He feels as if his jaw drops open. Nobody does anything for nothing. He fidgets, pulls his feet together to rise.

"That doesn't mean you have to leave. It's one of *my* choices."

Chase swallows, manages a grin. He came in here tense, resentful, now he's beginning to let some little thing go, seep out of his joints, his tissues. "One of those God things, I guess."

"Hey, you know that might be right. We can talk about what we believe and don't believe next time if you want to."

"Next time?"

"I hope you'll come back to see me."

"I don't know about taking so much of your time."

"I'm glad when I can help someone a little, Chase. We've scratched the surface today, don't you think? We wouldn't want that to go to waste."

"No, sir."

"Okay. Marsha will work with you to set another time if you like."

They stand, shake hands. Dr. Hagen walks him to the door, opens it for him. "See you soon. Take care."

Chase breathes a sigh of relief as he exits the double doors and steps out into the open air. The hardest part is over, he thinks. First session, blundering awkwardness. He'd assumed it would be the one and only session, a single concession to Uncle Mitchell. Now he isn't so certain. Hagen has surprised him. Not stuffy, not pushy, loose. Maybe he'll come again. Maybe he'll even talk Devin into coming.

As he moves down the walkway past the wrought-iron fountain, a mid-age couple come by, speak pleasantly. A group of teenagers holding books and papers move aside onto the edge of grass. One of the girls glances up, smiles as he passes. Not threatening. Not threatened by him. Willing to acknowledge that they, after all, are all pretty much alike.

* * *

After school, Bryan Upchurch drives him to the library. "Hey, buddy, I can come back. No problem."

"Thanks," says Chase. "Mitchell's picking me up on his way home."

"Okay, see you tomorrow."

He walks up the steps, the glass double door swings open, automatically triggered by an electric eye. Technology at work, making life easier. The library is hushed, though there are a number of people in every department, especially in research. He has a sense of irony. Upon these august shelves are the most depraved and the most eloquent thoughts of man, theory, ideas, conspiracies, confessions, political outrage, philosophical reason, religious persuasion. He wonders how one word, one paragraph can shape his or any individual's life, how all this knowledge is so blatantly defeated by chance.

As he looks down from the window a young couple ambles along, crosses the bridge, stops to kiss. An expression of love. He turns away, not wanting to invade their privacy, waiting for the clutch of aloneness to come. But it doesn't come; instead there is a second of intrigue, warmth. His heart smiles. Something new like a warm breeze. He allows it to flood over him, unquestioning, a sweet self-awareness he has all but forgotten.

As he enters the reference department, his scoping glance homes in almost at once on a girl standing on a stool, reaching up, trying to dislodge a book crammed tight into the shelf. It is Kimberly Compass. She is wearing a skirt, a light sweater, a pale green shirt. She has kicked off her shoes, stretching up on her toes. Painted nails, nice calves, curved hips. A startling, unexpected *whack!* slams through him. It is unnerving but also pleasant, a sensual springhead crying, *I am alive!* He thinks, *Yes!* At the same time he feels awkward, inept, starts to turn away. She has caught her tongue between her teeth, straining upward. Clumsy as he feels, he cannot allow this. He hurries over, touches her on the arm. "Let me do it."

"Okay, thanks." She drops down from the stool, lands on her toes with a slight bounce like a dance step. He takes the stool, dislodges the book and brings it down. *Index to English.* Hardly required reading. As he hands it to her she says, "The advantage of height. You're what? Six feet?"

"About."

"I'm trying to win an argument with my English teacher. When *none* is plural and when it is singular."

"Good luck. Why bother?"

"I think I'm right. I want to prove it."

"What if you miss?"

"Then I need to know." She smiles impishly. "It is *so* important whether you say none was or none *were*."

He smiles. "Yeah, I guess it means the world." His hands feel wet, sticky. She has ceased to smile and looks into his eyes soberly, unblinking. Waiting. Her lips are closed, shaped like a gull's wings. A year ago he had bantered with girls unselfconsciously. Now he feels juvenile, idiotic. He says, "You going to check it out?" It is a stupid question. He knows books can't leave the reference department.

"Can't. I'll find what I want, though, before I leave."

"Well, ah, I'll be somewhere. To put it back for you."

"All right. Thanks, Chase."

Again the faintest of smiles. Chase. Whoever said he had

such a sweet name? It is moist, husky, a whisper. Chase. He feels silly, stupid. Still, any new feeling or any old feeling rekindled is welcome. Anything to drive a chink in the hardened shell of resistance.

"Excuse me." Someone nudges between them, looking for a book on the same shelf. Kimberly fades off to a table, starts digging through the text. Head down, hair haloing her face, slender arms circular as a basket hoop. She has given over a little of herself to be nice to him, yet there is something pensive about her, too, tentative. Is this what draws him to her, two emotional cripples seeking one-kindness? Once you get used to it is it more comfortable to be *un*comfortable?

He finds his own reference books, settles down at a table where he can keep an eye on her. It is hard to concentrate. Pen remains poised over paper, sentences blur. His glance catches a man behind a counter, a library personnel, perhaps a volunteer, an ex-schoolteacher who assists patrons in the reference department. He has shaggy, grey hair, abrupt gestures. He gestures impatiently at a teenage boy who has evidently asked a frustrating question. His mouth turns down at the corners. It reminds Chase of his father. Once his father had been playing golf with a regular foursome when something happened to make him furious. He slammed a club against a tree; it broke, and the head struck him a vicious blow to the mouth, bursting his lips. For a week he was a rage to live with. One by one his golf partners withdrew, formed a new foursome—unwilling, evidently, to tolerate another outburst of rage. He hopes he and Devin will not have to face their father again, won't have to testify at a trial. Maybe someday, he will be able to look him in the eye, ask, "Why did you do it? At least give us that!"

He glances up at the man again. At the counter now the teenager has disappeared and a young woman is asking something. The man smiles, jumps up and goes to help her as if she has made his moment. The difference is night and day. His father must have been a little like that, charm sugar coating dangerous undercurrents. And women—did he kill Kelly so he could chase women, have affairs, escape the expensive process of divorce? How can any man physically abuse a woman he makes love to?

He forces the thoughts aside, looks over at Kimberly again, and is struck with disappointment. She is talking to a football jock who has easily replaced the book for her. He turns his eyes down, shading his face. What does he expect? He blows it every time. Why is he stuck in one place? He'd like to put his head on a pillow and rest. He'd like the sick dissatisfaction to go away. He'd like to believe he has some sort of purpose in life.

He remembers a brief, sketchy discussion with his mother when he was about thirteen. Sex is the most intimate of human experiences, she said. Yet night after night she slept with a man who snatched her life away. Rioting as his own libido is, it frightens him to think of getting that close, of using someone, hurting someone. What's going on here? His sexual desires are raging tortuously. Back home he pretty much had his choice of girlfriends. Two, three in a single year. He enjoyed the kissing, the petting. Some girls were looser than others. Sometimes if you pretended to really care for them, love them, they would allow things to please you. But he hated the lies. It was so false to use a girl's emotions without feeling something. And he cannot open his heart to feeling ever again. What is it he fears? Rejection, aloneness, loss of stability, loss of order. And hurting someone else.

A voice says, "I'm leaving now, Chase."

He starts, looks up to find her standing beside him. He scrambles to his feet, blunders, "Sure. Right. Look, I would…"

"You would what?"

"I don't know. Ask if you want to go for a burger or something. Except—"

"Except what?"

"I don't have a car."

"I have a car, Chase." She does not smile. She peers right into his face, her eyes steady, cool.

"Then would you consider—"

"Why don't we?"

He slides his chair under the table, then returns the reference books to the shelves. He joins her and they walk out together.

* * *

They settle on Dinglewood, just up the hill, another after-school hangout. It is a balmy December afternoon, sweater weather, mild temperatures, a light southeastern breeze. As they speed up Wynn's Hill a car passes, horn tooting, occupants waving. Friends of Kimberly's. On good days she is liked, on bad ones people shy away from her. He knows from experience and from observation. She has a pretty profile, long lashes. The only reason she is not swamped by boys has to be these inner forces which nudge them away. Standing at the counter, she orders a hot dog. "Hold the onions, please. Lots of ketchup." Polite but firm.

They get a booth, sip their diet cokes. "So you don't drive," she says.

"I do drive, just don't have my own wheels, and I'm not crazy about asking my aunt and uncle for theirs."

"Wouldn't they get you a car?"

"Yeah, I don't want to expect too much."

She takes the straw into her mouth, holding the cup in both hands. Her lips form a cupid's bow. Her fingernails are opalescent burgundy, lip gloss matching. She says, "Is it hard living with relatives? Being yourself?"

"I guess so. Depends on which self you are at any given moment."

"I know what you mean. There are countless ones, aren't there? I'd hate to try for good conduct every day."

"Probably it's not so hard for you."

"I'm sure you know better. I can be a witch. But I'm pretty certain I won't get thrown out." There is a change in her expression. "I'm sorry. That wasn't a very thoughtful thing to say."

"It's okay."

"What I mean is sometimes the hardest thing in the world is to act civil when you feel a terror. I don't even know why I'm wretched."

"You aren't wretched now?"

She smiles, her lower lip curving out a little. "No, not now."

The hotdogs arrive, other high schoolers come in, a couple with two small children, a mid-aged woman picking up a prescription. For decades, this pharmacy has been known for its soda fountain, chili dogs, home delivery. It is one of the first traditional gathering holes to which he was introduced when arriving from Raleigh. He goes over, grabs a bag of potato chips, shares them. As she eats, her motions are deliberate, experimental.

"I'm glad you and Bryan have become friends," she says. "He's a cool guy."

"Bryan's popular," says Chase. "Like you."

"I bet if you asked he'd tell you he can count his true friends on one hand. And what about girls? I hardly ever see you talking to girls."

It surprises him. He looks up suspiciously. "I'm feeling my way," he murmurs.

"To what? Liking them? Avoiding them?"

"Avoid getting carried away."

"Just as I thought. You're afraid of getting hurt. Or hurting someone."

"Something like that."

"You know, if you gave them half a chance, girls would be all over you."

He laughs. "Oh, yes, I'd have to drive them away."

"You're intelligent, serious and good-looking. Do you realize how handsome you are?"

"I've never been impressed with my looks," he says.

"Then stop being hard on yourself. Any girl would find you attractive."

"And what about you? You got a little whip in that purse?"

"I think boys are afraid of me," she says.

"Because they can't conceive of making it with such a knock-out."

"Because sometimes I go for days not even wanting to speak to anybody. Or love anybody."

"Why? What causes it?"

"Who knows? Medication helps a while, then doesn't. Sometimes in the morning I feel great, then by noon can't stand myself or anybody else. I'm not bipolar, though."

"Bryan tells me you were in a bad accident once."

"Yes."

"What happened?"

She cocks her head to one side. "I was with my cousin. She was just seventeen. I don't remember much about it. We ran off the road, there was a steep incline and the next thing I knew a big tree was coming at me."

"Was she hurt?"

"We were both fortunate. The car was totaled. She had a broken arm. I had a concussion, a bad cut on my forehead. After the tree the next thing I remember is waking up in the hospital."

"Do you think the concussion..."

"Has something to do with my mood swings? Maybe. I don't think I was so weird before that. Maybe I was. I could have been killed. I should feel very grateful."

"You have nice parents, don't you?"

"It's not my home life," she says.

"Home life is so damn important, but most kids don't get that."

"What happened to your parents?"

It jolts him. He is not expecting this. His inclination is to avoid the issue, but she has been so straightforward with him. He stops eating, can't take another bite. All the tables have filled now, there is a bustle all about. A group of girls and boys barge in squealing—happy freedom, after school. He hardens himself, lets something iron-like slowly arm him like a shield. His voice is remote, not quite his own. "One night my mother was there then she wasn't. They found her two weeks later."

"But what did your father *say*?"

"For about two weeks he pretended to search as hard as anyone, kept insisting she'd come back. Pretended to be crazy worried. He'd tied weights and thrown her into a deep creek. Some fishermen found her."

She gasps. "Chase, I...I..." Tears spring into her eyes suddenly, "I'm sorry."

"It's all right. I've been through it a thousand times. It took them just days to charge him."

"But why? *Why?*

"I don't know."

"Did he want somebody else? Why didn't he just walk away?"

"That's a question I've asked myself a thousand times. Why didn't he just leave? I guess he couldn't stand alimony and child support."

"But how could he have done that? I mean,..." She blinks hard, pressing a closed knuckle to her eyes. "Maybe he just went crazy—thinking about himself."

"Yeah, I guess so."

"How do you get over something like that?"

He looks at her but feels disoriented. It's really the same line as with Dr. Hagen but somehow with Kimberly things become clearer to him. "You struggle to figure out what you did," he says, "or could have done. The therapists call it the rotten kid syndrome."

"You blame yourself?"

"Same thing happens in divorces, I guess. The kids just thrash themselves. It's harder on my little brother."

"But you've decided not to blame yourself, haven't you? That isn't the problem, is it?"

He narrows his eyes. "What would you say is the problem?"

"Whether or not you can be loved again. Whether you'd just invite more heartache."

"Something like that, I guess. People try to heal you with things. Words, gifts. These help but what you really want is to believe in yourself. Everybody strives to be different, but you don't want to be a weird specimen."

As she gazes at him a strange thing happens in her eyes. First there is tender sympathy, then a stoic resolve, driving distance between them. It is as if she decides she cannot let herself be touched—her own defense mechanism, he suspects. Her tone becomes firm, objective. "I'm sorry for what happened to your mother, Chase. I hope you'll be okay."

It has the sound of hopeless dismissal. He feels rebuffed. He feels something give way, sag in his chest. There is a moment of awkward silence. He wants to recapture the sense of painful intimacy, but his own emotional fatigue hammers down, drives a wider distance between them. For months he's guarded against exposing even a small portion of his emotions. Now he doesn't know what he is most afraid of, losing this beautiful thing he's almost touched or driving another wedge into his own heart. He asks, "Will you run me back to the library? My uncle's picking me up there."

"Of course."

She grabs her purse, they walk out and drive down the hill together. He wants to say something, hang onto the moment. As he gets out of the car he says lamely, "You coming in?"

She shakes her head. "I have to go home."

"Well, look." He gropes, almost panicky. "Would you like to get together sometime? I mean for a date?"

"A date? A real date?"

He exhales heavily. "Well, sort of. We could just fake it at first."

She smiles. "Except I think my parents would insist that my date pick me up."

"I will. This is motivation."

"You'll get a car?"

"Theirs or my own."

"Then call me. Or see me in school. I'll try to get you my schedule."

"I know your schedule," he says. "By heart."

She smiles again. "All right. Thanks for the talk, Chase, and the food. See you soon."

He stands aside as she drives off, hoping he has not let something slip away.

8

Several times Mitchell telephones the Raleigh district attorney's office to inquire about the Solomon case. What he would really like is to grab Robert by the neck, demand some answers. Why did you do this? Was it insurance, another woman? Just tell us—why!

"We have enough evidence that the grand jury has indicted Robert," the DA says. "Trial date hasn't been set."

"You think the sons will have to testify?"

"Probably not but we don't know yet."

Mitchell has hoped this can be avoided. What could the boys tell them? What they need now is to put this horror in their lives behind. He does not mention his calls to Chase and Devin.

Each morning after the nephews are dropped off, he arrives at the office for a regular meeting with his partners. Lowry Shields, the senior partner, is a former bank president with many irons in the fire. He is a tall, slim, erect man with distinguished grey hair and piercing green eyes. He participates in all kinds of civic projects, political issues, charitable functions. W. G. Rhymes is about five years Mitchell's senior, a former Georgia Bulldog, who looks back on the early days of sports with affection but some disdain for the place to which it has ascended. He views the management of money as an intriguing game. "It's in my blood," he laughs, "from childhood ventures into Monopoly."

Following this regular morning session, W. G. walks Mitchell to his office. "Your heart doing okay now? You seem to be getting back to normal."

"I'd say eighty percent," says Mitchell.

"You sounded a bit distracted today."

"Did I? I don't feel distracted."

"Any problems with your clients? Something I can do to help?"

"No, the business is fine."

"How are things at home? The boys disrupting everything?"

"No, home is fine, too."

As they pause at Mitchell's door, W. G. says, "I swear, the older I get the less I care about the old passions, you know? I used to canoe, golf, hike. Wouldn't it be nice to get excited about something?"

"Decide to and maybe it'll happen."

"Anyway, I'm not just talking about this morning. It just seems to me you've been a little out of it lately."

"I don't mean to be."

"I know you had to give the nephews a home. But why can't you just let them sort of freewheel? They're old enough."

"We give them every liberty. We never tried to straightjacket our own children."

"What I'm talking about is straightjacketing yourselves. Back off. You can't undo what happened."

Uncomfortable, Mitchell says, "I don't want those boys falling through the cracks, W. G. They could, you know. Why should they believe in anything?"

"How about Paula? She as involved as you? This her life now?"

"I didn't say it's my life." He suspects W. G. has picked up on something. "They're boys. Naturally, the relationship isn't going to be the same."

"Okay. None of my business, I guess. I just know sometimes when a mother or a relative comes to live with you it can play havoc. Remember, in just a few years they'll be off to school or whatever. Then it's just you and Paula again."

"I understand, W. G. Thanks for your concern."

"Okay. Paula knows you best, I guess. If anybody knows anybody. They learn to love us for our frailties, I'm told. It just seems to me if you're going to live the rest of your lives together..."

"So now you're a marriage counselor."

W. G. laughs nervously. "No, but I'm about five years older than you, that makes me wiser, doesn't it? I don't always practice what I preach, but after all the year's ups and downs, my wife and I finally see that it pretty much comes down to just the two of us."

"Is this something you're supposed to tell me?"

"Hell, no. I haven't talked to anybody. I've known you a long time, Mitchell. A few years back, my marriage nearly fell apart. I just want what's best for you."

"Well, I'm listening to your advice."

"Take a trip. Time's your most valuable asset."

The secretaries are arriving, bringing doughnuts, heading for the breakroom to make coffee. Mitchell has always admired his partner for looking at the bright side of things.

W. G. reminds him a little of Kelly. She always made the best of everything, at least during all her young adulthood. Once when they were at the beach, he in his teens, Kelly preteen and more adventuresome, she insisted that they go up on a parasail with a tandem seat. He reluctantly agreed, but once they were airborne he was sorry. Height was not his passion. He felt himself turning pale, the blood draining from his face, torso, legs, toes. He clamped his lips shut. As Kelly cried, "Wheee! Open your eyes, Mitchell, look at the beach! I think I see Dad!" she shook him by the arm. "Don't you dare throw up on me!"

Finally it was over, they floated down, made a smooth landing. Excitement burst from her, exhilaration lingering on her cheeks. "Wow! I hope we can do that again!"

Slowly he got his legs back. "Not me. Once is enough."

"Oh, just to be a seagull for one day!" Such experiences whetted her adventuresome spirit, her quest for life. Was it possible that her boys would ever be able to grasp their mother's joy?

* * *

Paula understands how determined Mitchell is to get Chase his own wheels and finally Chase agrees. He chooses an F-150 pickup and when they set a day to bring it home, Mitchell says, "We should do something special, don't you think? This can be an advanced seventeenth birthday present."

"I don't know that he wants to make so much of it," says Paula.

"Why not? It's a rite of passage."

She is uncertain but proceeds with a candlelit dinner, best china, silver, even encourages Chase to invite a friend. "You can share this if you like. What about Bryan Upchurch?"

"No, it's all right," he says. "You don't have to do this, you know."

"We want to, and why not? I can't imagine not having a car of my own. It's a human right," she laughs.

At dinner, Devin is the most animated. His brother driving

may be the next best thing to his own freedom — the two of them without adults.

As they finish the meal she nods and Mitchell tosses over a ring with two keys, one for each of their cars, his and hers. "Now we have three vehicles, you get to choose."

"I don't know..." Chase hesitates.

"This is the van, this the Volvo," Mitchell says.

Paula speaks lightly. "It seems funny to me, I see more kids driving pickups."

"Yeah, it's the trend." Chase inspects the keys as if they are strange insects, appears to be holding his eagerness in check. He grins. "If my date doesn't like my truck she can find another stud."

"I remember when Grant and Leslie got their first car we couldn't hold them back," Mitchell says. "Always wanting to flit somewhere. This'll be a help to us."

"Sure, I can go places for you. But I need to buy my own gas. I'm looking for a job."

Paula begins to clear the table, bringing strawberry shortcake dessert. "We don't mind helping you, Chase."

He nods, seems eager to get this over. "I'll pass on dessert if it's all right. Think I might christen my new wheels."

"Go ahead." They follow him to the door, stand watching him back out. Paula has no doubt Chase will be a good driver, hopefully won't speed like a madman. Still, all through the celebration dinner she's sensed a reluctance, a kind of shadow pressing down against any little aspect of happiness.

They return to the table, talk to Devin a while, then when they are alone, Mitchell says, "His own transportation. I was hoping it'd be a big thing."

"A car isn't the problem," she says.

"What *is* the problem?"

"I wish I understood. Maybe they feel so obligated to us we suffocate them. Maybe they're just frightened to experience *anything*. Maybe they feel guilty, because they lived and their mother didn't."

"You mean they can't let happiness take the place of guilt."

"I'm just wondering," she says. "But, Mitchell, there always seems to be such an air of tension. What happened to their parents—they can't hold that against us."

"Why would you say such a thing?"

"Because I know there is only so much we can do for them, and they know this. I feel so sorry for them, but I'm afraid we have a long hard road ahead."

Mitchell remains silent a few minutes. "But you do think he was excited, don't you? Getting his truck and all?"

"Yes, I think he was excited," she says. "But don't ever expect people to respond exactly as you'd like. Usually you'll be disappointed."

* * *

One afternoon Dr. Hagen calls, says, "What do you think of my stopping by to see you and the boys?"

"I think it would be okay," says Paula. "We just don't want to hit them over the head."

"I know. Been there, done that. Why don't you ask their permission first? Chase is a fine young man, and I'd like to meet Devin."

"I'd like you to. I'll ask. Thank you."

She is still thinking about it a couple of days later after retrieving mail from their post box. She is in the den, perplexed, peering at an envelope, when Mitchell arrives home from the office. She gives him a long look and then hands him the envelope. "Look at this."

It is addressed to Chase and Devin Solomon, in care of the Ingrams. In the upper left corner is the name Robert Solomon, no return address.

"It's from their father," she says.

"Why, after all these months ..."

"You tell me. I'm just wondering if we should give it to them."

As he muses over the envelope, she thinks of how loud and boisterous Robert was, yet how scrunched up and stiff his handwriting. A sudden thought occurs to Paula. Kelly was always so sure of herself, so inquisitive and bold. Perhaps in time she overshadowed Robert; perhaps he found some nondescript woman who fed his ego, made him feel strong. It is a question to which they may never have an answer. Mitchell says, "I guess we don't have a choice. It's their mail."

"You think maybe you should read it first?"

He is uncertain. "Guess I better not."

"You know I would never suggest reading anyone's mail. It's just that I'm afraid of how it might affect them. Maybe he just enclosed a few dollars and said nothing at all."

She takes the letter and places it against the base of a lamp where they leave mail. "If we could get all this uncertainty behind. Why it takes so long to bring a case to trial."

She waits as he goes up, finds the boys in their rooms, the omnipresent music playing, brings them down to the den. Mitchell points to the envelope. "That appears to be a letter from your father. You can open and read it or, if you wish, I can read it first. Paula and I want what's best for you."

The tension is palpable. It springs into the room like something alive. Chase's lips are thin, his handsome face clouds against a fierce assault of rage and bitterness. Devin stands motionless, shoulders, arms, fists tightened into a rigid wall of defense. They cannot forgive Robert for what he has done, yet he is their father. If there is one thing Robert could do, one thing he could say that would relieve their pain, they would cling to his words. But they are held by dread.

Chase says finally, "You read it, Uncle Mitchell."

"Are you sure? Devin?"

Devin nods.

Paula stands silent as her husband opens the envelope. Inside are two notes, both in the cramped script, both on identical white unlined paper. He hands them to her. The first says simply: "Mitchell and Paula. I hope you are ok with the boys. They're good kids. I would send money if I could. They're better off with you. I know you will help them forget me." She reads the note once, twice, passes it to Chase. To the nephew he says, "This one is to us. You can read it." She waits as Chase and Devin read together, then toss it onto the table.

As she reads the second letter, she is overwhelmed with disgust. She raises her eyes to look at the boys. They are tense, silent, inscrutable. Aloud she reads: "Chase and Devin, I hope you are ok. Mitchell and Paula will take good care of you. I know you don't want ever to see me again. My lawyer tells me it is better not to say anything. Maybe someday you won't hate me. I'm sorry for everything."

She tries to pass the letter to Chase, but he refuses to take it, even to look at it. Remotely, like a man drugged, he mutters, "That's all he has to say to us."

There is an impenetrable wall of silence. It would be better if someone screamed. Finally Paula says, "If it makes you feel better, remember this. He has nothing but misery to look forward to."

Chase says through tight lips, "He can burn in hell!"

Mitchell asks, "Do you really feel that way, Chase? You have to look for closure on this. Maybe someday you'll be able to make peace with him."

Devin looks as if he could die. His face is deathly pale, the pall of disappointment so overwhelming he could be sick. He fixes his eyes on his brother and remains silent, lost, confused. Chase says coldly, "Okay, so he wrote us. I hope that clears his conscience." He turns, walks out and Devin follows.

Paula says, "Why do you think Robert bothered to do this? How could he possibly think it would help?"

"I guess he thought it would help *him*. I have an idea he doesn't realize what hell his life is going to be."

She hesitates, and then says, "I'm going up to see Devin. If only we could help them, know what to do."

Paula goes up, taps on the door, walks in. Devin is sitting at the desk staring at the floor, his face an inscrutable mask. She stands silently a moment. "Devin, Dr. Hagen called, asking to drop by and see us."

"What's the point?"

"I don't know. Just talk. Maybe we can help each other see things more clearly. Isn't it worth a try?"

"He's just an old church man."

"I think he's more than that. Counselors witness all parts of life."

"I didn't know doctors make house calls."

She smiles. "This kind does."

For a time there is silence. When Devin answers, there is no resonance in his tone, only dully anesthetized resolve. "If you say so."

* * *

Paula arranges for Hagen to come in the afternoon when Chase isn't there. She knows younger brothers will usually defer to the older and hopes one-on-one will encourage Devin to open up. She says, "It's all right to talk about what's happened, Devin. It's all right to cry, too. This man understands crying."

"He'll think I'm a baby."

"No, you think that. This is not about anything you have or haven't done."

Hagen arrives, the men shake hands, decide to walk through the house out onto the patio. It is a crisp, stimulating Georgia fall day when the sky doesn't know whether to portend winter or spring. Paula sits down with them a moment then says, "I'll bring something to drink. I make great tea." She leaves them alone and goes inside.

Hagen says, "Isn't it nice out here? I've been cooped up all day."

"Uncle Mitchell says we could use some rain."

"He's right. We're beginning to get the fall pollen and rain always helps."

Devin notices that Dr. Hagen keeps his feet flat on the floor. His posture is relaxed as though he hasn't anything in the world to do.

"How are things going, Devin? How's school? Your teachers?"

"School's okay," he says. "They're all about the same, I guess. I do have trouble with one thing."

"What's that?"

"Phys-ed. I can't get into it. Crossbones thinks I'm just lazy."

"Crossbones?"

"I'm sorry." He feels his face flush. "Mr. Zachery. I didn't give him that name."

Hagen laughs. "Oh, don't think we didn't have nicknames for our teachers. One was Arrowhead. She heard me call her that once and made me write, 'I shall never refer to Miss Singleton as Arrowhead again' two hundred times. I think it took about three hours."

"Did you ever call her that again?"

"Probably. But the next year we got along pretty well. Miss Singleton and my mother became friends and she occasionally visited our home."

Devin smiles, begins to feel a little looser.

"Tell me about *your* mother," says Hagen. "What was she like?"

He looks at an acorn spear on the patio at his feet. It has the shape of a flower. He says, "I wish I'd never said mean things to her. Once I told her I hated her. I wish I could take that back."

"Every child says stuff like that at one time or another."

"What made me do it? I can't even remember what I was mad about. There must be something really hateful in me."

"I have an idea, Devin," says Hagen. "Why don't you see if you can replace thinking about that with something like a time you were kind to her."

Devin digs his fingers into the chair arms, tenses his thighs. He's been through this before. "Once when she was really sick I took care of her, brought her soup and stuff. I read to her, too."

"Okay. Doesn't it make you feel better to think about things like that?"

"I guess so."

"You've heard this before. We can't change things, and we really can't forget them. What we can do is replace bad thoughts with good ones."

"I've tried that with my daddy. It doesn't work."

"Why do you think it doesn't?"

"Because all I can remember is how he must have hated us!" The piercing regret comes so unexpectedly, it is a sharp pain in his head—a thought, a memory so hurtful he cries out, "I wonder why he didn't kill us too!" Then without warning tears gush forth like water. He hates this, wishes he didn't have to go through it again. It is the last thing he wants, he'd been determined not to let it get him this time. He struggles to hold it back.

Dr. Hagen says, "You think that's what you deserve, Devin? If you are hated you should not live?"

"I don't know!"

"How do you even know it was hate? People lose their grasp on reality sometimes. How does that equal you and your brother causing things to happen?"

"He had to hate us to take our mother away!"

"Okay, let's say for some distorted reason he ceased to love you. That means you're the guilty one?"

"I don't know!"

"I'll tell you something I've discovered," says Hagen. "Sometimes when we're hurt or sad or depressed we blame ourselves, make ourselves the villain. You think this is rational? Does that really explain anything?"

He feels as if his throat will burst. Gropingly he says, "I just want to understand…"

Hagen's expression is calm, uncensoring. "Tell me about some things your mother and father did together. Did they take walks? Go on trips?"

Devin tries to relax, let out the tension, remembers some good things. "He taught us to ride bikes, skate. I thought we were a good family ..." Suddenly something turns loose, crashes down, something vile and repugnant long held back. "I hate him! He should be dead too! He ... he choked her! My mother! He put her in a river!" He buries his face in his hands, feels himself about to be sick. He opens his mouth, gulps air.

Dr. Hagen does not speak.

After a while Devin sits back exhausted. When he opens his eyes there is a handkerchief in his lap. He wipes his cheeks, his eyes. "I'm sorry ..."

"There is nothing to be sorry for."

"It's all a lie anyway. I don't want him dead. I want ... I want ..."

"What?"

"I want what he did to stop hurting so much!"

Hagen leans forward, looks at him with compelling clear eyes. "Devin, you're a smart young man. You've learned too much about life too soon. I want to give you something to think about."

"Okay."

"Everybody who's ever been born has one mother and one father, right? No more. And in this country we're free to think, to act, to feel. Are you with me?"

He nods.

"But every day we are affected by what we see and hear. I think we might view life outside our circumstances, but it takes work. Nothing in the world can calm the emptiness you feel, but I think you have an inner strength that can take you beyond circumstances."

Devin says grimly, "All the prayers in the world won't make these feelings go away."

"Maybe not, but you're alive. You laugh and you cry. You can feel rotten and still have hope."

"I guess I don't know how, then."

"Well, don't expect it all to come at once. As long as we look for happiness in conditions, we're not likely to find it. Everything in life doesn't tickle."

Devin turns in his chair, looks away. He hears the words but they are not getting through to him. The man has learned to say all the right things. It is not even his brain that betrays him, he can think all day about this mysterious inner strength—it is the uncontrollable despair in the pit of his stomach. He is relieved when Paula comes out with the tea. Hagen gestures and she sits with them, talk about the yard, sports, the weather. He is relieved that it is time for Hagen to leave.

The pastor says gently, "You want to talk again sometime, Devin?"

Something in him reaches out, something drops away. "I don't think it helps," he mutters.

"Maybe given time, some of what we've said will sink in. There are people around who love you."

"I know. I'll try. Thanks."

He watches Paula walk Hagen back through the house. When she returns, he is still sitting glumly on the patio. He notices her inquiring look, her hopeful expression. She is doing her best, he knows; she and Mitchell are offering everything they can. He wants to stop feeling sorry for himself. He thinks Dr. Hagen has helped Chase, but he just doesn't know—perhaps it is harder for him to let things out.

When Paula asks, "Would you like something to eat, Devin?" he shakes his head.

But then he sits up straighter, looks down, looks up. "I still have Dr. Hagen's hanky."

"I don't think he'll mind," she says.

"I guess maybe I could eat something, Aunt Paula."

"Okay, I'll bring it out here and you can keep soaking up the sun. It'll start getting cold soon."

9

Bryan Upchurch says, "Hey, you missed a spot."

"I did not miss a spot. It's just running off." Nevertheless Chase doubles back with his soapy towel. They are washing vehicles in Bryan's driveway. It is another mild, warm Chattahoochee Valley afternoon. Everywhere people are hurrying to the parks, cycling, jogging. The sky is cerulean blue with pinkish cotton clouds. The trees, still shedding their southern fall leaves, throw down shade like patchy ground covers.

Bryan drives a four-wheel-drive Toyota pickup, and they have agreed to vacuum and wash together. The strikingly beautiful Saturday afternoon floods through Chase's bones, his tissues. He cannot explain, but feels ineffably buoyant. It is such a precious feeling, he must constrain his impulse to run, to shout. They get the routine down quickly, one with bucket and towels, brushes, the other hosing off. They have both taken off shoes, socks. The sudsy water collects between their toes, bubbles under their feet.

"Now you have your wheels," says Bryan, "you gonna really start dating?"

Chase doesn't answer, feigns serious contemplation.

"Come on, it ain't natural not to chase girls." Bryan flips the spray with his wrist, the drops are a brief shock on Chase's neck, arms, quickly dissipating. "Chase," says Bryan. "What a misnomer."

"Not necessarily. Depends on the quarry. You know most animals won't expend energy pursuing prey that's unattainable?"

"And what about prey just waiting to be taken?"

"I guess I don't know any like that."

"Maybe you need a Compass to show you the way," says Bryan.

"Bad joke, I'm told."

"She's heard that?"

"Uh-huh. A million times, she says,"

"What else does she say? About you? About me?"

"She says...she says I'm good looking."

"God, the girl ain't got no taste." Bryan flicks him again with the hose, he returns with a spray of suds. "Actually, on a scale of one to ten I'd say you rate about a nine. But what do boys know about boys?"

"Apparently a lot, in our culture. You? Let me think. I don't believe she mentioned you at all."

Bryan feigns a heart attack, staggers against the car. "I can't believe it! Bury me with an apple."

"Why an apple?"

"I don't know. It just sounds appropriate."

"Now that you're dead, I do remember she said you're a nice guy. One of the few."

"Yeah, yeah. Sounds like you covered adequate ground over a hotdog. What about a real date?"

"I don't know," says Chase. "I mentioned it to her."

"And she said?"

"She didn't turn me off."

"Listen, chum, a dozen boys have missed with Kimberly

Compass. This thing with her crazy moods, and all that. My advice is to strike while the iron's hot."

"Why Kimberly?"

"Why? Because she's a girl of mystery. And you have the hots for her."

Chase is soaping the front, meticulously running his cloth into the fluted grille. Gravely, he says, "Kimberly deserves not to be hurt. In any way."

"You're afraid you'll break her heart?"

"You never know about the chemistry. You involve someone, then something happens and…well, somebody suffers. I can't let that happen."

"Look." Bryan becomes serious. "Pain is a possibility, but you're over-thinking things. Won't hurt to try one date at least."

"I can't take a chance on getting involved. Especially with Kimberly."

"Who *would* you choose if you decided to get involved?"

"Kimberly."

Bryan laughs, "Maybe she's the reason you're here. Maybe she's your purpose?"

"My purpose?"

"We all have a purpose, don't you know that?"

"Was my father's purpose to murder my mother?" He does not mean to say this. It just tumbles out, stark interruption to lightweight discussion. Still, it is something to think about. *Does life have a purpose? Is it possible monsters are created to ravish the defenseless? Or is everything really circumstantial, evil minds and harsh nature?* He thinks about this, decides to drop it. "What about the guys Kimberly's turned off?"

"Ah," says Bryan, "you *are* snagged. I don't know. They come and go. One in particular is a dude named Gene Holbrook. You know him?"

"Maybe. Passing in the hall."

"Loud mouth. Rioting hormones. We call him Snatch. You figure why."

"And Kimberly? She likes?"

"He makes her laugh. Something she needs, I think. But she keeps her distance. If he gets too close she backs away."

"Just wondered. Probably I couldn't make her laugh."

"Probably you could. You know what I think? Our parents haven't taught us kids how to laugh at ourselves."

"Well, you're a good-natured level-headed boy," Chase says patronizingly. "What does your girlfriend Jessica say about *you*?"

"Jessica says I'm a good-natured level-headed boy." Another swish of the cold flecks, droplets join the sweat on Chase's t-shirt, brow. "We've known each other a long time. Enjoy talking, doing things together. Agreed to keep it pretty casual. At least she has. Casual means wait and see. Drives me nuts sometimes."

They finish washing and start drying, working together. "My dad never dried," says Bryan. "But if you don't, you tend to have little spots." They use large old towels, take long strokes, see their blurred pudgy reflections in the shine. There is a pleasant clean small of water and suds, dampened concrete, runoff into the grass along the edges of the driveway. One of the car doors is open, from the player comes the voice of Nick Lachey. The sun has warmed the water beneath their wet feet, they slosh through the little puddles, sanding their pads on the scratchy concrete. Bryan says, "This here truck looks A-OK. Ain't you pleased?"

"I guess. Now I can maybe run errands for them, try to earn some points."

"Driving gives you a positive advantage."

"I hope it'll make things better for Devin, too."

"Yeah, it's shitty being a kid without a mother."

"How would you know?"

"I'll tell you. I did volunteer work one summer for the boys' ranch—maybe one like you went to. Thought it'd look good on my resume. College. Let me ask you." Upchurch pauses, towel in hand, looks at him steadily. "Is it worse to have your mother wasted or walk off and leave you?"

The question is too logical, too academic. "I don't know," says Chase.

"I think the latter. But maybe they end up hating the mother, and that's protection. What they learn, though, is you don't have to be blood to be loved. I was impressed."

"With Devin, I've been scared," says Chase. "What if he gets to depend on me too much? I don't know if I can handle it. But I think, hey, this is my job. My little brother. Maybe the one good thing I can do is keep him from utter destruction."

"Right. But not your only job."

"It's tough sometimes. How am I supposed to do that when half the time I don't even know myself?"

"I guess you concentrate on how much he depends on you."

"It's weird. I guess everybody wants to be needed, but being needed can be a load. I guess—" He sweeps the towel vigorously, the muscles in his arms flexing. "I guess that's why friends are hard right now. Especially girls."

"You don't have to defend yourself with me," Bryan says. "I just want to see you loosen up a little. We try to work with what we have."

Chase leans down deep, drying the sides, hiding his face.

He remembers the really hard times, the times he was not even sure he wanted to live. The time in the farm he stuck pins in his feet, hoping physical pain would mitigate the inner despair. Bryan would never understand this, the unbearable torture of grief, of aloneness. He knows all over the world kids are seeing their families blown to pieces, mostly in the name of some insane cause. He carries this burden, too. Yet this is the kind of day his mother lived for, a day when she would have kicked off her shoes, grabbed them by the arms, and run barefoot in the grass. He suddenly feels his youth renewed, feels the vital impulse of hope. He hopes it'll last.

They finish the washing, roll in the hose, pick up cloths, buckets. "Man, I'm hungry," says Bryan. "What about a grilled cheese?"

"Sure, okay."

"Coffee?"

"Yeah, I like coffee. I sorta got hooked on double mocha lattes."

"No kidding?"

"Back in Raleigh a lot of kids went to Starbucks every afternoon."

"Well, I ain't promising you no Starbucks."

"And I ain't promising you no tip, either."

They go into the house, shoeless, wet, feeling accomplished. Glad of spirit.

* * *

He enters Barnes and Noble and searches the aisles for Kimberly. He finds her standing between two high banks of shelves, a book cradled in her arms, her hip thrown slightly out. Her look is thoughtful, even perplexed. After a moment, she returns the book to the shelf and moves to another aisle. He decides to hang back. She does not appear to be looking for anything in particular. She reaches up, chooses a book at random, flips over into the middle and begins reading. Now her expression is lighter; there appears to be a faint smile on her lips. Evidently feeling his presence, she looks up suddenly. "Chase! Hi! How long have you been here?"

"I've followed you all over the store."

"You haven't! Why would you?"

"Just to see what you'd do."

She lowers her lashes at him. "Like that first day in the hall at school. You were spellbound, I assume."

"That's exactly the word. Spellbound."

She returns the book to the shelf, folds her arms across her chest. "One day I spent six hours in this store just by myself."

"What are you looking for?"

"Nothing. Anything. Sometimes I just choose books at random and read a few pages. It'll make you cry one moment, laugh the next. It can be fascinating."

"Sounds pretty disjointed to me."

"Yes, it is! Like life!"

They walk together toward the sandwich shop. He says, "I've never been good at amusing myself."

"Oh, as a child I learned to play alone. Have you ever played the telephone game?"

"I don't think so."

"Come, I'll show you."

She leads him over to one of the sales desks, asks the young man, "May I borrow your telephone book a second."

"Sure."

She takes the book, moves to one side, and flips to the yellow pages. "What you do is read opposite headings and see what you get. Like Computers/Concrete." She turns the pages rapidly. "Furniture/Garbage." She thrusts the book on him. "Now you."

"Aw," he says.

"No, go ahead."

He flips the yellow pages, grins. "Prosthetic/Publishers."

"There, you see! Isn't this *great* fun!"

She speaks enthusiastically, but there are no dancing lights in her eyes. He feels instinctively this is not a good Saturday for her. She is trying to keep up a front. He is disappointed, had hoped this would be a great time for them to get together.

He asks, "What would you like to eat? Drink?"

"Do you think I could have chai tea?"

"Most definitely."

They get a table and as she slips in across from him, he notices her hands. Slender fingers, dimpled knuckles, pretty nails painted with red. He has an urge to take her hands, wants them to touch him. It is a dumb idea, he knows, a premature move which would probably drive a wedge between them. She is wearing a white shirt, black pants with a wide belt—a sharp-looking outfit.

She says, "Aren't you glad now that you're driving?"

"It has its advantages."

"I got my license the day I turned sixteen. I could hardly wait." She tilts her head, closes her lips around the straw. It makes a pretty evocative O. Her lowered lashes are dark, curled, her nose slender, nicely symmetrical. He marvels at how good-looking she is, yet how few boys have been determined enough to pursue her.

She says, "Tell me about your friends back home, Chase. Was it traumatic pulling up roots and leaving?"

"Yeah, I guess so. Everything comes apart. It's amazing how

so-called friends scatter after the initial shock. Probably it was better to wipe that slate clean."

"Still, you remember how it was. Favorite places. Favorite people. Familiarity is a kind of security, I think."

"Yes."

"Sometimes I want to just fly away from everything. Other times, it terrifies me to think of things changing."

"I guess it's that way with everybody."

"Is there any one special person you'd like to see? Talk to? A girl maybe?"

He remembers those months in foster care. There were girls in a different dorm, one in particular whose name was Alicia. A pretty girl, dark hair, scintillating blue eyes. Her parents had split, her mother had become hooked on drugs, lost all grasp on reality. He always wondered secretly if his father had been on drugs, if that was why he did it. But the cops never said so. He and Alicia used to talk, about movies, school, their old lives, making friends...no commitments, nothing threatening between them. Still, away from her he thought of her running through the rain, of her wet clothes clinging to her chest, her whimsical, sad smile. Then one day she was gone. Vanished. No farewells, no apologetic goodbyes. Just gone, like his mother. He missed Alicia, had not realized how her absence would tug at his heart. Another of those small cruel infractions which instructed him not to feel, not to open himself...

He does not like this conversation, decides to change direction, asks, "You sing, don't you?"

"Yes," says Kimberly. "Why don't you join the choral group? You have a sweet tenor voice."

He forces a grin. "Thanks. I'm not ready for that. I like music, though. It's an escape."

"My father encourages me to sing. I think when they hear me singing it keeps them from worrying so much."

"About you?"

"About the moods I get in. One day deliriously happy, the next so wretched I could die. And nothing happening to cause the difference."

"I know the feeling."

"Do you?"

He feels slightly rebuffed. Why does she think she has an edge on suffering? He says, "Well, probably not so deeply as you."

The faintest apology darts across her eyes. "I didn't mean it that way." She smiles. "I think I've lost some of my communication skills."

"It's okay."

"I don't think I was so moody before the accident. Just don't ever have a concussion."

"What about your father?" he asks. "You talk a lot?"

"Oh, I guess so. I definitely realize I'm fortunate to have both parents."

"Yes? Why?"

"What you get from your dad is different from what you get from your mom. I have to tell you, though, some days I'm frightened of ever losing them, others I think if I could only get away…"

"I think every kid feels like that." He grins. "It's the hormones."

"Exactly! How well you understand me!" Her eyes are bright, beautiful, yet the fire is missing. He knows she feels as tentative as he. From the sandwich shop come the scents of coffee, cinnamon, pastries. At a table across from them is a young couple talking earnestly, some serious development scrolled across their

152

faces. The boy tries to take the girl's hand, she jerks away. Chase feels sympathy for him, sensitive to rejection. When he focuses on Kimberly again he finds her looking steadily at him. Waiting. The first time is always so hard. He asks, "What do you want for Christmas?"

"Oh, I want to be happy."

Of course. Who doesn't?

She says, "And I want you happy."

"Okay. That's a pretty general ambition."

"Well, at least it would be nice to hear a few pleasant things. Tell me one role model that makes us think life is fulfilling." Suddenly she pushes her glass away, sits up straighter. "I'm sorry. I'm not much fun today, Chase. It's my fault. Are you sorry we came?"

He smiles. "No, I'm glad we came. It's just that I'm not good at this."

She reaches across the table and draws his hand to her. A shock of thrill shimmers through him. Her eyes kindle and her pretty mouth softens. "Let's do something. Skating, bowling, a movie. Maybe we can talk then."

He jumps up, relieved, helps with her chair. "You make the call. Anything's fine with me."

"Anything?"

"Long as I'm with you."

She smiles brightly. "You do know the right things to say."

* * *

There are about eight screens, two of which are showing the same movie, different times. At the box office, he asks, "Which one?"

Kimberly shrugs. "I've heard *Dead End* is pretty good."

"Okay."

Unthinking, he buys the tickets. As they walk past the concession booth, he says, "Want something?"

"No thanks, you go ahead."

"I'll pass."

Their timing is about right—two-thirds of the way through the previews and advertisements. They stand a moment letting their eyes adjust to the darkness, then make their way down the aisle to find seats. He takes her hand and a firm warmth passes through him. He knows nothing about *Dead End* but realizes right away that he has let his vigilance slip. For months he has avoided violent movies. Now the scene opens with the stereotypical car chase in which a character's arm is brutally severed. He winces, clamps his jaw together. A couple of sequences later a young man is stabbed, there is blood gushing. He feels his arms and legs tensing, looks over at Kimberly. She watches the screen with casual detachment. A violent fist fight takes place, the so-called hero bashing the head of his antagonist. The brutality is graphic, relentless. He turns away, presses himself back against the seat, his thighs straining, the veins in his arm bulging. Why is this happening to him now? Because he has broken the rules, exposed one little part of himself. He thinks, *Not now! Please don't let the thoughts come now!*

He closes his eyes, but it doesn't help, only brings the old bitter images closer. He concentrates on Kimberly, her slim fingers entwined with his, the contour of her crossed legs. But cruel memory forces past his brain to twist and knot his stomach. He sinks back and remembers ...

It is late afternoon when the detectives come. The first warning that the news is bad is when Detective McClendon suggests Devin leave the room. "We're sorry, Mr. Solomon, we've found your wife."

"Found her?" His father is outraged, or pretends to be. "What do you mean, found her?"

"It's a homicide. She was thrown off a bridge."

"It can't be Mom!" Chase cries. "It can't be Mom! She's alive!"

"We'll need DNA for positive identification."

Chase turns aside, stumbles blindly to Devin's room, sinks down on the floor beside him. All night they stay together crying, sleepless. In the morning the investigation team arrives, takes swabs from their mouths, sends samples for DNA tests. But they do not have to wait. They know it is their mother.

How he and Devin get through the next days, Chase can hardly fathom. His father arranges a memorial service. How they bathe, dress, ride with him to the chapel, he doesn't know. Silently, friends file in, volunteers who had helped with the search. They cannot even see their mother. Devin whispers, "She didn't want to leave us!" Their father wears a face of stone. The frantic searching, the terrible uncertainty is over.

Chase sits through the black wall of the service, registering almost nothing. He knows an organ is playing, a solo is sung. The pastor talks about Kelly, what she liked to do, the kind of person she was. "We have never known a freer spirit. Our children love her drawings. She could always find something hopeful in every situation..." He hears few words, only sees his mother running, hiking, painting. He inhales the scent of flowers, knows he will never again smell flowers without thinking of her. When he peers over at his little brother, his heart is just torn. Devin looks so terrified, so lost, he wants pathetically to do something, but cannot utter a word. After the funeral, the calls of sympathy and concern dry up, even their school friends can think of nothing to say to them.

They do not know how bitterly the blinding blows of anguish can strike until just a few days later when their father is charged with the murder. He is arrested, led away in handcuffs. Devin looks as if his own life has been suffocated. "Why did he do it, Chase! Why!"

"I don't know! God, I don't know!"

All these months now he has been unable to stop wondering what he could have done to make things different, why he had been away that night. The guilt is unbearable, the self-accusation relentless. Why wasn't he there, how could he have let it happen!

He feels people looking, curious about him. The freakishness, the progeny of a monster who strangled his wife. The stares. He thinks, Leave me alone, dammit! Fuck you, go away! It blasts his brain, sharp shards of garbled sounds, flashes of confusion, pain. If only he could say, *I love you, Mom, you're a good mother...*

"Chase!" Kimberly whispers. "Chase!"

"What!"

"You're squeezing my hand to death."

He jerks loose, she withdraws, massages her fingers. He fixes his eyes on the screen but feels her looking at him. Relax. Relax. Breathe deeply, let the tension drain from your forehead, your shoulders, arms, legs, toes. Feel the tenseness seep from your body, run off across the floor. It's hard, like struggling for rebirth.

She reaches, takes his arm, pulls it over her shoulder. It brings a great relief of tension. He is grateful, thrilled. Why has she done this? Seeking security? Offering him security? Is there anything romantic about it, sexual? Or merely a gesture of acceptance? Perhaps we will learn to talk, but for now you can put your arm around me because I'm okay with that.

Now with his arm over her shoulders, things go fast; it is over too soon, he is sorry to see the movie end. They walk out with the audience, blinking against the sharper lights. The horror of his dark thoughts has faded with the sweet feel of her, the scent of her hair. She has opened her arms to him, made herself a joyous potion. Why? Because he is being himself. For the first time in nearly a year he does not want to be closed off, wants to experience everything, know everything...

As they get into the car, she says, "I thought that was so-so. What about you?"

"I could have lived without it."

"Maybe we should have gone bowling."

It is late afternoon, the sun canting to the west. She stretches, yawns. "Do you know why you yawn after you've been to a movie?"

"No, tell me."

"Because you forget to yawn when you're in."

He laughs. "You base that, I assume, on empirical research."

"Of course." She laughs too. "I would never brainwash you with hypothesis."

"But you would brainwash me?"

"Oh, I would. To fit all my wishes."

"Well, go ahead, try."

"And you'll be putty in my hands?"

"Pure putty. The silly kind."

"Well, Mr. Chase Solomon, you just might not know what you're in for."

He is deliriously happy, something about his old self has

slipped into the car with them. Her mood is lighter. She, too, has undergone transformation. They talk about friends and non-friends, Bryan Upchurch, snobs. All the time he is feeling better about himself. There is such a relief from the black memories of the movie it is like getting over a stomach virus. Kimberly feels this, too. He thinks she may be inspired by his lightened mood. "There may be hope for us after all," she says. "Don't you think there's hope?"

"Anything's possible."

As he pulls up into her driveway he grasps the remaining minutes, keeping the attitude upbeat. Kimberly teases and giggles, but then she sits up straight in alarm. "Oh, no!" she cries. "The jerk!"

"Who?"

In her driveway is a strange car, no one inside.

"Gene Holbrook. I've *told* him not to come without calling."

"Oh." He remembers Bryan mentioning Snatch Holbrook, boy on the make, primitive woman chaser. "What's he doing here?"

"Well, he came to see me, of course."

"Uninvited? Unannounced?"

"You would never do that, Chase, I realize. This is just unacceptable.:"

"Why does he think he can do it?"

She looks at him, her eyes steady, unflagging. "I don't encourage it, if that's what you mean."

"Still, here he is."

"Chase, listen, I don't blame you for being upset. I didn't know he'd show up. I told him not to do this."

Stubbornly he says, "Maybe not in a way that he gets it."

"Oh, don't accuse me!" she cries. "I am not *flattered* by this!" She sinks back suddenly. "At least he hasn't given up on me. What about you? How easy do you give up?"

There is a wild hammering in his breast. Still, it is feeling. *Feeling.* No numbness, no vague disorientation. "I don't know," he says. "I'll walk you to the door."

He wonders what will happen now. If he leaves she could spend who knows how long with a notorious woman chaser. Well, what is it to him? She must encourage this, subconsciously or otherwise. Maybe Holbrook challenges and excites her. Chase's nice feelings about himself turn sour, resentful. All he wants now is to get her to the door, make a clean break. But just as they reach the porch Holbrook comes out. He's been inside charming her mother probably.

Kimberly, scarcely acknowledging him, says coolly, "You know each other, don't you? Gene Holbrook, Chase Solomon."

Holbrook smiles broadly, evidencing no sign of hostility. He's a big guy, broad-shouldered, sturdily built, a linebacker. But there is something faintly spurious about him, something blatantly presumptuous. Kimberly's mother, Mrs. Compass, follows him to the door, looks out smiling. Fascinated, it appears.

"Chase," Kimberly says, "this is my mother. Mother, Chase Solomon."

"Hello, Mrs. Compass."

"Hello, Chase, how was your afternoon?"

"Pretty good, I guess."

"Hey, dude, what's happening?" Holbrook asks. His tone indicates he couldn't care less.

"Fine. Wonderful," says Chase. "Everything's lovely."

It's bad chemistry and everybody knows it.

"I gotta go," Chase says. "I promised my uncle ... "

"Chase." Kimberly follows him down the steps, appealing to him with her eyes. "I had a very nice time. Thank you."

"Yeah, well, me too."

"Will you call me tonight? I want you to."

"I don't know what the Ingrams have planned ... "

She fixes him with a cool blue gaze, her lower lip turned out faintly. "Call me." Invitation or command? He doesn't know, but somehow her determination lifts his spirits, his step is not so labored as he turns from them and strides out to the car.

* * *

At home he closes his door, hopes no one will bother him. He is excited, tense. In less than eight hours he has been high, low, high, and low again. Roller coaster emotions, forcing himself out of focus on himself.

He thinks of holding Kimberly in his arms, of her tender touch, the light brushing of her hair against his cheek, a stirring along his thighs. Thank God, it is still there! For months intimacy, physical contact seemed abusive to him, almost vile. All he could think of was what happened between his mother and father—lovemaking, violence, then death.

Now he senses a burning in his groin, something outside his conscious will pressing, taking life of its own. So much of that had been lost, erotic intimacy seemed such a lie. Now thinking of Kimberly he experiences none of the old repercussions of guilt. Still, he wonders how vulnerable Kimberly is, how much she might be persuaded by reckless abandon, by a reputation of sexual bravado, like Holbrook: cynical, chauvinistic, full of self;

self-assured and arrogant. So different from he, Chase Solomon, who fumbles over words and feelings, who is afraid to allow himself almost any emotion, anything that will pierce the hard shell in which he has managed to encase himself.

He slips downstairs, walks out into the Ingram's back yard. Looking up, he wonders how many stars there are, what little role each plays, if there is some identifying force which distinguishes everyone from any other. In the rear of the garage is Mitchell's storage and workroom. Here are Grant's and Leslie's early lives recapitulated, crammed full of old memorabilia. He sits down in a patio chair. The metal is cold, damp, through his clothes. He can smell the grass. He knows he should go in and call Kimberly, but it is probably too late now. He wonders what she wants, what she might expect of him. Or herself. He knows he would never hurt her. Never hurt her even if it meant never touching her. But this is not all. As he presses himself down into the hard chair he thinks, Don't hurt *me!* Don't hurt *me!*

10

Devin and Will are working on their bicycles, scrubbing them down, filling tires, oiling sprockets and chains. The December sun is spring-like, the Chattahoochee Valley flooded with silver light under cloudless blue skies. The deciduous trees open themselves to the false new season with an occasional stirring of wind. It is typical Georgia weather for this time of year, variable day by day, hour by hour, electronic thermometers on banks and billboards skittering twenty degrees in a single day. It brings people out, stimulates a hopeful mood, just as the first colors of fall had two months earlier.

Will says, "Sometimes my dad and I ride to the Riverwalk and back. You can go with us if you want to."

"Your mom rides?"

"Once in a while. Usually she'll walk."

"My mother used to take us hiking," says Devin. "Chase doesn't think she was ever sorry she didn't have a daughter. She made the best of us boys."

Devin feels lighter than he has in a long time, alive and real. Probably some of Chase's optimism has rubbed off on him. The sun warms his back, tingles down his arms. He guards against the shadows lurking in the recesses of his mind.

Mrs. Lasiter, car keys in hand, walks out into the yard, smiles, "You doing all right, Devin? How's your aunt and uncle?"

"Fine, thanks."

"I haven't seen Paula in ages. Tell her I said hello, will you?"

Mrs. Lasiter has her hair cut short, her nose is narrow, and while she is plumpish her features are delicate. The earrings she wears make her look pert and lively, and she seldom lacks a friendly word for everyone. He's glad she has decided to like him, or accept him at least, though he still feels awkward around her.

"I have to run a brief errand, Will. Won't be gone long. Devin, you're welcome to stay and have dinner with us if you like."

"Thank you."

As she walks out to the car Will says, "My mother is so organized. Drives my dad crazy sometimes."

"Aunt Paula is that way, too. Nothing should ever be out of place. Including us." He laughs but does not feel mirthful.

Turning their bikes one way then another they check parts, cables, gears. "At one time we had a little compressor," says Will, "but it got zapped. This'll do, I guess."

They employ an old-fashioned hand pump to inflate the tires. Devin says, "We used to clean these gummy parts with gas. I could use some now."

"Look in the storage room," says Will.

Devin finds a red gas can, a small scrub brush, but no container. He hesitates, then decides to try the house. He walks into the kitchen, rummages around, discovers several containers in a bottom cabinet. Choosing one, he goes out, pours in the gas, dips the brush and scrubs the gunk from his chain and sprockets. Will looks up, says abruptly, "Where'd you get that?"

"The house."

"I don't know if Mom's gonna like that."

A small barb of rejection pricks his nerves but he keeps on with his task. The gas is black now, the container oily and grime-streaked. "Want to clean yours too?"

Uncertain, Will says, "May as well now that it's ruined anyway."

"I can clean this up."

"I don't think so. That stuff's all through the plastic."

"Maybe we'd better get rid of it, then."

"Yeah, but then if she ever asked about it I'd have to lie. And I don't like lying to my parents. They have a way of finding out."

Will takes the brush and begins cleaning sprockets and chains. They work side by side. They do not hear Mrs. Lasiter until she walks up, says, "Just wanted to let you know I'm back, Will. Everything okay?"

"We're just about finished."

"Is that gas you're using? Don't you think—Will!" she cries. "That's my best container!"

He dips his head, brush suspended.

"Where did you get that?"

"Kitchen," he mumbles.

"You've dumped dirty gas into my best container?"

"Not me. I" He looks desperately at Devin.

She turns, peers down at him. "Did you take that from my kitchen, Devin?"

He doesn't answer, holding rigid.

"Did anyone give you permission to do that?"

"No, ma'am. I was going to put it back."

"I certainly hope you wouldn't do that."

It is amazing how swiftly the hot choking pressure closes on him. "I'll get you another one!" he exclaims. "I'll bring it to you—"

"I don't expect you to do that. I would simply suggest you not take things without asking—"

"I won't ever again! I won't take anything that belongs to you—" He jerks his bike up, throws his leg over. "I have to go!"

"Devin, wait a minute."

"I'm sorry, Will. I'm sorry I came ..."

"Hey, man, listen—"

He flings his weight forward, digs in.

"Devin!" cries Mrs. Lasiter.

He pumps hard, hits the driveway, pedals furiously out to the street. There is a hard pounding in his chest. Behind him Will yells, but he is not about to go back. He doesn't belong here, he should have remembered that he doesn't belong anywhere.

* * *

He slams down his bicycle, manages to get into the house without anyone seeing him. In his room, he closes the door and the blinds; the nightlight beneath the window blinks on. He kicks off his shoes, throws himself onto the bed and pulls up protective covers. The tiny light casts weird patterns onto the dresser, the bath door, a triangle of ceiling above. Why does everything he touches turn sour? Is he nothing but a fuck-up? He wants his mother. His yearning for her is intense, wretched. He is not a child anymore, yet chronology has deceived him, made him older inside like the strange disease which ages children to make them resemble old men.

He draws the covers closer. For a while after his mother's death it was as if she'd simply gone away. Some obscure and fathomless and soon to be righted destiny. For months, he was physically sick.

He starts, jerks his eyes open. He sees the form of his knees and feet beneath the covers. If he tries to move even an inch, it will tear him apart. He tries to surface, to make himself fully conscious, then he lets himself go down deeper until darkness passes and day exposes everything for what it really is. Half asleep in a drugged twilight of uncertainty, he sinks, sinks until he doesn't want to come back, his lead-like legs and arms going deeper while a kind of spiritual element ascends, taking him high above everything. He looks down on his physical shape, indifferent to its imperfections, to the blasts it receives from the world. From here he sees everything clearly, the air, the sun, a pure beginning of himself, righteous and unscathed. His heart sings, untouched by earth's misery. He is everywhere, in command of boundless space, he breathes time, purity, sunlight, soars joyously above the earth like an endless brilliant white cloud.

Once when he was very small, he broke his father's big work lamp. It had a huge globe, a large green horn-shaped canopy. It could be hung or set on a table. They were in the workshop behind the garage. "Don't touch that light," his father had warned. He did anyway, the bright globe fell, came crashing down, pieces of glass scattering like slivers of broken ice. His father whacked him viciously on the back. "You bad boy! You bad boy!"

He wakens with a start, a cold cruel moon shattering the windowsill. He has slept, not slept. Dazed, he tries to stretch his arms out to the air, the heavens, but he is dragged back down, tumbling to earth. Voices cry Bad boy! Bad boy! Like satanic angels fleeing through the sky.

* * *

When his Uncle Mitchell enters the room, he is up, TV on, books scattered across the bed. He moves zombie-like among the disarray, his mind a mask. Mitchell locates the TV control, punches the mute button, drops casually down onto the bed.

"How're things going, Dev?"

He is jolted back to reality. "Okay, I guess."

"School work coming along?"

"I'm not failing."

"Mrs. Lasiter called tonight."

It hits him with a shock, a slamming wall of regret.

"She says you got upset today."

He drops his chin, stares down at the floor. "What'd she tell you?"

"Not much, really. Just checking on you."

"I guess I was disrespectful."

"That doesn't sound like you, Devin. Want to tell me what happened?"

"Whatever she said."

"All she said was you got upset and wanted me to tell you she is sorry."

He looks up, confused.

"I spoke to Will, too. He asked you to come over tomorrow and finish your bikes."

"He did? Why?"

"I guess he wants to be your friend."

He fights tears, miserable, yet feeling the load lift a little. "I did a stupid thing. I ruined one of her containers. That wasn't the worst though. I yelled at her."

"Are you sorry?"

"Yes, sir."

"Well, you can tell her, then forget it."

"It wasn't that she was that mad at me. I say things I don't mean. It's something coming out I don't even know. I'm bad, I guess."

"You are not bad, Devin," he says. "You're not a rotten kid, either, if that's what you're thinking."

"Then what makes me do these things?"

"What do you think?"

"Because of what happened to my mother, I guess. I don't know. I'm not like *him*. Neither is Chase."

"You're not like anybody," says Mitchell. "You're an individual, one of a kind. You were made to be exactly as you are."

"What is this…this poison in me, then?"

"Look, Devin, life is seldom easy. A lot depends on how we react to things that happen to us."

Devin looks down again, clenching his hands together. "I don't think I can ever go back there!"

His uncle stands, comes around beside him. "You have to forgive yourself. And forgive others, too. That's not easy either."

"You don't think Mrs. Lasiter's mad at me?"

"She isn't mad. She's sorry you got upset and that she scolded you"

He remains silent a moment. He's been a jerk, he knows that. Lashing out without provocation, twisting things around because he knows they think something is wrong with him, something mean and ugly…

He says, "Thanks for telling me."

"Chase is home now," Mitchell says. "Why don't you go pester him?"

"I think he gets tired of me."

"Probably, sometimes. But that's okay. Stop being so hard on yourself." Mitchell puts a hand on his shoulder. "You're a fine young man. You have to believe that. No one can tell you."

He waits until his uncle goes out, then finds a tissue, blows his nose, washes his face, works on forgiving himself.

11

The day has been set aside for testing—aptitude, personality. In the halls and cafeteria, Chase sees people he seldom encounters except at games. Lunch becomes a sort of excited havoc, students yelling across the big room, scrambling for a table with friends. He and Bryan Upchurch find a place together, keep their dishes and drinks on the trays, easier than reloading for drop-off on the way out. Bryan reaches for the salt, makes certain the top is screwed on securely. Everyone has been victim of the loosened top that dumps an entire shaker onto their food.

"Man," he says, "I know I shouldn't have this stuff. But something in my system just cries for salt."

"If you didn't have it you'd get used to doing without," says Chase.

"There are worse things. Look at the NutraSweet in these diet drinks. Ossifies the brain." Bryan laughs. "Course, I think about half the brains in this room have turned into bone."

People call out to Bryan, slap him on the shoulder. He is well-liked, well-mannered, courteous. Chase cannot resist a small spark of jealousy. Jealousy is an emotion. Bryan has led a comfortable, unthreatening life. But this is unfair, Chase knows. Why is everything so blurred, every relationship tainted by self-doubt? He is sick of feeling stamped and forged by something unnatural, yet wants to be noticed...

Beside him a voice says, "Why haven't you called me?"

He is startled, recognizes the pulsing octaves of her voice before he looks up into those clear frank eyes. He stands. "I was going to. I am."

"My mother would like to know you. I've told her how nice you are."

Bryan says, "Hullo, Kimberly."

"Hi." She looks down, smiles. "You fail the career test?"

He laughs. "How'd you know?"

"Me too. Anytime they ask the same question three ways I give three answers. Is that to confuse them or because there are three me's?"

"Both. Mostly three me's."

"Maybe they'll choose the best and give me a star for that." She turns back to Chase. "You take that test yet?"

"No. After lunch, I guess."

"Introvert or extrovert?"

He manages a smile, too, though he feels nervous. "Like you. One one day, one the next."

"You could do well in anything," she says. "Strong personality. Strong will. There's strength to be tapped there."

"I've got you fooled, I guess," he says.

"You just have to believe in yourself."

"Like you?"

"Like I'm trying to."

From seemingly nowhere an arm slips around her, squeezes her close. "Drop these nerds, Kimberly, come sit with me."

Without turning her head she says, "Speaking of someone who can benefit from A Search for Identity."

Snatch Holbrook and a couple of his cronies seem to suck up all the air around the table. Holbrook looks bigger, stronger, robust. He's probably filling the gap from football at the gym, working out. About his expression is a kind of aloof cynicism one might envy. How liberating to live in a world which revolves around Self, Chase thinks.

"Hang around with losers," he quips, "and you lose. Come on, Kimberly, we look good together."

She tries to turn away but he holds her firmly. Chase remains standing, rigid, raw nerves tightening. Bryan says amiably, "Control yourself, Snatch, failure is inevitable here."

He laughs and continues, "I haven't failed yet, have I, Kimberly?" He leans as if to kiss her, but she makes a sort of pirouette and frees herself of his grip. "Not like some people I know." He looks at Chase.

"I have to go," she says. "How nice to see all three of you at once." Caustic. Ironic.

As she walks away Holbrook scrunches his nose, winks lecherously. "Tell me, Solomon, how is it really with Compass?"

Chase holds steady, fists clenched.

"Is she good? Easy? A tease?"

The boys snicker. Chase feels something in his brain about to explode, blind and dangerous.

"Tell you what," Snatch adds, "you let me know about Compass, I'll let you in on a couple of my old rejects."

Bryan says, "You're a stupid prick, Snatch."

They laugh, move away.

"Take him for what he is, Chase. Don't let him freak you."

He forces tension from his body, forces control. "What can she possibly see in him?"

"Maybe she's just waiting to cut him down a peg."

"All she'll ever get from Holbrook is abuse."

Bryan fixes him with a skeptical glance. "Kimberly isn't an angel, Chase. None of us is."

"Compared to him she is."

"You think she can't take care of herself?"

"No, I don't. He's a liar and a bully. If she wanted to she could tell him to piss off."

"Maybe, maybe not. Hey, man, she's fractious, you know? Like thin glass. Afraid of anything shattering."

"He can't be anything but shattering."

"I guess most of us can use any little admiration we get."

The bell rings, they gobble the last few bites and head for the tray deposit. Chase slams his into the window with silent fury, surprised to find the veins in his hand bulging. This anger frightens him. How can he trust his own feelings? He wishes he were bold enough right in front of God and everybody to take Kimberly into his arms. But he is terrified of rejection, of inflicting pain — and of his own violent heritage.

* * *

The halls are noisy with catcalls, slamming locker doors. When the bell rings they all crash into their desks, listen to instructions, receive papers. The girl next to Chase smiles; he can smell her perfume. Behind him two boys are grumbling, profanely resenting these stupid tests. He tries to close them all out, fixing his gaze on his shoelaces, his fingernails. In the desk before him a heart had been carved, highlighted with red pen. This had to be done years ago; no knives are brought to school now. The "A" in the initials is turned out with a cross — "A+!"

At his desk, paper before him, pen in hand, his breath heavy, he struggles to understand the meaning, to untangle the confused questions. "Write the first words that come to mind when you think…" He comprehends nothing, the pen held poised, untrustworthy. What has set this off? Snatch Holbrook, of course. And Kimberly. Every encounter threatening, dangerous. Images unlocked from the black vault of agony…His mom struggling to suck in the last thread of air, her beautiful eyes glaring out blindly, her mouth a grimace of terror…My boys! My boys! The madman who slept with his mother nearly twenty years, who appeared to lead a normal life…

Slumping down at his desk, blurred paper before him, Chase feels sick. His face is burning hot, his body shaking.

Beside him, bending close to his ear, a voice whispers, "You okay, Chase?"

He does not answer, does not look up. His eyes are stinging, there is a wet splotch on his paper.

"Hey, listen, relax," Mr. Mosley says. "This is no big deal."

He jumps up suddenly, rushes blindly to the door, bursts out into the hall. The girls' locker room is closest. He heads there, hoping everyone is in class. In the lavatory he is sick, once, twice, a violent retching in his stomach so overwhelming he is terrified. At last he is exhausted, steadies himself against the sink, washes down the bowl, splashes cold water into his face. He walks quickly down the corridor, slams open the double door. Outside, he sinks down on the steps, his head in his arms. No one comes, no one speaks to him. He loses touch with time, doesn't know how long he sits there trying not to think, not to feel, care. The damn memories! The bastard memories that shatter him at the most unexpected moments! After a while the bell rings, the period is over. He pulls himself up by the rail, returns to the empty classroom to get his books. Mr. Mosley looks up from his desk, puzzled, frowning. "Another day we'll do this, Chase. Don't worry about it."

"Yes, sir. I'm sorry. I didn't mean—"

"Forget it. You okay now? Want to go home?"

"No." He hesitates, says not so much to the teacher as to himself. "It's not the first time. Sometimes I...don't...think the right things."

"We all do that, don't we?" says Mr. Mosley. "You want to talk to a school counselor?"

"I'm seeing someone, thanks. Nobody can help you but yourself, I guess."

"Maybe, maybe not. Don't give up on yourself."

"Yes, sir. Sometimes when you lean on somebody else you get—ambushed."

He collects his books, leaves Mr. Mosley sitting at his desk, still puzzled, frowning. He works his way through the maze of incoming students, moves almost blindly up the hall. Mr. Mosley is all right, he thinks, most of the teachers are all right. Keeping their distance, trying not to get personally involved. They feel disconnected, too, he supposes. Still, Mosley has picked up on something, gone out of his way to offer a little reassurance. Why should he bother? Why should anyone bother with Chase Solomon, genetically connected to accused murderer, whose single most intense objective in this moment is to justify a reason for his own existence? Who yearns for a tender touch, yet is frightened by jealous rage—the part that cannot be him, must not be him. The part he knows will make him hate himself. And more than anything right now, he knows he needs to love himself.

* * *

As he drives home he turns up the street and notices a man going in and out of a house transporting what appear to be heavy boxes. Out in front a sign on a white panel truck says "Chattahoochee Flooring." On a hunch Chase pulls up, catches the man as he lifts another box from the truck, mumbles, "Hi."

The man looks up, nods. "How're you?"

"I was just noticing…You seem to be working hard."

"I'm working my ass off."

He laughs nervously. "I was wondering…if you could use some help."

The man pauses, rests his foot on the truck bumper, rests the box on his leg. "You looking for work?"

"Yes, sir."

"I ain't no sir. My name is Mac."

Chase extends his hand. "I'm Chase. I applied for a job at Chick-fil-A but nothing's come through yet."

"Here." Without warning Mac pushes over the box to him. "See how you handle this."

Chase takes the box. It isn't large, about twelve by twelve inches, but it is much heavier than it appears. After the initial surprise, he gets a better grip, says, "What is it?"

"Tile. What if you had to carry about a hundred of these a day?"

"I can do it."

Mac looks at him a moment, squinting. "Okay. You wanna start now?"

"You mean like right now? Working?"

"You said you wanted a job."

He hesitates, grins. "Well, okay, sure. What am I supposed to do?"

"Just follow me. We gotta get about a dozen houses finished before the end of the year."

Mac lifts another box from the truck, then pauses. "Look, Chase, I understand you want to make a few bucks. But this is what you'd be doing every day. Bringing stuff in, taking stuff out. Tile, carpet and so on. It's a tough job. How old are you anyway?"

"Just turned seventeen."

"Well, you look sturdy enough, but this ain't no easy work. You sure you don't want to keep looking?"

"I need a job for the holidays."

"Okay. Why don't you try it the next couple of hours then decide."

"I'll be working for you?"

"I ain't the boss. After today he'll be paying you, if you decide to stick. I already told him we need somebody."

For the next two hours Chase works with the man unloading the truck, transporting the boxes and carpet into the house, placing them in different rooms. He feels it all in his arms and legs but when the van is empty at last he sucks in a deep breath, leans back, experiences a moment of pure self-assurance.

"Okay," says Mac, "we done it. Now how are you about doing this all day?"

"It'll make a hulk of me, I guess," he laughs.

"Okay. Good enough." Mac pulls a twenty dollar bill from his wallet, hands it to him. "The pay's twelve an hour. That's the going rate around here. I'm giving you a little extra today. That sound okay with you?"

"Sure. Twelve."

"When can you start?"

He thinks, calculates when school is out, gives him a date.

"Okay, we'll figure on that following Monday," says Mac. "You drive? Got a way to get to the office?"

"That's my truck over there."

"Good. I won't have to pick you up."

"Thanks, Mac. I'll be ready."

They shake hands, sealing the pact. He slips the twenty into his wallet. Darkness is descending, the air is cool, fresh. His flesh is warm and tingling, he feels good about himself, what he has done and can do. He realizes suddenly that he has less dread for the upcoming holidays.

* * *

On the last day of school Chase hurries to his locker, retrieves what he needs and rushes out to where Kimberly parks. About the time he reaches her car, she exits the big doors on the north end of the building, books cradled in her arms like a basket. Her sweater is thrown over her shoulders and her step is swift and resolute. She sees him, cries, "Chase! Hi! I'm glad you waited. I had a couple of things to do."

"I just got here. Thought I'd missed you."

"Yeah, everybody's bent on escape, aren't they? Clearing out as fast as we can." She tosses her books into the car. "Well, we survived the first half. Now we have a couple of weeks of bliss."

"What are your plans?"

"Oh, I don't know." She looks at him with amusement. "Why do you so seldom call me, Chase?"

"I *do* call."

"Sometimes, but it's not as if you're dying to talk to me."

He laughs. "That's the problem. I die when I talk to you."

She tosses her hair, smiles. "Do you say such beautiful things to all the girls?"

"I didn't realize there were other girls."

"I've noticed you haven't been in the greatest of rushes."

"Don't think it's because I don't want to. I'm just afraid—"

"What? That you'll fall in love with me?"

It hits him with a shock. "No. Yes. I—"

She laughs. "You're sputtering. I can think of a worse fate in case you want my opinion."

There is a flush all through his skin, a pleasant tingling sensation.

"Tell you what," she says, "I have to go now. But during the holidays I want you to learn how to use the phone."

He opens her door, watches the nice firm curve of her legs as she slips in. "I hope we can get together," he says. "I guess it sort of depends on my job."

"You have a job?"

"Yeah, helping some flooring guys. I think we'll be working late."

She catches her lip, turns her eyes up coquettishly to him. "You'll work me in if you want to. Then maybe I can do the same." She laughs again, reaches over and squeezes his arm. "I do hope this is a good time for you, Chase. Please let me know how you're doing."

"All I wanted was to hear you say so."

"Well, I'm saying so. I really got nervous when you don't call me."

Before he can answer, she is backing out.

On the balls of his feet, fairly airborne, he hurries back to the south end of the building where Bryan is waiting. "Sorry, I was talking to Kimberly."

"No problem. She okay?"

"Yeah, she's okay. Problem is, I got this job and don't know if I'm going to have much time off. I need the money, though."

"I'll be working for my dad the next couple of weeks," Bryan says. "Maybe we can get together and do something, though."

"Good. Holidays tend to be ... depressing." He asks tentatively, "You decided what you'll get Jessica for Christmas?"

"One of those chain rings, I think. Circles of love. Kind of pricey, though."

"She'll love that. I'd like to give Kimberly something, but ..."

"But what?"

"I don't know how personal to get. Then there's a matter of money ..."

"She won't care what it costs, Chase. Just get her something you'd choose yourself."

"Right. Okay, thanks. Now that I've got my transportation I'll pick you up sometime."

"No problem. We'll talk in a day or two."

The Ingrams take them out for pizza Friday night, then on Saturday Chase finds a baseball and a couple of old gloves out in the storage room, remnants of Grant's high school days. He fetches Devin and they pitch as they used to. He is out of practice, still he has something of his old touch, is able to put the ball over the patio chair cushion which serves as home plate. He fights off the sadness, remembering how things once were, the sheer act of throwing and catching, a physical reprieve which, God knows, helps detour round the shadowy thoughts. Devin shoots him a few make-believe signals, but they don't talk much, just concentrate on the practice. It is just possible he'll get into baseball again.

The weekend passes quickly enough and on Monday his job begins. Mac and Chase drive out to one of the new outlying subdivisions where the streets are rolling; new trees have been planted everywhere and all the mailboxes are of a kind. These upper price houses are of brick, dryvit and stone, L-shaped, two-story, split-level, with and without enclosed garages. All up and down the streets new houses are under construction, there are pickup trucks, panel trucks, dump trucks, and an assortment of painters, carpet layers, electricians, landscapers and cabinet makers scurrying about as if they, too, are driven by the imminent interruption of the holidays.

As they pull up in front of a half completed contemporary style brick house with dormer windows, Mac says, "Okay, young fellow, show me what you have."

All through the day Chase works around men stripping floors and laying pads, carpet, hard tile. "I could learn to do that," he says.

"Course you could," says Mac. "But you don't want to spend your life laying floor covering."

Hauling heavy boxes and rolls of carpet is not easy, but as the days pass Chase feels his stamina improving, his arms and back growing stronger. Mac, chewing tobacco, cursing, and spitting is okay to work with, a scrawny man of about forty with sinewy arms strong as a horse.

After a string of twelve-hour days, Chase collapses into bed bone-tired and weary, but with an increasing sense of accomplishment. Hardly ever does he stop thinking of Kimberly Compass, excuses himself by deciding he is too tired or nervous to call her. It is a copout, he knows. He is pretty sure Bryan Upchurch sees or talks to his girlfriend every day. He thinks of Kimberly yawning, stretching, crawling sleepily into or from bed. He wonders what she sleeps in, imagines shorty pajamas or just panties and sheer top. There is a quiet unexpected stirring in his groin which he is both grateful for and skeptical of. It is not how he thinks of her exactly, sex is part of it, but repetitive thoughts of intimacy seem frightening. He wonders if he desires her or loves her. Both, maybe, but love must come first.

A couple of times Mitchell asks, "You sure you want to work like this all through the holidays, Chase. You deserve a little break."

"It's good for me. Look." He flexes his arm. "I'm building muscle."

"Okay, I admire your determination."

Bit by bit the shattered pieces of life seem to be coming back together. He doesn't trust them yet, but even for a day, a few hours, feelings of self-satisfaction provide a spark of reassurance.

* * *

Paula asks, "When are we going to meet Kimberly, Chase?"

It catches him by surprise. "I don't know. Things aren't that serious."

"They don't have to be serious for us to meet her."

"Well, soon, maybe. The next time we have a date."

"We'd like to get to know your friends. And what about Christmas? Are you going to exchange gifts?"

"I'd like to, but I'm not sure yet."

"What are you not sure of?"

He hesitates, but she evidently picks up on something. She reaches for her purse, pulls out her wallet. "Here's my charge card. Why don't you get her something nice?"

He looks at the card, looks at her. "You really want me to? You sure?"

"I'm sure. If I were Kimberly, I'd be very disappointed if you didn't get me something."

He walks over, puts his arm around her shoulder, half expecting her to draw away. Instead, she slips her arm around him, too. "Thanks, Paula."

She laughs. "A hug is okay, Chase. Don't be afraid of touching."

He turns quickly away.

It is after work, late and almost closing time before he can get home, change, and drive to the mall. He takes his clue from Bryan Upchurch, walks through the jewelry departments of Parisians, Saks, a few other stores. He has decided on a bracelet, girls always like jewelry, things they can wear and keep for life. It does not take long to confirm his decision. The bracelet he chooses is tri-color gold, interwoven like a ponytail. It is pricy, but taking Paula at her word, he hands over the charge card. The salesperson asks, "Is this a gift? Would you like it wrapped?"

"I would. Thanks."

She wraps it in pretty spruce green foil with a large red bow—his choice. Back home he returns the charge card, says, "I hope I didn't spend too much."

"It's all right," Paula says. "I'm sure your girlfriend will be pleased."

"I don't know if she's my girlfriend."

"Well, whatever you call them now."

He telephones Kimberly, asks when he can come over. "Probably tomorrow night is the best time," she says. "Sorta late, though. We're having relatives for dinner. They should be gone by nine or so."

"You're sure it's okay? I wouldn't want to interfere."

"It's fine. I want you to come."

He works next day, hurries home, showers, dresses, and drives over. There are several cars in the driveway. Apparently everybody is staying late. He rings the bell anyway, and when Kimberly opens the door, says, "Sorry. I see your company is still here."

"It doesn't matter. Come on in."

"It's okay. I just wanted to give you something."

"Don't be silly. Come in. We'll go into the den."

He follows her, hears voices and laughter from the dining room, and knows his time is crunched. As Kimberly slips down close beside him on the sofa, she says, "I thought they'd be gone by now."

"It's all right. I have to get going early tomorrow anyway. I just wanted to give you this."

He hands over the gift. She gives an excited little squeal. "Wait, I'll get yours." She scampers over to the big lighted tree and puts her hands on a package. "I was counting on giving you your present early."

"Hey, thanks. Should we wait until Christmas or open them now?"

"Now!"

He watches as she tears into the box, lifts out the bracelet. "Chase, it's beautiful!"

"You really like it?"

"I love it! It's the prettiest bracelet I've ever seen."

She hands him the bracelet, holds out her arm. Obediently, he fastens it on her wrist. She presses it to her cheek, then kisses it. "Okay, you now."

He tears off the wrappings, pulls out a handsome pewter grey North Face jacket. "Well, look at that. This is great."

"You really like it?"

"I love the color."

"Try it on. We can exchange it if it doesn't fit."

He stands, tugs the jacket on. "It feels fine."

"You look so handsome!" She stands, too, kisses him quickly on the lips. Then hearing the scuffle of feet and the clatter of chairs, she complains, "Shoot! They're getting ready to leave."

"That's okay," he says. "Let me get out first, so you can tell them goodbye."

She takes his hand, walks him to the door. He wants to make a quick escape to avoid having to meet anyone. She leans up, presses her cheek against his. "Thank you again for the bracelet, Chase. It's lovely."

"Thank you for the jacket."

"I would have been very upset if you hadn't called."

He wears his North Face jacket home, tosses the old one onto the seat. All through the neighborhood the Christmas lights look warm and friendly. It is a high time for him. It occurs to him that there are no secret formulas to courage. It is just something you discover about yourself. He can survive, he knows, he can endure—because he is who he is.

12

Mitchell usually walks early in the morning, before breakfast. It is his quiet time. He would never consider plugging into earphones as many walkers and joggers do. Sometimes he begins early enough to see the sunrise, the soundless stirring of light which seems to come not from over there somewhere, but simply to glow from within the earth as a light within a globe. Indistinguishable trees begin to emerge one by one, taking shape like sentinels. He hears the first bird. The scents are pure, clean as distilled water. There is something different about observing the earth light up instead of simply stepping into it after it happens — to glance behind and exult in his own footprints in the frostbitten grass, or pause to watch filaments of smoke curling up from a chimney. Life, he thinks, has to be more than a string of sequential events against which all preparation, all expectation, is futile. He wonders if he can ever make Chase and especially Devin understand that all through life he will do wrong things, say wrong things, but these do not make him bad or ugly or unlovable. One's view of the world does not change things, it changes him.

He and Paula have behind them now nearly thirty years of self-expression and familiarity, of challenge and resolution, a complex fabric woven with laughter and tears, with expectation and hope. What makes couples split after most of the lessons have been learned, most of the ambitions solved or forgotten? Yet, he is poignantly conscious of Paula's unrest.

"Why don't we drive up to Gatlinburg," she said, "Smithgall Woods. Build a fire. Go antiquing."

"That would be nice."

She peered at him, shrugged. "Oh, well, I guess we won't go anywhere before we're too old."

What is he afraid of? That the boys could feel abandoned, not part of it all…He wants them to draw closer, not apart. But he realizes that sometimes the noblest of intentions turn sour, are twisted into repercussions never foreseen.

When he and Paula were young, dating and carefree, they did silly things—scavenger hunts, trailing one another through strange neighborhoods with the clues of arrows chalked onto the sidewalk. He knows that chronological age should be no deterrent to romance. What Paula needs now is reassurance, a gesture, a special touch. By the time he returns home, the rising sun warm on his back, he has decided to send his wife a bouquet of red roses, her favorite.

* * *

At dinner Paula asks, "What do you boys think? A big Christmas tree, or small, one that'll sit on the table."

"Big," says Devin. "All the way to the ceiling."

"They'll have Frazier fir and balsam," says Mitchell. "Or we could get Virginia pine. They grow these right here in the valley."

"Frazier fir," Paula decides. "It's the one that smells most

Christmassy. Unless we pull our artificial tree down from the attic."

"What about it, men?" asks Mitchell.

"It'll be fun decorating a live tree," says Chase.

"Well, it's settled, then," Paula says. "We'll have to move furniture around."

They drive through neighborhoods where decorations are out. One house is wonderfully ornate, the entire cornice traced with jagged white icicles, a big red Santa Claus mounting the chimney and in the yard a carousel, reindeer pulling a sleigh, a manger scene, elves arranging toys , illuminated walkways, doves suspended from wires. "Wow," says Devin, "this homeowner loves Christmas."

It has turned cold and they zip up their jackets. They stop at a corner lot where there are trees. A southeasterly wind brings to them the scents of greenery, needles, sap, of sawdust thrown onto spongy surfaces, of coffee and apple cider and cocoa.

As they walk through Mitchell asks, "How about this one?"

"It has a gap on one side," says Paula.

"We could turn that toward the wall."

"Look, I like this one," Devin says.

"Lord, it must be twelve feet tall."

"I told him it's too big." Chase, Paula notices, looks at the price tags. A good sign, she thinks, fiscal responsibility.

"She stops at a pretty tree. I like this one."

"I'd have to trim off the lower limbs," Mitchell says.

"I can use them on the mantle. Chase, Devin, what do you think? You like?"

They walk around, inspecting from all angles. "Looks fine to me," says Chase. He examines the tag, whistles. "Seventy-five bucks? For a little tree?"

"Must be a seller's market," says Mitchell. "Stand here and guard. I'll find some help." They wait as he locates one of the attendants wrapping and loading trees. Paula remembers the Christmases Leslie and Grant received their first trikes, their first bikes, their first car keys. They would never have dreamed that someday they would have a kind of starting over with his sister's younger sons. The attendant runs the tree through a netting machine and as Mitchell pays, Paula stamps her feet and hugs herself. "Where did all this *weather* come from? We'll have hot chocolate when we get home, you can count on that."

As they enter the driveway Chase takes charge. "Devin and I'll get the tree, Uncle Mitchell."

"Sure you can handle it? Got something to cut the cords?"

"I'll get a trimmer from the garage. I can put the stand on out here, too. Keep from dropping needles all over the floor."

"Sounds like a winner to me," says Paula.

They leave the boys with the tree and just as they enter the house the sudden blast of heat makes them shiver. Paula looks at Mitchell, he reaches out and she comes into his arms. They embrace, share a moment of romance, then hurry to the den to move furniture.

* * *

By the time the nephews bring in the tree, they have arranged space for it. The den is accented in blue tones, with double windows admitting plenty of light, white, full-length draperies, stippled grey blue carpet. There is a sofa, a love seat, end tables and lamps, a fireplace and mantle, one entire wall shelves with books, a built-in television, pictures. They place the tree in the corner, blue green spatulas robust and stark against the white draperies.

Chase says, "I only had to remove a few bottom limbs to get the stand on. Run and get them, will you, Devin?"

When Devin returns Paula places selected cuttings on the mantle with Christmas balls. The men string lights, passing the rolled strings from one to another.

"Make sure you put lights inside the tree," she says, "not just on the ends."

She is meticulous about laying out the ornaments to avoid grouping the same kinds together—feathered birds, crystal-line round balls, golden stars and carriages, delicate glass canes, weightless snowmen, Santas, globes with ice skaters inside, min-iature dolls and sleighs and soldiers blowing tapered horns—a menagerie organized under her orderly hand.

"All right," she says, "you can start the decorations while I make chocolate. Don't forget, the angel on top, Mitchell."

"Marshmallows, too?" says Devin.

"Absolutely. What is hot chocolate without marshmallows?"

She goes to the kitchen, leaving the three hanging ornaments, not without first noticing that Devin is the meticulous one. He places the balls just so, making certain they do not drag the limb below. Chase is less precise, looser, yet with an eye for symme-try—spacing uniform, colors and shapes varied, ornaments flow-ing in and out of the branches, pretty much according to her own tastes. She sees the glow of red and green and blue in their faces, and hopes that this moment will be happy for them.

She makes chocolate, returns with a tray, four cups of choc-olate. "It's really a pretty tree. I hope it stays cold like this for Christmas."

The boys are staring at the brilliantly colored lights, and she wonders what they are remembering.

* * *

Grant and Leslie arrive, unexpectedly, a day early. It is evening, the doorbell rings, though they both have keys, and there they are, arms full of presents, Grant wearing a Santa hat, Leslie with her new short hairstyle she has told them about, clunky earrings dangling against her pale cheeks. Squealing, Paula throws her arms around them both at the same time. "Why didn't you tell us you could come early?"

"Oh, no, that would have spoiled the surprise."

"Hey, you look like someone who used to live here," Mitchell says.

They relieve Grant of packages, and talking and giggling, stack the presents under the tree, then go out to bring in the luggage. There is a moment of palpable hesitation as they drop the bags onto the floor of the kitchen instead of heading straight to their old rooms. Paula asks, "Well, how did you manage this? Arriving at the same time a day early?"

"We planned it a while," says Grant. "Then hooked up at Cracker Barrel and tailgated down."

"Have you eaten?"

"We have. I need to use the bathroom." Leslie looks at her mother. "Which one?"

"Downstairs, I guess."

"Where are Chase and Devin?" Grant asks.

"They're up there somewhere. They didn't know you were coming."

"How are they doing? How are *you* doing?"

"Very well. Adjusting. Looks like you've put on a few pounds, my boy. You needed it."

"It's not junk food, either," says Grant. "I'm eating right, getting exercise. I'm planning to get back into golf. Think I'll take my old clubs with me."

Grant is a slim, good-natured, non-worrier. He is less sensitive to the quirks of human aggravations than his sister and mother. Since his early high school years he has been interested in history and politics, reading *National Review*, *Time*, and other publications, then forming his own opinions and sticking with them.

Leslie has long mysterious eyelashes, high cheekbones, a perky nose. She is pragmatic, intelligent, less staunch in her views but no less insistent on her personal space. Once when she was a teenager, she discovered that she'd been shortchanged a dollar at one of the fast food windows. "Darn!" she said. "I have to go back."

"Forget it," says her father. "It's not worth the dollar."

"Oh, no, I have to call them on this. They need to be more responsible."

This is Leslie, exact, square-dealing. Like Paula, she has always looked younger than she is — fair complexion, large brown eyes, slender hips and shoulders. As she returns from the bathroom Paula says, "Come see the tree. The boys did a grand job."

They walk into the den together. Leslie exclaims, "It's beautiful!" and Grant laughs, "Why don't you get a few thousand more lights?"

Chase and Devin come downstairs, tentative, feeling their way. Paula has a moment of apprehension, knowing they have never quite convinced themselves they should be here. She is grateful when Grant takes the lead.

"Hey, man, how you doing?"

"Fine," says Chase. "Great."

"How about you, Dev?"

"Okay." Devin takes the hand that's offered, keeps his head down.

"School's out for the holidays, I guess," says Leslie. "Two weeks of R and R, huh?"

"I got a job," says Chase.

"Oh! You like?"

"It's okay. Just until school starts back."

"I worked a couple of Christmases," she says. "Remember, Mom? In Victoria's Secret."

"I remember you took nearly all your salary in merchandise."

The conversation is polite, though Paula suspects that Leslie and Grant don't really like this sparring for space, denied the freedom they used to enjoy coming home — the long lazy mornings, their own rooms, the familiar surroundings and a few days escape. She says, "I'd planned to arrange the rooms tomorrow. We can do it tonight, though, if everybody helps."

"Where am I sleeping?" asks Leslie.

"Your own room. I was thinking Chase and Devin can double up, you can have your room and Grant can either take the den or I'll come over with you and he can double up with your father."

"I'm thrown out of my own room!" cries Grant. He makes fake mockery of it.

"Can anyone think of a better arrangement?" asks Paula.

"I can't sleep with Chase," says Devin. "I don't want to sleep with anybody."

"Well, that's a luxury we can't demand right now," Paula says.

"I'll throw my sleeping bag down somewhere."

Chase says, "We need to let them have the rooms. They came first."

"Now this is nonsense," says Mitchell.

"No, look," says Chase. He's gentle but firm. "Devin can use his sleeping bag. I'll take the sofa. We always did things like that when we traveled."

Fighting exasperation, Paula says, "Why are we making this complicated? It's just two or three days. Can't we enjoy it?"

She notices that Devin's eyes are troubled. He lifts his head as if looking for a place to hide. "Maybe I could sleep over at Will's," he says.

"Grant! Leslie!" She appeals to them.

"Well, anything's okay with me," Leslie says. "Just show me a pad . Maybe we made a mistake coming early."

"Of course we want you here as long as you can stay." Paula looks at Mitchell, her eyes accusing. "Can someone offer me a solution?"

"Yes." She is thankful that he takes control, speaks in a tone that clearly defies challenge. "I'll take the sofa bed in my office. It was meant to be a bedroom anyway. You and Leslie take a room and Grant and the boys can take the other two rooms."

Devin says stubbornly, "I'll throw my sleeping bag down."

"Fine," says Mitchell, "you do that. But in the room with Chase."

"I just wish I weren't here!"

"Yes?" says Paula. "Well, where would you like to be?"

"Paula," Mitchell says.

"I'm just in the way!" Devin's lips tremble, his eyes watery. "I'm sorry you ever had to take me!"

"Did we have to, or did we choose to?" Paula asks.

"I don't know what made you! We don't belong here!"

"Devin—" Mitchell says.

"That's okay." Chase takes Devin by the arm, draws him to the door. "We'll move our stuff around, so you can get in. It's only right that Grant and Leslie have their old rooms. We'll take your office, if that's okay, Mitchell." He pulls Devin out.

Grant says, "We don't mean to disrupt things."

"You're *not* disrupting things." Paula is standing with her arms straight down by her sides. "This is your home. We *want* you here."

Leslie says, "I'm okay with anything, really. You sort it out. Can I use your big shower, Mom?"

"Sure, go ahead."

"They may as well leave their stuff where it is," Grant says. "We're here only two, three days."

"They don't feel that they belong here," says Mitchell, "or any-where else."

"Maybe not," Paula says, "but I didn't see them bending over to cooperate."

"I can't say any of us bent over tonight."

Grant decides to shrug it off. "I'll go and tell them to clear the beds, that's all."

As Paula and Mitchell are left alone, she says, "I knew some-thing like this would happen."

"I don't see that it was necessary."

"Are you blaming me?"

"Of course I'm not blaming anybody. Grant and Leslie do have their own apartments now."

"Oh, but they think of this as home. I hope they always will."

"So do I. Does that mean we're never supposed to touch their rooms?"

"What it means is we can never give them the idea it's incon-venient for them to come home. I couldn't stand that."

"Still, I think they can see there's no better way to open our home to two needy kids."

"Don't expect too much too soon," she says. "Everybody's a little jealous of their space. They feel as if *they're* the intruders."

"Now isn't that strange?" Mitchell speaks with irony. "Four young people all thinking they're interfering. If they'd stop looking at themselves a moment and consider the effects on others, they might be a little more sympathetic."

"I want to do whatever we can for your nephews," she says, "but my children come first. Any mother would feel that way."

"Sometimes we have to be more than mothers and fathers, Paula. We're expected to make sacrifices for others. I'm thinking about how those boys have lost their home, their parents..."

"Maybe you think of them too much, even more than they want you to."

"What does that mean?"

"We're not their mother and father. I don't know if we'll ever be more than benevolent strangers to them."

"I don't see it that way," he says. "They're reaching out. Maybe they don't yet know what they're reaching out for. Us. Love. God. A purpose for living. I just want us to do what little we can to help them."

"I don't think they want to be smothered, though."

"And I don't think what they felt tonight exactly convinces them of their welcome."

"Well, they have to make an effort, too."

They hear Chase coming, break off suddenly as he appears at the door. "Sorry about Devin," he says. "Kid brothers can be a pain."

"When people are unhappy," Mitchell answers softly, "they often react with anger. I don't think he means to be ugly."

"You don't get to see your kids every day. Devin and I will try to give you some slack." As quickly as he appeared he turns away.

Mitchell mumbles, "Funny, now I wonder if Leslie and Grant will be jealous that we got Chase a nice truck."

"Of course not," says Paula. "All kids get cars nowadays."

"Too bad we can't all look out of ourselves and be happy for each other."

She knows her husband has a point. Especially since the heart surgery Mitchell has been more sympathetic, more giving. She cannot help but wonder, though, what and how much will be demanded of her. Where is that freedom, that self-expression that she has so long yearned for? Still, her own maternal instincts shame her when she feels she somehow has let the nephews down.

Grant and Leslie return from their showers. They sit down before the sparkling tree and it is like old times when they came home from college. Leslie says suddenly, "I'm going up and get Chase and Devin. They need to be down here with us." She bounds upstairs.

Paula smiles. Her daughter. The air becomes lighter.

13

Christmas morning. Chase wakens, his eyes so wide and alert it is as if he hasn't slept at all. He lies motionless, staring at the ceiling. Everything feels strange. The room. The house, the season. It is the worst time of year. Christmas. When they were small, he and Devin rushed to the tree at first light, tore into packages and ribbons as Mother and Father looked on. Always he'd managed to save enough of his own money for presents for the three of them. It was as exciting to see how they liked what he gave as to open his own gifts. Today he doesn't know what to expect. The house is noiseless, everyone is sleeping late. Grant and Leslie have come home to bomb out. He turns onto his side, staring at the window where a dull morning is breaking. After an hour or so he hears someone stirring, knows he should get up. Fighting the blue doom of depression, he walks over to Devin's sleeping bag, nudges him with his toe. "Time to rise, sleepyhead."

There is a low growl, a barely audible voice. "For what?"

"It's Christmas."

"So?"

A tough day. He feels sorry for Devin, knows he must keep up a good face if only for his little brother.

"They're not opening presents, you know," says Devin.

"Why wouldn't they?"

"They're waiting until this afternoon, when Paula's parents arrive."

"Well, maybe they'll let you open one little one."

"I don't want to," Devin says.

"Why not?"

"I didn't get anybody very much."

Chase sits down beside the sleeping bag, wraps his arms around his knees. "You didn't need to."

"I spent every penny Mitchell gave me on presents, but it didn't go far." Their uncle had given them each two hundred dollars to spend as they liked on gifts. Chase accepted it reluctantly, sorry he hadn't yet made enough money of his own. He hates the idea of buying gifts for Mitchell and Paula with their money. He says, "At least we're here, Devin. With family. You'll feel better when you get up, have breakfast. Grandmother and Granddaddy Atwood are coming."

"They aren't our grandmother and granddaddy."

"Well, let's not be negative, huh?"

In the bathroom Chase washes his face, dresses. His facial hair is becoming more than fuzz, he shaves once or twice a week, likes the aftershave, the woodsy smell. His expression is grave, but it is Christmas and he concentrates on remembering the joyful past.

As Devin struggles out of the sleeping bag he loosens up, begins to chat about little things. "What's that smell, turkey?" he asks. "Aunt Paula must have put it on early."

"Probably. Right now I guess we'll have a big breakfast."

"What do you think of Grant and Leslie?"

"They seem fine. I'd say it's pretty tough giving up your room, seeing your stuff moved out."

"Leslie's pretty. You think she'll get married?"

"Of course, someday."

They find aunt and uncle in the den beside the lighted tree, having coffee. Mitchell says, "You guys hungry?"

"Yes, sir, I guess so."

"We'll give the travelers another few minutes."

They settle down on the floor beside the tree, then hear movements and a little later Grant and Leslie come in.

"Good morning, Rip van Winkle," says Mitchell.

"You needed the rest," says Paula. But now we can eat."

They all move to the breakfast room where Paula insists on serving a big spread of ham and cheese omelet, hot fruit, cinnamon rolls and hash browns and juice which she has gone to some effort to prepare. "Eat lots," she says. "Our next meal will be late." Devin, Chase notices, keeps raising his eyes to glance at Leslie and Grant, wondering, probably, if they can ever be friends.

Grant says, "When are Grandmom and Granddad coming?"

"About oneish, I should think. We'll have dinner around two."

"I guess they'll bring a carload of stuff."

"Maybe not. Shopping's not that easy for them now, and I insisted on no more than one or two gifts each."

Devin says, "I got a football from Will. He gave it to me last day of school. Want to throw it?" The invitation's directed to Grant who answers easily, "Sure. Why not?"

After breakfast they go out into the yard, where Devin shows off with jump passes, running catches. The crystalline tips of grass sparkle like glass straws, the odors of someone's wood-burning fireplace wafts across the lawn. Uncle Mitchell handles the football easily, teasing them with crazy tosses. Grant responds, challenging Devin with wobbling receptions and exchanging quips with his father.

Waiting for the ball to come his way, Chase thinks of Kimberly Compass, wonders how she feels this Christmas morning, whether it is a hard time for her or if she can open her arms to expressions of concern, to such gifts as those near her might give. He thinks of calling her, decides he'd better wait, not interrupt their family Christmas morning. As he jumps to receive a high pass, he wishes he and his little brother could be carefree and natural as he hopes all the kids around them are.

* * *

The Atwoods arrive bearing gifts which are heaped on the stacks beneath the tree. Everybody hugs, even Chase and Devin hug them tentatively and are greeted with warmth. Both Bob and Clara Atwood, slender, athletic, look too young to be grandparents of twenty-odd-year-olds. Both play tennis, it is where Paula has learned the game, growing up on the courts. Bob is wearing a tan pullover sweater, khakis, loafers, his hair mostly a rich grey, his hands large, his movements confident. Clara is more outgoing, her eyes friendly and inquisitive, hair tinted dark brown, gestures expressive, with a slight but palpable tendency to monitor everything. It is from her that Paula gets her personality, her looks, Chase thinks, a demand for clarity, the avoidance of innuendo and suggestion. Once or twice he catches Grandmother Atwood looking at him or at Devin and imagines she is weighing the significance of their presence here, how it affects lives, what kind of boys these are who derive from such a sordid background. Still, they appear to be very fond of Mitchell and must realize the nephews are of his blood.

In midafternoon they sit down to a big holiday spread, turkey and dressing, honey baked ham with raisin sauce, broccoli casserole, squash casserole, sweet potato soufflé, beans and several other dishes. Paula has gone all out and Grandmother Atwood has brought dishes as well. Just before they go into the dining room, Devin edges close to Chase. "I don't think I can eat," he whispers.

"Why not? Sometimes you're ravenous," says Chase.

"I don't know. My stomach is queasy."

"Well, just pretend. Maybe when you start you'll develop an appetite."

Someone says, "What do you think, Chase?" He sees Leslie looking at him. "Should I get a kitten or not?"

"A kitten? Well, sure if you want one."

"Who's going to take care of it and feed it when you aren't home?" asks Grandmother Atwood. "You live in an apartment. Do they allow pets in apartments?"

"Well, yes and no."

"Does that mean you think you could hide it?"

"Not exactly. I know the resident manager…"

"She's implicating *him* in deception," laughs Grant.

"I'm waiting for Chase to answer. He's a disinterested party here."

"I guess a kitten would be good company for you," he says.

"Maybe you should get a dog," says Devin. "Then he could go places with you."

"Like where?" Leslie laughs. "Restaurants and work?"

"Hikes and stuff. I wanted a dog, but Daddy would never let us have one. He said all dogs are good at is chewing up garden hoses and plants." With a helpless appeal, he says, "A dog's your friend."

"Well, Devin," says Mitchell, "maybe we'll consider getting you a dog."

"I don't know about that," says Paula. "What do you do with a pet when you go on trips?"

"I'd take care of him," says Devin.

Grandfather Atwood remarks quietly, "The Carolinas have beautiful hiking trails. You have some here, too, up in North Georgia. Is this town very different for you, Devin?"

"It's not home." This slips out, there is a noticeable struggle as he adds hastily, "It's okay, though. I guess things are about what you make them."

"Now that is a very mature observation," says Mitchell.

Paula has set a beautiful table with reds and greens, candles, holiday centerpiece, and Christmas music in the background.

"This is a wonderful meal, Paula," says Grandmother Atwood. "You did too much."

"Remember who taught me to cook."

"Not me," says her father. "I give your mother credit for that. I taught you everything else, though."

Following the meal there is general confusion as everyone pitches in to clean up, then an hour's lull before they head for the den and presents. There are gifts for everyone, piles of them. Chase, sitting on the floor, is surrounded by packages. Devin, across from him, stacks his gifts neatly as they are handed out by Grant and Leslie, all to be opened together. When Grant says, "Okay, let's go!" they tear into ribbons and wrappings, crying, "Oh, you shouldn't have!" and "Just what I wanted!" Mostly they get clothes. Chase receives a new baseball glove—to encourage him to join the team in the spring, he imagines—Devin, a Walkman and a couple of video games. Mitchell keeps torn wrappings and ribbons swept up, stuffing them into fifty-gallon garbage bags. The four cousins exchange small gifts, Chase remembering that what he and Devin give Grant and Leslie has been bought with their parents' money.

Politely, Devin says, "Thank you for my gifts," but there is something furtive about his eyes; he struggles to appreciate every little favor. Chase understands—it all seems so pointless, so uncentered. He struggles to be cheerful, knows on this first Christmas after their mother's death, his little brother is just tortured inside.

As the gift exchange winds down, Paula gives Mitchell a look and he says, "Oh, there's just one other thing. Something for Leslie too large to wrap."

He and Grant go to the master bedroom and bring back a beautiful piece of furniture, a combination jewelry cabinet and dressing table. In the center is a tall mirror, on either side, drawers and doors for jewelry. "It's lovely!" exclaims Leslie. "What a creative arrangement!"

"We've had it for weeks," Paula beams. "Last time we were in your apartment I noticed how unorganized your things were."

"Now I can see to dress!"

"How're we getting it back in your car?" asks Grant.

"It breaks down." Mitchell points out pivots and connections. "The two of you can carry it in, then reassemble it. Look, the mirror tilts. Have to be careful, though, it's not that sturdy."

"I'd love to be able to do lathe work like this." Bob Atwood runs his fingers across the top of the mirror which is scrolled, beveled.

"A piece like this will go with any kind of furniture," says Clara. "Modern or contemporary. It's really lovely."

As they all admire it, Devin begins to investigate, opening doors and drawers. "Where's the secret compartment? There's always a secret compartment."

"Never mind, Devin," says Leslie, "we don't need your fingerprints over everything."

Mischievous, he quickly slides out one tray then another, dodging her as she tries to catch his arms. "Is it here?"

"Get away! It's none of your business."

As they spar, there is a devilish grin on his face, and something insistent, too. Leslie's lips clamp in determined resistance, she intercepts his groping fingers with counteractions just as obstinate as his. There is a swift, frenetic struggle as he reaches for drawers and doors, laughing, and she grabs his arms. It is when he knocks her hand aside that her wrist crashes against the mirror. It breaks, there is the sound of smashing glass, and she cries, "Oh!" She jumps back, a gash oozes blood down her wrist.

"My God!" says Paula.

"Devin!" exclaims Grandmother Atwood.

His expression is frozen in horror. He stands humiliated as Paula bursts out, "Mitchell!"

Mitchell hurries over, lifts Leslie's arm, looks at it. "It isn't bad. Just a little cut. We can fix that."

Devin spins, runs from the room, runs upstairs. They hear his door slam. Chase stands helpless. "I'm sorry. He was just—"

"Come on, Leslie, let's get that bandaged."

Paula goes with them. There is a moment of intense silence before Grandfather Atwood says, "Let's clean up this glass. Where do they keep their stuff, Grant?"

"I'll get it."

As Grant goes out, Chase drops to his knees, picks up the shards which are mostly large, with a few small slivers. The majority of the mirror remains held by the frame. Bob Atwood says, "At least they won't have to worry about breaking it carting the thing up to Atlanta."

"We need to get all the glass out," says Clara. "No use inviting more cuts."

As they take command, Chase slips out, goes up to the bedroom he and Devin have shared these few days. He finds him standing by the window, rigid. His arms, his shoulders stiffen more as the door opens. "Devin," he says.

"What!"

"It was an accident."

"I don't care!"

"Nobody's mad at you. Leslie isn't mad."

"I don't care!"

He walks over, stands beside him. Devin's head is pressed down, there are tears on his cheeks. "It'll be better if you come on back. You can apologize if you want to."

"They hate me!"

"Nobody hates you."

"I'm no good! I can't *talk* to them!"

"Yes, you can. You just have to stop being so touchy." He reaches his arm out. Devin recoils, moves away.

"Just leave me alone!"

"No, dammit, you're going to talk to me!"

Devin's fists open, close. His body is coiled, ready to lash out. His teeth grind so hard the tendons in his neck bulge. "I should have stopped him," he murmurs.

"What? Who?"

"That night. I should have stopped him! I was there!"

"Devin, no!"

"Why didn't I hear something! Why didn't I feel something!"

"It's not your fault."

"Because I was asleep! I was fucking asleep!"

"It's not your fault, Devin!"

"He did it right there in the house! He killed her! Why didn't I hear something!"

"It's not your fault, Devin!"

"Why didn't I stop him!" A great anguished sob racks his body. He shudders, there is a tortured wail. "Because I'm no fucking good! I'm no good to anybody! I should kill myself!"

"Don't say that! Don't you *dare* say that! Ever!" Devin slams his head hard against the window. His head snaps back, there is a gasp of pain. He slams it again.

Chase grabs him, locking his arms tightly. They struggle, rage infusing the young body with extraordinary strength. Chase holds on, fighting him back against the wall. They crash into the dresser, knocking the lamp over. "It's not your fault, Devin! It's not your fault!"

Devin lashes out, trying to strike with his fists.

Then the fight goes out of him, and his body seems to collapse. Chase holds him up, refusing to let him give in. Another bitter sob racks through the fragile tissues, he drops his arms, then hangs there held close, sobbing. "When am I going to stop crying, Chase? When am I going to laugh again?"

"You will," Chase says. "God help us, you will!"

At last his little brother pulls away, sinks down onto the bed, buries his face in the covers. "Just let me sleep. I'm so tired, so tired…"

Chase stands unmoving. He knows he must go downstairs, try to patch things up. He does not want be sent back to the ranch for homeless children. He will not go back, even if means running away. But he cannot run away with a kid brother. What would happen to Devin? And why at seventeen does he feel so old?

* * *

Mitchell says, "Just a little cut. You'll live."

"I can handle the cut," says Leslie. "What about my mirror?"

"Not to worry. As soon as you set your furniture up, I'll have a new one installed."

"At least *we* won't break it," smiles Grant.

Mitchell cleans the wound, swabs on Polysporin and applies two Band-Aids.

"Oh, don't make it look more dramatic than it is," laughs Leslie. "You just want to doctor me like you used to."

"Right. Another opportunity for Daddy to remind you you're still his little girl." Putting away the medicines, Mitchell says, "I know Devin feels miserable."

"Well, he needn't," says Leslie. "He was acting like a jerk, but at eleven I probably did too."

"Something like that happened to me once," says Mitchell.

"Really? What?"

"I was horsing around with my mother. We were walking. Two or three times she told me to cut it out, but I paid no attention. I accidentally tripped her and made her fall. She suffered a badly sprained wrist."

"Well, I'm sure you didn't mean to make her fall."

"No, but I blamed myself. She couldn't talk me out of it, either, no matter how hard she insisted it was all right. I was gloomy for days."

"Well, I'll let him suffer a while, then go and make him feel better," Leslie smiles impishly. "Girls have a way with boys."

Paula has gone back into the den to join her parents, who are cleaning up. Leslie and Grant go, too, as Mitchell hangs back. Something has made him remember the days he and Paula were Leslie's, Grant's age. He had just worked his way through college and married Paula when his sister Kelly was entering the university and needed his financial support more than ever. Those were difficult, thin years, but he recalls actually being happier and more carefree at Grant's age than later when they had money and did not have to pull so hard to make ends meet. A broken mirror, a lacerated wrist is not nearly so momentous to Grant and Leslie as to the adults. They have the much heralded—and he thinks often overrated—extravagance of youth on their side. He wonders what he would do differently if he could go back to the age his children are now, or even if he would choose to go back. He knows he would try harder to give something to the world, not merely take from it.

He walks upstairs to the bedroom where Chase has just left Devin. He finds the younger nephew slumped on the bed, hands hanging listlessly before him, head bowed. "Devin, everything's squared away now. You can come on back."

"I don't want to."

"Nonsense. You choose to isolate yourself in this room all day?" Mitchell walks over, stands close. "Look, we all know you're sorry about the mirror. Nobody's angry about that. Especially Leslie. The best remedy now is to forget it and enjoy our time together. Otherwise we'll all just keep wondering about you."

"Nobody'll wonder about *me*."

"Listen, Devin, this is time for our family together. You're part of the family and you're coming back to join us."

Devin looks up, the cloud lifting a little. "I am? Part of the family?"

"You know you are. Now I'll give you five minutes to wash your face, then I want you back in there."

Devin nods, says meekly, "Yes, sir."

Mitchell smiles. They are making progress. He returns downstairs, wondering if people can really learn to live beyond the troubles of circumstances. He doesn't know. Somehow they must if they are to survive. In a few hours Christmas day will be over.

14

Kimberly Compass answers the phone in an airy, husky voice which at the same time is faintly distant. "Hello?" It sends a thrill through him. "Hello" like the wind through cane reed. "Hello" like the persuasive command of all seductive madness. "Hello," she says.

"Kimberly? It's Chase."

"Hi, Chase. I was wondering when you'd call."

"Well, you know. Work, the holiday rush. How was Christmas?"

"Okay. Fine. Yours?"

"Up and down."

"Your cousins came?"

"Yeah, they left last night. What've you been doing?"

"Oh, sleeping. Eating. Chatting with boys — if they call me." She is coy. "What is it we have now before school?"

"About five days, I guess."

"Time just flies. Scary isn't it?" Her tone becomes coquettish. "Especially when you don't make a move."

"Who, you? Me?"

"You. Boys make the move, usually."

He feels pleasantly cajoled yet anxious, says, "I got a new glove. Maybe we could throw ball sometimes."

She laughs. "Oh, of course, I think Bryan might be better at that. I like golf though."

"I hadn't thought of you as a golfer."

"Not a very good one, but I enjoy it. My dad says ballplayers make good golfers. The swing, I guess."

"So I've heard. Maybe you could give me some pointers."

She starts to say something, interrupts herself. "Chase, I'm sorry, I have to go. I promised Mother I'd do something with her."

"I understand. Look, now that the hustle is over, maybe we could catch a movie or something."

"Okay, when?"

The "when" comes across as her "hello" had. Airy yet direct, a demand for specifics. "When," as if she had known all the time there would be no if, only the cautious step by step maneuvering toward the when.

"Tomorrow night?"

"All right. Say around seven. It'll be fun."

This last in a slightly insistent tone, as if she does not entirely trust herself to make it so.

* * *

He has his own set of keys, one to each of the cars, but always asks in advance if he can take one of the cars instead of the truck. Mitchell and Paula make every effort to juggle their schedules. The better-off kids at school of driving age have sharp little Mustangs and Coopers and VW's, or monster SUV's and trucks with gigantic tires layered with Georgia red mud. As he dresses for his date and then walks into the den, Mitchell looks up. "Hey, you look great. Especially the jacket."

"Thanks. You can wear it sometime."

"I guess we're pretty close to the same size. Besides, fit is no longer in style, is it?"

He grins. "Sloppy and baggy. Crazy, I guess. The girls' stuff gets tighter and tighter, the boys' hang like sacks." He presents himself in profile. "Kimberly gave me this jacket."

"I would say she has very nice taste."

"Thanks again for all our Christmas presents. Devin's too."

"Our pleasure."

Chase perches on the arm of a chair. "Mom said shopping for boys is harder than for girls."

"That so? Well, maybe. I admit Paula picks out most of the clothes. Mine too."

"She does everything pretty well, doesn't she?"

Mitchell laughs. "Efficiency is one of her assets. Prefers things columnized, clear and balanced."

"You sound like an accountant."

"Investment advisor. She got it from her mother, I think. Say what you mean, mean what you say. No hidden agendas."

"That's great. First you have to know how you feel."

"Right. Now that can be an issue." Mitchell lays his book aside, a bad sign, Chase thinks, ready to talk. "You feel good about this date? This girl?"

"Kimberly? Yeah, I think so. *She* has issues."

"Does she?"

"Highs and lows, you know? Life's great, life's the pits, that sort of thing." He hesitates. "Like me, I guess. Good for each other, bad for each other—I can't say yet."

"There's an old saying. Seize the day. Live the moment. Don't explain, don't second guess. Just be here now. You might try that."

Chase manages another grin. "Is that religious?"

"Not necessarily. It leans toward appreciating others. Appreciating self. You and Kimberly have youth on your side. That's a plus."

"It's okay, then, the car and everything?"

"You know it is. Is Kimberly not okay with your truck?"

"She is. It's just that it seems to me a car might be more…intimate." He grins self-consciously.

Before he leaves his uncle hands him an extra twenty. He protests, insists he has money, but then accepts graciously. This is one thing he has begun to learn. Be grateful for every small favor, every kind word. And express appreciation. Gratitude rewards the receiver and the giver.

* * *

They decide on one of the dozens of Chinese restaurants in town. Kimberly is wearing a V-neck blood-red sweater, a gold chain with a diamond and ruby heart, black slacks and shoes. She always looks good in black. Her hair falls loosely about her shoulders and her eyes are searching and alive. Her cheeks are vital, rosy, as though she has just stepped out of a shower, her fingernails painted to match her lip gloss. She has a funny way of turning her mouth to one side, a minor distraction, he thinks, but she is especially pretty on this starless December night, one of the best-looking girls in school. When she first opens the door she exclaims, "Ah! You do look good in that jacket."

"I like it better than any other I've ever had."

"I'm so glad. The color's just right for your hair."

They talk about taking in a movie but she says, "I'd just as soon not unless you especially want to."

At the restaurant they are seated in a small alcove secluded behind reedlike curtains. He starts to slip in beside her, decides to sit across where he can see her better.

"Well, what'd you get for Christmas?"

"Oh, clothes," she says. "Most everything I have on." She turns her torso a little each way to model.

"You're gorgeous," he says.

"Thank you. I got a new cell phone. They're making them smaller and smaller. Easy to carry, easy to lose."

"Devin and I got phones," he says. "We're all in a sequence of numbers."

"That makes them easy to remember. Tell me about your job."

"Not much to tell. No talent required. Just labor, hauling stuff around, cleaning up, but I like the money. And there's something to be said for using your muscles not your brains."

She laughs. "Don't all therapists say the way out of the blahs is to use your hands?"

"I guess so."

"Plant a garden. Knit a sweater. Build a fence. It might sound pointless but it works."

"How do you know?"

"I was in therapy once. I learned how to make little bead bracelets and necklaces. It helped keep my mind off things. Before my accident life seemed less complicated. I think I need to be better with people. I confess now I don't try too hard to turn on the charm." She pushes her glass away, searches among the napkin holder for straws. "What about you? Are you talking to anybody now? I mean, like therapy?"

He hasn't expected this, says evasively, "Yes and no. I've had one session with a man Mitchell wanted me to see. I may go back."

"You think he can tell you something you can't figure out yourself?"

"Probably not. He may help speed things up a little, though. Besides, it makes my uncle feel better."

"We have to do that, don't we?" she says. "Things other people want us to do. If we didn't, I guess we'd just live all in our own heads and that isn't how it's supposed to be."

"How is it supposed to be?"

"Oh, I don't know. Try to help others along the way. Be nice. Give up a little of our precious self."

"And how did you arrive at this?"

"I don't know. After my brain got rattled in the accident, I guess. I could've died. I sort of came to the conclusion we can't always live every minute of every day only for ourselves."

She adjusts the collar of her sweater, the modestly plunging V, smoothing down the front. It is an unconscious casual gesture but his eyes follow along the stitched seam, the clear complexion, the heart, the contour of her bust. He sees in her the things he himself feels, the fear and uncertainty, the lightning fast change of mood, the hope for joy and confusion about what brings it, the erotic thirst and terror of heartbreak. In the muted light her hair is dark, haloing her face. She takes small, experimental bites of coconut shrimp, leaning slightly forward. Little crescents of lipstick form asymmetrical patterns on her napkin.

"Your mother was pretty, I bet," she says. "Do you look like her?"

"I don't know. I guess."

"What was your favorite thing about her?"

He shakes his head. "I never thought about it."

"I'm not surprised. Think about it now. Your favorite thing."

He pauses. "Well, she was always inquisitive. She liked to see things from different perspectives. She'd sketch something, then take out a mirror and look at it in reverse."

"What did she draw? People, figures?"

"The outdoors, mostly. Things we saw together. Birds sometimes, streams, rocks. Shapes, not detail. Little is more, she used to say."

"And you sketch, too."

"A little. It's good therapy."

"What do you like most?"

"Drawing and baseball, I guess."

"I think the thing I would remember most about my mother is how she saves everything. It's weird. Clothes, programs, ticket stubs. Every picture she's ever taken of me. All my little pinafores and dance shoes from the time I was about two."

"You must have a lot of storage space."

She laughs. "Oh, yes. The attic, high closet shelves. From time to time my father puts his foot down and they spend weekends going through boxes, trashing things. She's hyper-sentimental."

"You, too?"

"No," says Kimberly. "It's strange, isn't it? I don't keep anything. What's over's over. I guess it's rewarding to enjoy memories like she does."

There is a pensive look in her eyes. As they sit talking, the slim, black-haired, delicate-featured server comes to ask if they would like anything else. "She wants our table," says Kimberly. "We're denying her tips."

"People are waiting, too. Shall we be considerate and leave, or exercise our rights?"

"Let's be considerate and leave." She smiles, minute dimples forming beside her mouth, her lips faintly moist.

"We could go bowling," he says.

"Okay. I'm not very good at it."

"Doesn't matter. We can take out all our fury on the pins."

She laughs. "And they can't fight back."

* * *

He watches as Kimberly cocks her head, fixes her gaze on the pins. For several seconds she holds the ball close to her chest, then her arm drops and her approach is rhythmic, no awkward stumbling or swaying. Her hips are nicely curved, the strength in her thighs emphasized by the tight jeans. Her arm sweeps forward, she bends slightly on her toes, not throwing but gliding through. The ball passes right across the arrow she had targeted but halfway down begins to drift. Chase smiles as she snaps her feet together, tries with both hands in the air to nudge the ball over, feet, hips, torso making evocative movements to the left. No good, the ball tumbles right, catches a single pin before clattering into the pit. "Oh, darn!" she says, but without passion. She turns, lifts her brow, informs him, "I get a second chance."

"Indeed you do."

"You'll see."

On the second roll she is a bit more effective, taking out an additional seven pins. Just as the ball strikes she gives a little jump, using all her body language. As she turns triumphantly to him, she says, "What?"

"Nothing. I like the way you throw your heart into it."

"Well, you can never accuse me of half trying."

They bowl two games, then grab a soda and sit at a little round table. Some teenagers enter the alley, she lifts her arm to them. "I hope they don't come over. I don't want anyone joining us right now." They all wave back, then go on about the task of finding their balls. A couple of the girls are wearing low rise jeans and tank tops, with tattoos on their hips. Kimberly raises her brows. "What do you think of the tattoos?"

"They're okay," Chase says.

"But?"

"I don't know. I wouldn't want to stamp myself with anything for life."

She giggles. "I got one of these paste-on things, the kind that wash off, you know? I showed my parents and said, 'Some girls and I decided to go ahead and get tattoos. We had the hardest time deciding which ones.' My daddy fell for it and had a fit."

He laughs. "Well, I guess you know where he stands on tattoos."

"You see that girl in red? She's a wonderful actress. Hopes for a scholarship, then after college to study in New York."

"Like a million others," he says.

"True. So much depends on timing and luck. That's how it is in everything, isn't it?"

"Yeah, I guess so. First you gotta make up your mind to do it."

"Is that what happened when you finally started noticing me?"

"I noticed you all along. Nobody else."

"Aha! That's what all the girls say."

"What girls?"

"The girls who notice you not noticing."

"Oh, I bet, I don't—I couldn't even—"

She laughs. "Now you're sputtering again."

"I'm not sputtering."

"I know one thing. You and I are both very careful about the relationships we choose."

"Why do you think so?"

"Because we don't want to be the ones to make people happy or unhappy." She sighs. "It's a burden to carry. Especially with those you live with. I don't like thinking when I'm wretched they're wretched. It just makes things worse." She gazes at him with wide frank eyes. "Why didn't your mother leave your father?"

It is a blow he doesn't expect. "I don't know."

"Did she try? Did she stay because of you and Devin?"

"If we were an issue I didn't know it. I guess they did a helluva job hiding what was going on. Or he did."

"Does it hurt so much to talk about it?"

He looks away, looks back. "The screwy thing is most people are afraid to talk about it. They're embarrassed to bring it up. It makes you feel that maybe *you* drive them away. Not you, though. You don't skirt anything."

"Because when you've been so far down, nothing seems pathetic and shocking."

"You have your mother and father to support you," he says. "That's a lot to be thankful for."

"Did I ever tell you my father had great ambitions as a singer?"

"You've hardly told me anything about your parents."

"He has a beautiful baritone voice. But something happened to his hearing, a virus or something, and he had to give up hopes of ever making it big. He married Mama instead."

"And had you."

"And had me. Isn't he lucky?" There is irony in her tone, and a touch of sadness.

He says quickly, "And my bet is he's thankful every day for the way things turned out."

"Maybe. Are you thankful that what happened to you happened? That you had to leave Raleigh and come here?"

"No. Yes. I'm thankful I met you. And Bryan. And a few others."

"Do you think God put us here for you?"

"How does God come into this?"

"I guess half the kids around us never give God a thought. Others believe He's in everything."

"I guess it depends on how we look at life," Chase says.

"During my recovery I thought about it a lot. Why did that virus destroy my father's dreams and potential? Was it so he could marry Mama and have me?"

Chase smiles. "It was so he could have you, so you could have me."

"Ha! So you do believe."

"I don't know."

"Sometimes you do, sometimes you don't, is that right?"

"Something like that," he says. "Except that's the same as not believing, I guess. You either do or you don't. There's no in-between."

"I think you're right. Why aren't you sure?"

"Because of what happened to my mother, I guess. To us. Until then I was okay with it."

"Do you think it disappoints your uncle and aunt very much? That you aren't convinced."

"I guess. They're pretty sure trying to learn to love others is our best hope."

"I believe," she says.

"Okay."

"It's hard for me to think this life is the beginning and end of it all. That we just evolved. At least we can make the choice for ourselves."

She slips the straw into her mouth. He can see the faint distention of her throat as she swallows. Then she smiles suddenly. "Why don't we get out of here and go somewhere?"

"Where would you like to go?"

"My house maybe. My parents are away a couple of days. I'm not supposed to have boys over when they aren't there, but..."

"Maybe we shouldn't then."

"I guess this one time..."

She looks at him almost helplessly and there is a quick rush of his blood.

* * *

They leave the alley, slip on their coats, and hurry to the car. He pulls out and drives slowly, prolonging these minutes when they can laugh, talk, kid each other. He slips his hand across the seat, tentatively takes hers. Her fingers close around his — a good sign.

She asks, "Do you think you'll jump back into baseball?"

"Probably. I guess that's my best shot at becoming involved."

"You'll start back," she says. "This spring. I'll make you."

"You will?"

"It's easy to give up on things. But we have to have an interest in something."

He says in a husky pretend voice, "I have an interest in you."

"But not as a hobby."

It is dark, only a few porch lights burn encouragingly. The sky is clear, the stars glitter on charcoal paper streaked with glares of ghostly silver. As they turn into her driveway he kills the lights, feeling faintly clandestine and criminal. She rummages through her purse to find her keys, then they walk up to the door. She lets them in, closes the door behind.

"You have a pretty house," he says.

"Thanks. My father's the neat one. He wants everything nice and orderly. Mother's a little looser."

"It's just the opposite with my aunt and uncle. She's the rigid one. Takes both, I guess."

They settle on the sofa, turn on TV, keep the volume muted. "I've never brought a friend home with no one else here," she says.

"Why now?"

She looks at him without smiling, sober, faintly chagrined. "Where else could we go? I don't care that much for prowling shopping centers or parking lots."

He grins. "Right. Perfectly logical."

"Besides, it's been so long since anything seemed to matter, I just want to feel passionate about *something*."

"I know how you feel," he says. "Except I think I had it a long time ago. Then — " he hesitates, " — something closed down."

"How many kids do you think really care much about anything? My father gets so frustrated. You can't be depressed he says, you're the most favored generation the world has known."

"I'm not sure that's a plus. What about Snatch Holbrook?"

"Why does Snatch keep coming between us?"

"Why do you keep brushing him aside?"

"Gene plays games. Sometimes I'm attracted. Mostly not, though." Her look turns coy. "I don't mean to suggest I'm totally naïve, Chase."

"Really? How un-naïve are you?"

"Now you're making fun of me."

There is a brief standoff. Her lips part, the downturn appears to suggest challenge and defiance. It is amazing how swiftly desire whips through him. He leans toward her, hoping she won't turn away. She doesn't, her mouth is moist and warm and sweet. He draws her closer and she comes willingly, her tongue exploring. Her arm slips around to press their heads together. His blood hammering, all the pent-up desire and darkness seeking escape; he moves his hand up to stroke her breast. She allows this. He is about to explode, an irresistible current of passion rushing him blindly forward, forward toward a thundering shower of release.

Then there is an inexplicable agonizing drop, a great hole opens below and suddenly all the black distance jolts them apart. He thinks, Damn! Damn! As fear and anger and memory freeze his blood, an absolutely impotent frustration caves in upon him. He turns his face aside, gasping for breath.

"What's wrong?" she whispers.

"I don't know!"

"Is it me?"

"God, no, it's not you!"

They break apart, she sits back peering intently at him. "I don't expect anything, you know?" she whispers. "You're not sending me any false signals."

He leans forward, buries his face in his hands. "This can't just be about me! It can't!"

"It isn't, Chase. It's about me, too. Don't you know that?"

He clenches his jaw, confused, outraged by the defensive numbness that grips him. He cannot allow himself to turn loose, not his emotions, not his heart. He cannot take advantage of her. The pressure in the room seems to press upon him, squeezing his chest and head, his limbs.

Kimberly reaches over, draws his hand close to her, holds it gently. He knows she is as confused as he, as frustrated, yet reaching out, touched by instinctive tenderness. They sit silent, rigid, waiting for the tension to pass.

* * *

When it is time to go they part with a solemn goodnight kiss. Driving home he is pounded by self-incrimination. He blew it. The all-American screw-up. Failure sags his shoulders, shatters along his pent-up nerves. What kind of misfit is he? He pleads for liberation, yet a choking fist closes tightly upon everything he wants to feel.

In his room, the door closed, he opens the window and sits on the floor, the cold air blasting his face. The room is darker than the night; outside the street, trees, rooftops are silhouetted with a haunting moon. He experiences an urgent yearning, some fervent and helpless desire for a past—any past—when he thought he was happy.

He strains to look up the dark street as if some answer awaits him. A shadow slips by, an owl, he thinks. A moment later he hears the call. His mother loved owls. All over their house were sketches of them, figurines, monogrammed towels. What happened to these collections? Trashed, stored somewhere, dumped in a yard sale? Memory—he lets it come now, groping back for guidance, for closure, not the horrible images of her last days...

It was one of the few times he ever saw her sad, saw her cry. He was about thirteen. The six-year-old daughter of her best friend had just died of a malignant brain tumor. They'd held out hope until the last; the child was so bright, so lively, so loved. His mother, with her compassionate heart and almost always seeing good in everything, took it hard. He saw the pain in her eyes, the tears creeping down her cheeks.

He asked, "Why does something like this happen? It doesn't make sense."

Kelly dabbed her tears, looked at him bravely. "No one knows why things happen, Chase. Perhaps there is no reason. But I think sometimes it is to prepare us to help others who someday suffer the same thing…"

Cynically, he shook his head. "I think that sucks. Throwing away one life to make it a little easier for another."

She put her hand on his arm and looked at him with deep feeling. "It may seem unjust. But one never knows the value of the heart he is saving."

He slips down now, rests his arm on the windowsill, balls his fist and raps his knuckles on the side of his skull. Trying to clear his brain or hammer sense into it. He sees no sense at all in what has happened to him, to Devin, to anybody.

15

Final bell. First day back at school is over with great splash and rush.
Lockers slam, echoes reverberate through the halls. Pupils shout
to one another, splintering the decorum the principal insists on
during school hours. A kind of rebellion or mere release of tension? Christmas presents fly by—new sweaters, new jeans, bracelets, watches, Oakley sunglasses. Coats and jackets are thrown
over shoulders or tied around waists, arms encircle books like
iron hoops.

Teachers are just as eager to get the day behind, a few sit at
their desks, doors open; others rush from the building with the
same intense escape as their students. Ms. Magill, the French
teacher, bears a vase of flowers, headed out to her little two-seater
Mazda. Walking behind her, Chase inhales her perfume or perhaps it is the flowers. Something in him is stirred; he recognizes
the odor, wonders if his mother had worn the scent. Ms. Magill
is a petite woman, dark hair, smooth alabaster expressive arms, a
soundless stealthy walk like a tigress. He imagines her in various
poses of undress, shakes his head, turns away.

He exits the north corridor into the afternoon sunlight, bright,
cold. Midafternoon slams him. A Burger King coffee cup blows

across the driveway, but there is very little litter, Mr. Franklin's spies pounce on anybody caught discarding trash on the grounds. From the north wing where most of the students park, cars exit the paved lot, the dirt section beyond, pulling out from under the gigantic oaks. Kimberly has her own car and he knows exactly where she parks. Difficult as it is, the young drivers stake out their personal little spots, seldom vary more than a space or two. He feels a kind of quiet admiration for this tacit code of a generation not well known for civility and responsibility. He steps from the little stoop, crosses the paved driveway, weaves a maze through cars and pickups. Drivers are pulling out, others milling around, slouching on hoods, grabbing ten minutes of intimacy on back seats.

When he sees Kimberly exactly where he expects, an unexpected painful anger stabs him. She is in a fight with Snatch Holbrook. He has her by the arms, dragging her forward. She digs in her heels, but is no match. She tumbles forward, plants her legs, stumbles forward again. Above the honking and noises, he cannot hear her cries but knows she is shrieking, struggling. She falls toward Holbrook, jerks away and digs in again. His strength is taunting and arrogant; she is a mere twig to his gale force.

An irrational deep rage whips through Chase and he propels himself forward. With a will of their own, his legs rush him through the space of cars and pickups. He dips his head and hits Holbrook hard from the side. Holbrook staggers, his arms fling up, knocking Kimberly away. He tumbles back, trips, but does not lose his footing. Chase swings a vicious looping clenched fist to his nose. He feels bone to bone, there is a savage sweet pleasure as blood spurts from Holbrook's nostrils.

"God damn!" Snatch regains his footing, flings up his guard

against the hammer blows, whips his powerful arms out around Chase to send him spinning aside.

"Chase!" Kimberly cries. "Stop! He wasn't *doing* anything!"

He falls against the side of a car, crashes away and throws himself straight into a fierce driving punch to the head. A cannon blow, Holbrook's superior weight knocks him down. On his back, he lies a moment dazed, then pulls himself to his feet, his arms flailing now, wild, disoriented. They lock together, struggling, half cursing, half sobbing. He manages one fierce solid blow to Holbrook's gut before the huge deadly fists batter his chest, his stomach and body so murderously his head swoons, his knees buckle and he goes down again. Towering over him, enraged, bleeding, Holbrook bellows, "Get up, you fucking bastard!"

He rolls to his side, tries to rise but something is pushing him down, there is pressure on his chest. Kimberly cries, "Chase, stop! Stop! He wasn't *doing* anything!" she repeats. All her weight is down against him, her arms pinning his, her hands pressed to his face, his shoulders.

"What?"

"We were just cutting up!"

He struggles, she holds tight, her body thrusting down against his. Vaguely he realizes Holbrook has disappeared, along with those who'd run over to watch. A teacher or maintenance man is hurrying across the yard to break up the fight. Too late, the man glares down as Kimberly moves aside, Chase sits up. He rubs his face, opens and closes his fists, checking to see if anything is broken.

"You kids get out of here before I haul you in to Mr. Franklin!" The man turns on his heels, retreats.

Kimberly stands, reaches down. Chase accepts her hand, allows her to help him up. She fixes her steady gaze on his face. "What made you do that? What made you, Chase?"

"I want him to keep his damn hands off you!"

"You acted crazy."

The words hit him like another blow. Crazy. Maybe he is. Maybe there is something cruel and savage lurking beneath the surface. He feels his stomach roil, feels he is about to throw up.

Gently she says, "Are you all right? Did he hurt you?"

"I'm okay. I thought he was—"

"I know." She reaches, takes his hand. "Do you want to come home with me? You're pretty shaken up."

"No. Thanks."

"You're bleeding." She touches his cheek.

He draws her hand down, holds it a moment. "It's okay."

"All right. I'll get your books." She goes over, collects the books where he's flung them. As she hands them to him she leans, kisses him on the cheek. "See you tomorrow."

She walks away quickly, something both reflective and uncertain in her step. He stands unmoving while she backs her car out, heads down the drive. Then he realizes all the cars are gone, the grounds are empty. There is no one in sight.

* * *

He is halfway down the east driveway when Bryan comes hurrying to meet him. Bryan has heard about the fight, is looking for him. For the past five minutes Chase has hardly felt anything, his body and emotions anesthetized. Now it all crashes into focus, the raw aching knuckles, the burning split lip and cut over his right eye. The self-incrimination, fear of losing control. And control is everything, he knows. Of emotions, of words, heart. The safest way is to live in a tight, constricted little ball, a fetal position of inaccessibility. If he understands this why does he lash out, in a mindless explosion of bitterness?

Tensely, Bryan says, "Blood's all over your jacket."

He doesn't answer, fixes his gaze straight ahead.

"What happened?"

"Nothing."

"Nothing. You look like you ran into a truck."

He keeps walking, offering no excuse, feeling Bryan's disapproval.

"I don't believe in fighting Chase. It's stupid and pointless. People battering each other with their fists. Juvenile, too."

"So?"

"So why do it? Especially with a creep like Snatch. It just brings you down to his level."

"Maybe that's the only level he understands."

"It makes you look as dumb as he is."

They reach Chase's truck, stand beside it. "There are other ways of settling differences," Bryan says. "You're capable of rising above that."

"Somebody has to shut his foul mouth."

"You think this is Snatch's first fight? It's what he wanted, to bring you down to his terms. What are you going to tell your aunt and uncle?"

"Whatever I have to."

"I'd try to clean up a bit. Put something on those cuts. Cold water will help the bloodstains."

There is a moment of tense silence. As Chase opens his car door, Upchurch says again, "I don't believe in fighting, Chase."

It strikes him as an ultimatum, a kiss off. He responds coolly, "Okay, I read you."

Bryan nods. "I just want you to think about it."

"Sure. I'll think about it."

Chase gets in, slams the door, drives home. No cars are here, he is relieved, needs some time. He enters through the side door, moves quickly upstairs. As he passes Devin's room he is disappointed and irked when his brother hears him, calls, "Hi, Chase."

He starts to hurry on, thinks better of it, pauses. Averting his glance, his shoulder half turned into the room, he says, "I thought no one was here."

"Aunt Paula dropped me off then went somewhere. What's that on your jacket?"

He jerks the garment off, crumbles it beneath his arms. "Nothing." As he turns away, Devin runs to the door. "What happened to your face?"

He hesitates, too tired to hide anything. "Fight," he says.

"Who with?"

"Boy at school. You don't know him."

"Wow. You have a cut over your eye. Lip, too."

"Yeah. He got in a few licks."

"What about? A girl I bet."

"Yes and no. The guy's a jerk."

Devin stares at him, his expression awed and anxious. "You almost never had fights."

"Well, it's a dumb idea, so let this be a lesson to you. Walk away whenever you can."

"Did you try to walk away?"

"No, I went after him."

Devin steps back, his eyes wide and wondering. "Why did you do it?"

Chase feels tension along the back of his palms. "I guess I went a little crazy, like trying to save Mother from Daddy…a bully and an innocent victim. I couldn't let it happen again."

"Wow," Devin says. "Did you win?"

"You ask a lot of questions, don't you? No, I didn't win. Nobody does in something like this. I probably look worse than he does."

"Wonder what Paula and Mitchell will say?"

"Look, Dev, I've got to clean up. Just let them find out themselves, okay?"

"I bet you'll have a black eye."

He lays the bloody jacket on the vanity, takes a damp cloth and removes some of the stains. The cleaners can finish it. In the mirror he examines his face. Devin is right, his eye is beginning to swell, the lower area tinging blue. He has a puffy lip, realizes he must have bitten his tongue, it stings to run his tongue over his teeth. He strips off his shirt, washes his face gently, then goes downstairs to the kitchen. He fills a Ziploc with ice and returns to his room. Lying on his back, he holds the pack against his eye and mouth, alternating as it becomes too cold. A sudden weariness caves in upon him. The bed feels alien—Grant's bed on loan to a wild-assed cousin. He thinks of his own room back in Raleigh, his baseball paraphernalia, his pictures, posters. He remembers how he used to be, how he took great pleasure in buying birthday presents for his mother and father, secreting them behind clothes in his closet until the eventful day; how he anguished over a dog's broken leg, talked boys out of fighting and almost never got into a fight himself. Who was he then? Who is he now?

He remembers his first brutal blow into Holbrook's nose and

a warm vengeful satisfaction settles over him. Then, pressing the ice bag on his eye, he feels ashamed and afraid. What kind of monster is he that he takes pleasure in inflicting pain, even deserved pain? His distrust of himself, and of his emotions, are only deepened. And now he is afraid that even Bryan distrusts him. Bryan who admittedly is no angel, but is the closest thing he knows to reason and responsibility in their own little teenage circle. His closest connection to a friend, too; though he knows even with Bryan there has always been a separation, a gap wedged open by his own inner turmoil.

When he hears his aunt and uncle enter the house he gets up, dumps the ice into the lavatory, disposes of the Ziploc, strips and takes a shower. Meticulously he grooms his hair, the brush abrasive against chafed skin, then does all he can to disguise the damage. The ice has helped, the laceration over his eye not so bad, his lip still puffy, but beginning to recede. He decides not to wait for Mitchell to come up on his usual pilgrimage of good will. Instead, he takes a deep breath, walks down to the kitchen. Paula is arranging canned goods and boxes in cabinets. Mitchell stands at the table looking over the mail. As he enters they both glance up, speak, then she exclaims, "Chase! What happened!"

He shrugs, crosses to the sink and draws a glass of water. Looking closely at him, Mitchell says, "You been in a fight?"

He nods, having decided against lying. He steadies himself for rebuke.

"Why were you fighting?" asks Paula.

"It's a long story. Not worth telling."

"Just two of you?" says Mitchell.

He nods, wishing he could say it was a group quarrel, making it somehow less personal.

"Why were you fighting?" Paula repeats. "Who started it?"

"I don't know. Him. Me. I struck the first blow, if that's what you mean."

"Let me see that eye." Mitchell comes close. Chase starts to resist, decides to submit, stands unmoving as his uncle examines the cut.

Paula leaves off arranging the groceries and stands with her arms straight down by her side. "I can't remember Grant ever getting into a fight."

Abject disgust surges through him. He looks at her coolly. "Well, maybe he never had anything worth fighting for."

"Or maybe it just wasn't in him."

Mitchell asks quickly, "What about the other guy? He okay?"

"He knocked me down. I expect he's satisfied."

"Well, look, it happens. Boys get into fights. It's part of growing up."

"Is it?" Paula is not persuaded. "Fighting is not the way to settle disputes. I want no part in it."

"This has nothing to do with you," says Chase.

"Anything that happens in this house has to do with me."

"Yeah. How can I forget?"

"And you're still mad, aren't you?"

Awkwardly he walks to the sink, dumps the rest of the water. With exaggerated respect, he says, "Anything I can do to help?"

"No," she says. "We'll call you when dinner's ready."

"What about Devin?" Mitchell asks. "He up there?"

"In his room. Or Leslie's room I should say." He knows this is a cutting barb, is sorry but can't resist. He's acting like a prick and knows it. If his aunt and uncle hadn't brought them here to live, where in hell would they be now?

He leaves the kitchen, starts upstairs then stops, backs up a few steps and stands listening. It is something he has never done before. His mother long ago taught them never to eavesdrop, to steal another's private conversation, but a gut feeling holds him, he knows intuitively they'll talk about him.

Paula says gravely, "I knew something like this would happen."

"Like what?" Mitchell's voice is distant. "It doesn't mean anything."

"Doesn't it? Doesn't it mean they have something of their father in them?"

"Paula, damn it, no! Don't blow this out of proportion! When I was a kid I had fights. It's not genetic, believe me."

"Maybe not. How do we know this isn't just the beginning?"

"The beginning of what? I swear, I don't understand what you're afraid of."

"I'm afraid of our lives being torn apart. I'm afraid of something really bad happening."

The heat seeps out of Mitchell's voice as he says, "You could look at it another way. Things could have got pretty dull around here. We could view the boys as an opportunity. God knows they need us."

She says quietly, "Dull like two people who no longer enjoy living together? Just the two of them doing things?" She falters slightly, then with resolution says, "I've said before and I say again I support you in this, Mitchell. I just pray nothing worse than this happens."

Chase turns, blows of regret driving him down the hall. What can he expect? He deserves her doubts. Every day he seems to make himself less lovable. He thinks again of getting out of their hair, but where would he go, what would it do to Devin? Mitchell and Paula offer them their best chance of putting their lives back together, but something bizarre and diabolical imprisons him. Or perhaps he is the prisoner who finds the cell door open but can't bring himself to rush through. There is something blackly secure in the cell, feeling nothing, invulnerable, untouchable. Something he despises but can't let go. Something that makes others suspicious and afraid. Something that keeps him from loving himself.

* * *

Marsha, Hagen's assistant, opens her door, motions him into her office. He is nervous, knows he is imposing. When he called earlier, she'd said, "Chase, I'm sorry, I don't know how Dr. Hagen could see you today."

"I really need to talk to him."

She hesitated, after a moment relented. "All right, I'll see what I can do."

In ten minutes she called back and at five o'clock Chase walks into the office, feeling guilty for making demands. Hagen comes out, says cheerfully, "Glad to see you, Chase. Come on in." He leads the way into his private office, closes the door, and says, "Excuse me a minute, will you?"

"Sure. Fine."

Hagen is wearing a black suit, black shoes, dark tie, more dressed up than he usually is on weekdays. Quite distinguished, thinks Chase. He disappears into his private bath and returns without the coat and tie, wearing a pale green V-neck sweater. "We had a funeral earlier," he says. "Don't tell anybody, but I hate wearing suits."

Chase forces a smile. "That's too bad. You look good in black."

"Thank you. It hasn't been that long since we all wore white shirts and ties. Now just about anything goes."

Chase drops down into the same chair he'd used before. "I'm sorry to bother you. I mean, after something like a funeral."

"No bother at all. It's quite normal for us to celebrate a birth in the morning, conduct a funeral in the afternoon." Hagen settles into his own chair, tugs the sleeves of his sweater. "Well, how's it going? You feeling better?"

Chase looks at his hands. "Sometimes yes, sometimes no. I'm tired of thinking everybody's watching me all the time."

"Why should they be watching? Because you're grotesque, hideously ugly? Because you look like Leonardo DiCaprio? Which do you see when you look into a mirror?"

"A little of both, I guess. I don't hate what I see, if that's what you mean. At least not physically."

"So. You hate your thoughts?"

"I hate feeling self-conscious and nervous all the time. Defensive, too."

"Why are you defensive? What are you defending?"

"I'm not sure. Defending myself against them or from them. Sometimes I want to yell, Leave me alone! Others, *Why* are you leaving me alone!"

"You know, I sometimes feel the same way," says Hagen. "Is this something new?"

"No, it's the same old sh — the same old stuff."

The pastor looks at him with patience. "Marsha said something seemed to be weighing pretty heavily on you."

He looks away, squirms. "I need you to help me figure something out. There was this fight. My fault. I started it."

"Why were you fighting?"

"I thought this big blowhard was hurting a girl. I had to stop him."

"Was he hurting her?"

"I found out later they were just playing around."

"So what are you feeling now? Guilt? Shame?"

He closes his fist, raises his hand and scrubs his forehead. "Not that exactly. I should have realized they were cutting up. Something made me go after him. I guess it was jealousy that just exploded in back of my head. I'm afraid it'll happen when…it could be worse."

"Well, how did you feel at the time? Were you angry? Letting off steam?"

"That's what scares me. I wasn't that mad. Resentful I guess. He's such an asshole. Excuse me." He glances at Hagen, is relieved to see him nod. "I hated it afterward. But there was something I liked about it, too."

"What did you like?"

"I'm not sure. I *felt* something. Nothing I'm proud of but *something*. Even feeling lousy sometimes is better than feeling nothing at all."

"Okay, I understand that. Let me ask you. You were letting out something. What is it you'd been keeping in?"

"I don't know. Rage, maybe. Hate."

"But you said you weren't that angry."

"I know, I know." He taps his head with his knuckles. "I gotta figure this out. What was I taking out on Holbrook? I need you to tell me."

Hagen leans forward. "You think maybe it's not that complicated? You're throwing too much into the mix? Think it might simply be pain?"

"No, no, that doesn't make sense."

"What doesn't make sense about it?"

A sudden burning sensation strikes him behind the eyes. "Things can't hurt forever. They can't!"

"You mean you can forget the past?"

"I have to!"

"How do you propose to do that?"

The stabbing fire goes down through his heart, his groin, thighs, the old and powerful recall that slams so swiftly into him it makes him sick. "I can't let it change me!" he says. "Not like that! Not taking it out on somebody with my fists! That's what…that's what *he* did…"

"Your father?"

"He would have done that to me too! He would have wiped me out!" Then it comes, the gale force of memory that will never release him. He fights it, he always fights it, but in a way he knows he must let it come. It is his only hope of ever escaping. He is back in Raleigh. As his father, released on bail, thundered into the house, Chase flung himself at him, fists wild, flailing. "Son of a bitch!"

His father grabbed him, struck back, threw him against the wall.

Screaming "Stop! Stop!" Devin ran to the phone to call for help.

In the painful violent minutes before the police arrived, Chase, hurting, gasping for breath, cried, "Why! Why! Just tell us why!"

His father slammed away, trying to get away from them. "Shut your fucking mouth! You don't know what you're talking about!"

"Why did you kill Mom! Tell us, dammit, at least give us that!"

"I didn't do a fucking thing!"

"You did! I know you did! I've always known!"

He pursued his father down the hall, into the bedroom, Devin following behind. "Just tell us why, damn you! There has to be a reason! What did she do to you! Tell us!"

"Shut up before I shut you up!"

"Yeah, why don't you do to me what you did to her! Why don't you kill us too! Chop us to pieces!"

"Damn you, Chase, you're asking for it!"

"Go ahead! What the fuck do I care! How did you do it! A pillow! Your hands! You took Mom away! Why!"

His father cursed, yelled at Devin. "Shut up! I hate that damn crying!"

Chase balled his fists again, swung wildly, useless, ineffectual blows on the shoulders, arms. His father slapped him hard, bursting his mouth. "Why did you do it! Oh God, please just tell us why! What did she do to you!"

"Get out of my sight!"

"You hate us, too, is that it! You're supposed to be our dad—!" He broke down completely, sobbing, racked with pain…"My God, my God, why did it have to be you!"

The room spins violently, shattered by guttural broken sounds, something alien and threatening. He realizes suddenly the sounds are coming from his own mouth, tries to muffle them against his arm. Dr. Hagen says quietly, "It's okay, Chase. Take all the time you need."

He digs his fingers into his temples. "I'm sorry…" Finally there is a great shuddering sigh, he is wrung out, his throat dry and aching, his body suddenly still as death.

Hagen does not speak, just slips a box of tissues over to him. He yanks one out, wipes his eyes, blows his nose. "I'm sorry. I didn't mean…"

"Chase, tell me. Is that what's bothering you? You think you need forgiveness?"

"I don't know!"

"Who would you say is supposed to forgive you? What are they to forgive you for?"

"We had to be partly to blame. He would never have done that — nobody would do that to another human unless — there had to be a reason."

"What if there is no reason? No answers, no confessions, no repentance? What if it just happened?"

"Nothing like that just happens. Not…not the way he did it."

"All right, let's just say your father can't *give* you a reason. Should you let that keep eating you? You'll waste your life waiting for an explanation. One thing you have to believe. It wasn't because you and Devin are rotten kids. You said so yourself."

Chase forces himself back against the chair, opens and closes his eyes, trying to stabilize, to bring shapes together into something substantial.

Hagen says, "What is it you're afraid of?"

"Aw, God, I don't know. Of ever feeling anything good again. Of letting myself hurt like this again."

"You know what I think? Hurting is part of life. And it's worth the risk. If we risk nothing with our friends, with those we love, we haven't much chance of ever experiencing 'good' things."

"You open yourself up somebody's gonna pour shit in." He shakes his head. "Sorry, pastor, I don't mean to use words like that."

"What if somebody does? Pours pain in? If you never risk feeling pain, will you ever feel anything else? Joy or beauty or goodness. Sure, there's pain all in the world, but love, too. Gratitude. Happiness. Can you close out one without closing out the rest?"

Chase looks down, the dried tears stinging his cheeks. Numbly, he says, "This girl I had the fight over. We're pretty stuck on each other."

"Good. That's a beginning."

"I think I could get really lost in her. Maybe people aren't supposed to get that deep into someone else. Especially kids like us."

"Age makes a difference?"

"For a lot of our generation everything is pretty superficial, you know? Love, sex. Nothing seems to mean very much."

"What do you think it's supposed to mean?"

"Something. It's supposed to mean something. If going to bed with someone doesn't mean much, what does?"

"I'd say that's thinking beyond your years. But what's scary about it meaning something?"

He squirms, looks at the bookcases, the baseball trophy, the framed photographs. "My father and mother were married eighteen years before he...he buried her." He fights the tears trying to erupt again. "I don't want ever to lie about loving someone. About making love to them."

"Chase, you know what I think? I think you have to trust yourself. Your own body, your own mind. Nobody else. Every person is different. Your mom, your dad—they're part of you but not you. You have to choose which part, sort it out and throw out the garbage. Does this make sense?"

"I don't know."

"Does it make sense to hate your father?"

"I can't help it. At one time...I loved him."

"Well, that's one of life's ironies, isn't it? We despise only that which has most aroused our passion. Does that make you feel better? Make him feel worse?"

"Yes. No. Sometimes I hate myself for hating him. It makes me...like him."

"Look, you say first you're afraid you'll never feel anything again, then you say you feel hatred. Seems to me you can't pick and choose. You want to feel love, romance, joy, you gotta experience pain, anger, too. You name the emotion, it's in this world."

"I know, I know."

"So why not let the hatred go? Listen to your own body. It's better at telling you what's best for you."

Chase sighs, feels dead tired, weary. He says, "I wish I had more faith."

"In what?"

"I don't know. Myself. God. Something."

"Faith is a gift," says Hagen, "but it can be sought and it can be found."

"Uncle Mitchell has it, I believe. To take this chance with us."

"You think that might provide you another opportunity?"

"What kind of opportunity?"

"To spend less time thinking of yourself than of someone who evidently considers you two very special young men."

"Yeah, maybe so." He lifts his head, breathes deeply. "Mostly talking never helped much. You're pretty good at this, you know."

Hagen laughs. "Am I? Well, I enjoy the intricacies of life. They're a feast if you're willing to try them."

"I guess you're right."

They stand and shake hands. Chase goes out into early darkness where sodium-vapor parking lights are burning. As he walks from one light toward another, his shadow becomes shorter and shorter until he steps through it.

* * *

He and Devin are working together to organize the storage room in the rear of the garage. Not since Grant and Leslie left has Uncle Mitchell bothered to get rid of the junk, the outgrown toys and unneeded tools and grade school mementos. Some of the stuff is worth saving. These items the brothers put to one side, to be hauled to Goodwill. Some of it is long since due for the trash bin. The rest—tools, fasteners, useful remnants of paint, they arrange neatly on shelves or hang on nails driven into the stud walls. Their labor will be rewarded. When they achieve an orderly restoration of the room, they will be able to bring more of their things down from Raleigh.

Devin asks, "What's happened to all our stuff back home?"

Chase picks up a yard broom, examines it, tosses it into the rubble pile. "Uncle Mitchell arranged for it all to be put into storage until we see how things go here."

"Sometimes I remember stuff I used to have. Nothing very important, just things. I miss them."

"Like what?"

"My old basketball hoop with a half-torn net. My first bike—"

"You outgrew that long ago."

"But I did love that bike, Chase. My books, too. Just because you outgrow them doesn't mean they aren't important to you."

"I know. But I wouldn't bring them here even if I could."

"Why not?"

"Maybe because I feel they're at home there. This is not where they live. Besides, why think about things that hurt? It doesn't change anything."

Devin leans against the door, hands in his jacket pocket. His lips are rose against pale cheeks. His dark hair is unkempt, unruly strands falling across his forehead. He asks, "Chase, do you think we could go back and see our house? Just look around, maybe ride through the neighborhood?"

"I imagine the house has been sold and people live in it. We don't know them."

"They'd probably let us in, though. Or not even that. Just look around the outside. Climb the old mimosa tree."

"No, I don't think so."

"Why not?"

"It isn't a good idea."

"Don't you think Uncle Mitchell would take us?"

"Maybe, if we asked. But it's no good, Devin. No, don't think about it."

With his toe Devin nudges a small box over to the door, his voice husky. "I wish I could go home just once. See what it's like. Maybe it wouldn't be..."

"What?"

"The way I remember. Maybe they've changed everything. Then it wouldn't be the same and I could try to forget."

"Don't you think it's better to remember the way things seemed to you?"

"Maybe. Except I want something to happen that'll make me stop thinking about it."

Chase picks up a box, takes it out to the stack for Goodwill. His young brother looks older than eleven. Strong jaw, straight, fine lips, a well-shaped nose. In a couple of weeks he'll have a birthday. He'll be a handsome young man, someday the girls will be eager to help restore his confidence. But to Chase he looks as fragile now as the ceramic figurines that have been tossed into the refuge box. Between them there has never been great sibling rivalry, perhaps because of the age difference, perhaps because their mother diligently taught them to respect one another. In a way it might have been better had they fought, Chase thinks, had they been grudged enemies. Then it may be easier for him to distance himself, to avoid the heavy burden of responsibility. Sometimes he has the awful sense that his life is not his own, that he has been given a charge of which he is not capable.

He says sternly, "What we had is gone, Dev. This is what we have now."

"I want to see my street, my room ..."

"Look." He takes his brother's arm and turns him to the clutter. "You see what a junk heap this is? That's how all our old stuff is now. Just so much junk crammed into a heap somewhere."

Devin jerks away, tears suddenly breaking through. "Why are you being mean to me!"

"I'm not being mean. I'm trying to get you to understand you can't live in the past. Damn it, Devin, I fight it, too, every day! Mom's gone, we have no father. So what, dammit! Thank God we're alive!"

"Who's God?"

"I don't know yet. Every once in a while I feel something inside. Maybe it's pure dumb hope. All I can tell you is it doesn't have anything to do with what's happened or might happen. It's beyond all that. It's *inside*, don't you see!"

He stands helpless, looking at Devin. He wishes he could help his brother get it all out, the fear, the anger and defenselessness. What is he supposed to do? It's too much to carry. He wishes he could show Devin how to turn it all loose, how to look neither forward nor backward but only toward today. He has finally begun to feel a glimmer of hope, at least enough to want to catch hold, cling to it. He doesn't know how to explain this, how to make his little brother feel it. Perhaps death, tragedy, suffering makes one look beyond circumstances and environment to something that is not entirely physical or worldly. God? An inner spirit that can be let in or kept out? Sometimes it is hard to pretend strength and hope that he doesn't feel, but he knows if he does pretend long enough it may become real to him and to Devin, too.

"Anyway," he says, "I'm just trying to get this myself. Everything we think and feel doesn't have to come from what happens to us."

Wiping his tears Devin says, "I have these feelings inside, too, Chase. Then I'm ashamed. How can things be all right when Mama never even got to see us grow up? How can I think it's okay to be happy sometimes?"

"Don't you think that's what she would want? When are you happy?"

"I don't know. When I do or say bad things and everyone tells me it's all right. When Aunt Paula takes me out for a snack or Mitchell throws ball with me. Little things."

"Then try to hang onto those. I think if Mom could speak to us she would say that more than anything she wants. More than anything she'd want us to have a good life. Maybe if you feel shame it could be because you're letting her down that way."

Devin bows his head, sighs deeply, then moves thoughtfully toward another shelf. Chase sees something happen in his look, his motions. It occurs slowly but his movements, his eyes are different. Perhaps at last it is resolved, a willingness to let go, maybe to believe in himself again. Strange how so much of life is decision. You're either greedy for the world or you recognize its limits, you decide to love or not to love. Maybe Devin is beginning to feel some of the things he himself feels, hope beyond things seen. For so long they both have felt alienated, disconnected, wanting to blend in. Maybe it's all right to be different. He knows he is right about one thing. Their mother would want them not merely to survive, but to live whole and constructive lives. And he knows Mitchell and Paula want that for them, too.

Devin says, "Okay, I don't need to go home. We can still bring some of our things here, though. This'll be my shelf, okay? Just for the stuff in my secret box."

Chase grins. "Your secret box. Yeah, I remember that. I bet it's full of love notes from the little girls."

"Maybe it will be someday," says Devin, "more than yours."

"Y'think so? In that case I better start teaching you some things."

He cuffs his little brother on the neck and they finish the cleaning, hang everything up and sweep the floor. When Paula calls them to lunch, they race in to wash up.

16

Paula is having lunch with her friend Marge. Their regular tennis games have become sporadic depending on the weather. As she waits, she orders water with a lemon wedge and looks at the frost on the restaurant windows. Crystalline beads are turning slowly liquid and running down the glass in thin rivulets, reflecting ambient earth colors, pastel hues of sienna, greens, yellows. It is deceptive, she knows, the glaring enticing sun on the cheerful panes, beyond which an anomalous cold bites to the bone. Warmth and coziness inside, a quarter of an inch away an ersatz deceiving brightness that is the true staggering version of the day.

As Marge enters and approaches the table, she looks better. Her smile radiates its usual simple warmth, a defenseless sincerity, and Paula wonders how she keeps up such a courageous front when inside pieces are sloughing off.

"Hello, Paula. Am I late?"

"No, you're fine. I was just thinking how inviting it looks outside until you venture into it."

"Oh, it won't last," says Marge. "In two days, it'll be warm again."

"What would you like? Let's eat something."

"No, you go ahead. Just coffee for me."

"I refuse to eat unless you do. And I'm hungry."

"Well, I don't know. I'll have onion soup, I guess."

They order, Marge shrugs out of her coat, lets it fall behind her. She has picked up a little weight, her face fuller. To Paula, this sends an encouraging message.

"How are you really now, Marge? Any better?"

"A little, I think. We're trying another antibiotic. It's at least got the infection stymied for a while. Probably a temporary reprieve but every little favor is appreciated."

"You seem to have more energy," says Paula.

"Eventually, though, antibiotics won't help, then I'll have to consider monthly infusions. I dread the day."

"It'll be worth it to get you well."

"Not well exactly, but at least not feeling so horrible. There's always the possibility of acquired diseases. Mad Cow for one."

"No!"

"It's one of the possible side effects. You have to sign all kinds of releases." Their coffee is brought, they remain silent until the server goes away. "It's scary," Marge says. "Still, the odds are pretty good. There are those who encounter far greater threats." She encircles her cup with both hands, letting the warmth flow through her fingers. "You know what I've decided, Paula? Life is so short. I'm learning to think of every single day as a gift. Just like Mitchell."

"That's hard to do, though, when there are so many things you've left behind."

"But aren't there a lot of those we can just give up? My expectations, the little impressions I have of others and want them to have of me—all the little ways disillusion and pain affect me—on my last day I refuse to be remorseful with disappointment and failure."

"I guess Adam is helping you with these decisions?" asks Paula.

Marge looks down at her coffee cup. "No, not really. In fact, I think Adam is getting a little tired of my illness. I don't blame him. Sometimes we don't communicate very well. You're so fortunate to know exactly where your husband stands on everything."

"The problem," says Paula, "is I don't know where *I* stand on everything. I want to support Mitchell, of course, but all he thinks about is those boys." She is silent a moment, says, "Chase got into a big fight."

"Anyone hurt?"

"He got bloodied up. I realize I'm probably making too much of it, but it scares me, remembering their father...Oh, I don't know, Marge. I guess I just have to make up my mind that we're in this for the long haul."

Their soup arrives. After the waitress leaves, Marge says, "It seems to me you could either let the boys wedge you apart or bring you closer. I know Mitchell's heart is in the right place. He's not thinking just of himself. I'm sure it's hard on him because first of all, he loves you."

"I love him, too, and I admit I'm thinking selfishly. This shouldn't be all about me, but about them, too."

"It's a decision, isn't it? So what will you do?"

"I don't know," Paula says. "Try to be good to them. Try to help them love again."

"Maybe the best thing for both of us is just to *be*. There's nothing to do or say. Just be."

"Is that another word for giving up?"

Marge smiles. "It sounds like a reasonable solution, doesn't it? Besides, what can we do to change the past?"

"Nothing, I guess."

"Nothing at all. All we can do is decide not to be miserable."

"That's basically what Mitchell tells the boys. But who can absolutely master their thoughts?"

"Mostly we do live all in ourselves. But you know, when you hit absolute bottom you really look hard to see what's left. I feel sorry for those who find nothing."

On the window the frost has all but disappeared, leaving one or two inches of frosty mountains and valleys along the sill. Coldness presses against the pane with clear freshness, quickens the walk of those crossing the parking lot. Paula feels a sudden unexplained vibrant strength in the air. Her friend Marge is going to make it, she knows. Why, how, she can't explain, Marge just is. And so is she. It is so easy to forget the important things, so easy to cave in to things that are not as one would choose them to be. What does one do? she wonders. Work on remembering the priorities.

* * *

When the Raleigh District Attorney's office calls Paula and Mitchell get on the extensions together. The case prosecutor informs them that two young women, strangers to one another, hearing about the indictment, had come forward to give a deposition that they were having affairs with Robert Solomon, swearing that they did not know he was married with children, and that he had promised them a permanent relationship as soon as he could get a few obstacles out of the way. Evidence revealed that with charm and deceit, Robert had won his wife Kelly over; he had won two or more lovers over, and accumulated considerable debt. The prosecutor informed them that right away Robert applied for Kelly's death insurance and swore violently when he learned she had dropped him as a beneficiary. "Our case is solid and his lawyer is initiating a plea bargain."

As they hang up the receivers Mitchell says, "I guess we should tell the boys before they hear it another way."

"You don't think Robert will contact them?"

"I doubt it. Probably he is stuck in denial. Maybe he thinks they are better off not to hear from him. My guess is if he is sorry at all it's because he got caught."

"It's just terrible, but maybe at least we're beginning to see some closure on this."

* * *

His cell phone rings, jolting Chase awake. Kimberly's voice is low, husky, choked with sobs. "Chase," she says.

"Huh? What? Who is this? Kimberly?"

"Chase, he's dead."

"What—who?"

"Gene Holbrook. He died an hour ago."

"But why—how?"

"One of those stupid, stupid things they do. Hood surfing. He fell and crushed his head on a curb."

"My God!"

She cries quietly. "Can you come over?"

He blinks sleep from his eyes, looks at the clock. "It's nearly 2 a.m."

"I need you. I need to talk to somebody."

"Yes, well—" His mind is alert now, racing. Everyone is asleep. The house is quiet, dark. He struggles a moment to reconstruct the timeframe. He saw her Friday night. It is Saturday. He says, "Give me twenty minutes."

"Okay." Helpless. Submissive.

"Kimberly, are your parents with you? Do they know you called?"

"They think I'm asleep finally. I need to talk to…to someone else. Will you come? Please?"

"Twenty minutes. Look, hold on, huh? Will they mind if I…"

"Don't knock or ring the bell. I'll come out."

He scrubs his face with cold water, dresses stealthily. Grabbing his coat, he moves through the house quietly, then pauses, makes a decision, returns to his room. At his little work desk he writes a quick note, just in case they wake before he returns. "Sorry, had to go out. Be back soon." In the kitchen he places the note on the counter beside the coffee pot, where they will see it first thing. Then he leaves the house, lets his eyes adjust to the darkness and slips into the truck, easing the door shut. For ten seconds, he holds his breath hoping no lights will come on. Then he starts the vehicle, backs out before turning on headlights and drives slowly up the street.

The night is cold. Tree limbs and the few remaining leaves look stiff and brittle. A chilling south wind whips up an occasional whirl, spinning leaves and debris along the street. Most of the traffic lights are blinking yellow or red. At each intersection he slows to a crawl, checks both ways. The last thing he wants is to be pulled over by a cop at two in the morning.

Snatch Holbrook dead. It's hard to grasp. For no reason at

all. Some wild-assed bravado that makes no sense. Why do kids do such things? Standing in a football crouch on the hood of a moving car. Challenging chance, balance. Why? Out of boredom, rebellion, wanting to make a name. Kids who have absolutely everything the world offers, finding it not enough. Restless, unsatisfied. What have they missed.

A pang of regret sweeps through him. The last impression he has of Gene Holbrook is one of anger, violence. The fight on the school grounds. Bitter competitors, out for blood. He is ashamed of himself. That he started the fight, that he answered the loneliness in his own heart with a senseless attack. Out of guilt he suddenly sees Holbrook in a different light. One of cynicism and contempt, but also one of independent zest. The catcalls in the halls, the shameless flirtation with girls which repulsed them and intrigued them. His iconoclastic disregard for any sort of sexual morality, yet an electric magnetism which breathed life. He did not deserve to die. Chase wishes he could undo the fight, make up somehow. He had thought of calling Holbrook to apologize, thought of it but not done it. He is swept with regret.

At this hour there are few cars on the street. He is thrilled that Kimberly needs him, nervous about how little he can offer her. He declines to turn into her driveway, instead pulls up to the curb and kills the engine. He gulps a deep breath, steps out quickly and closes the door without slamming. Her house is dark but for the soft glow of a lamp in a downstairs window. The cold damp night presses in on him, shrouding him in blackness. A good thing, he assumes, no restless neighbor will see him moving hesitantly up her walkway.

Her voice strikes him from the darkness. "Chase."

Startled, he takes a misstep, almost stumbles. She is sitting on the steps, a heavy coat pulled about her. Her knees are pressed tightly together, her calves and ankles bare, light slippers on her feet. The faintest silhouette from the window halos her hair, angel-like. Her head is tilted up, watching him.

"How long have you been out here?"

"Just now. I saw the lights turn the corner and slipped out."

"It's too cold. You'll freeze like this."

"I need to be cold. I need to hurt."

"Nonsense. That's a crazy thing to say."

"It's better to feel something physical."

"That doesn't make the pain go away, Kimberly."

"How do you know?"

"I tried it once. I stuck pins all in my feet. A hundred of them."

"Where were you?"

"The children's farm. All it got me was heavy counseling. Don't ever tell Devin. He didn't know."

"Why did you hurt yourself?"

"I thought physical pain might help me get out of my mind, just for a while. It didn't. It won't help you either."

"But I'm a coward, you see. I can't hurt myself. I can only hope the cold will numb everything."

He drops down on the steps beside her. Her hair smells fresh as the night. He inhales the scent of her skin, her body lotion. There is an aching in his throat. He puts his arms around his legs, leans forward, trying to absorb her pain.

"It's so scary," she says. "One moment you're alive, the next…it happens so quickly."

"Yes."

"Nobody knows, do they? Nobody ever knows."

"But we never believe death can come to us. We're too young."

"I know we don't. Not even when we see it happening so close."

"I had a friend once," he says, "back in Raleigh. He was always speeding. One night he went off the road, plowed into a tree. It should have killed him but he survived. For a year he drove like an old lady. Then he just started speeding again. We forget. We forget so fast."

Softly she says, "I never went anywhere with Snatch. I wouldn't ride with him. He scared me a little, with his weird ways. But when someone really seems to like you … it's hard to resist. He was a bluff, a charmer. But he could be fun, too."

"Your mother liked him, didn't she?"

"I guess so. Yes. She didn't really know him. He was always so polite with adults."

"I feel sorry for his parents," says Chase. "One crazy, senseless mistake. And they're the ones who suffer."

"Do you think he's in heaven?"

"What? I don't know."

"Sometimes I wonder if this life is all we have. Why are we even born? I don't believe it is to suffer and hurt and die. There has to be a reason."

"Maybe not," he says. "Maybe things happen just because they do."

"Do you think you'll ever see your mother again?"

Something twists and turns in his breast. Inside is conflict, struggle. He closes his eyes, opens them against the black cold. "I guess I hope I will."

"You believe in heaven, then."

They sit silent. Negative space but not negative feeling. The quiet biding says everything. The night air charged with soundless emotion. Back in the house somewhere a clock chimes. Three a.m. It is amazing that through the closed doors they can hear, yet the faint clear tone is like a quiet promise, the promise that time will help. He feels Kimberly trembling, but not from the cold, realizes she is crying again. He wants to touch her but is afraid to. He does not know if he can ease her pain, hers and his, too. Then something occurs to him. It is his pain which *enables* him to bear hers. Perhaps that is even the reason for it, as his mother said. Perhaps the weight he has carried provides the strength for this moment, when he can lift just a little of her heaviness and carry it for her. He suddenly feels needed as he never has before.

At almost the same time he edges closer to her, she whispers, "Put your arms around me, Chase."

Through the heavy coat he can hardly feel her warmth but he is surprised by how fragile her shape is, how vulnerable. She is like a kitten with ever so much fur and beneath, delicate and defenseless bones. Still, as she drops her head onto his shoulder there is about her something strong and unconquerable. Since her concussion, she has suffered from highs and lows more dramatically than kids normally do. She says she would never hurt herself, but he isn't sure. Usually people can survive the worst times if they just wait. How does he know this? And how will he use this knowledge? He isn't certain, but it is as if Kimberly's pain infuses his own with a strange new strength, a determination to survive and to be useful. As she cries softly, he has never felt so needed, and it is not a physical thing at all but something that sweeps his own turmoil aside to clear the path he must help her along.

"Thank you, Chase," she murmurs, "for coming."

"I didn't know …" He falters.

"What?"

"I didn't even know I could do this. It's as if what you feel is more important than anything I feel."

She whispers brokenly, "I love you, Chase."

It rushes through him, startling and uplifting, as though she gives him a rare and self-sustaining gift. He says hoarsely, "I love you, too. Until now, I didn't know how much."

They sit huddled close against the cold, his arm around her, her head on his shoulder, not moving, not talking. When the clock chimes four she rises quietly, kisses him on the lips and steals into the house. He walks out to the truck, drives home as cautiously as he had come. In the kitchen he retrieves the note from the counter and is lying on his bed, clothes on, when the morning begins to stir. No one has missed him, has even known he'd gone. This treasure that he holds warmly in his breast has been given to him for special and private care. After a time he will share it with his aunt and uncle. For a while, they were all uncertain, but now he knows he can talk to them about everything.

* * *

After Chase tells them of the tragic death of Snatch Holbrook, of his time with Kimberly and of her confession of love, Paula says. "I think now it's time to tell them about their father."

Mitchell nods. "I guess you're right."

The four of them sit down together in the den. Paula is glad that Mitchell takes the lead, his voice strong, his look kind and sympathetic. After telling them about the trial and sentence he says, "You are great kids. Obviously, it is your mother who taught and guided you, but you must remember that Robert is your father; he helped bring you into the world, and you have every reason to believe you can live peaceful and fruitful lives."

They listen, remain silent.

"All we ask," says Paula, "is that you let us know what you need, what you think, what we can do for you."

"We hope someday there will be healing," Mitchell says. "People change. We have to forgive them their past mistakes. Whether you ever see or hear from your father you have to work on healing from this."

"It doesn't matter," says Chase. "I don't care if he is out of our lives forever. I hope he is."

"Me, too," murmurs Devin.

Paula says, "As you grow older and learn more you may feel differently. Try to remember the good things and what your uncle just said. You are fine young men and if you try hard you can rise above your past. And remember we love you."

Okay," says Chase. "We love you too."

"We do," Devin says.

They know the boys want to forget their father, what he had done, but they never want to forget Kelly. "You are her legacy," says Mitchell. "She would be proud to have brought you into the world. Live for yourselves and for her."

Paula watches their faces. This has been tough — on them all. But by their expressions she thinks they are one little step closer to reconciliation.

* * *

A couple of times a week Mitchell and his partners, W. G. and Lowry, get together for a morning pow-wow.

Sipping a cup of coffee, Lowry says, "What about Spandoffer, Mitchell? You okay with taking over his account?"

"You've managed him well for a decade," says Mitchell.

"I know. But now we just seem to have some sort of personality clash. He's a greedy old cuss."

Mitchell smiles. "Do you think people ever get rich enough, Lowry? Is that what life's about?"

"Yeah, I guess so. For most of us, that's what life is about."

Mitchell does not argue. Sometimes he feels he's in the wrong business, helping people strategize a worldly future when he sees how flimsy it all is. Still, he would never choose to go back to the time when he and Paula had to look over the prices on menus before they could go into a restaurant, when they had to call a hot, congested apartment home. Were they happier then? Only younger and poorer. In a certain respect it seems they were driven by loftier ideals, by appetites less insatiable. He knows Paula wants to get away, just the two of them, and more and more he wonders why not? What difference will it make? How could the world change during their absence? Still, he thinks that with the boys, a day, an instant can be fateful. He would like to get away, too, just he and Paula. But it would be fun with the boys, the antics and energy, if they could all go as a family. He remembers how it was with their own kids growing up. A romantic holiday is very appealing, but it worries him that the nephews might get the idea they are in the way. The older he grows, the more he wants his life to have significance, wants to make one worthwhile contribution. He wonders if the nephews are it.

"What about Spandoffer?" Lowry asks.

"Huh? Oh, well, sure, if he's okay with it."

"Where are you?"

"Just thinking."

"Thinking can kill you," Lowry says.

Driving home in the afternoon, Mitchell notices the holly trees, dark and green, with crisp faintly curled points and clusters of deep red berries. When he was a kid, they would find hollow cane poles, cut sections about twelve inches long, pick holly berries and chinaberries, and make pea shooters. With an explosion of breath, they took aim at birds, squirrels, chipmunks, missing of course. He wonders if the nephews have ever done this, if their father had ever shown them how to make pea shooters.

By the time he reaches home it has clouded over, begun to rain, portending a cold front. He finds Paula in the kitchen trying to put together a dinner that will please everybody. She is wearing pants, a fitted button-up shirt, and a light sweater. Her hair picks up glints of light, her motions and gestures still those of the young girl he had loved early. The pattering rain reminds him of something, and he says, "You remember a long time ago when I went on my one and only golf retreat?"

"I do."

"Well, the men left two days ahead of the women. We played one day but the next it poured down rain. I sat in a motel room all day staring out the window. It was miserable."

"I remember you telling me."

"It rained the next day, too, but you came in that night and I didn't mind the room at all. You being there made all the difference."

"I'm glad you're telling me again. Something like this means so much to a woman."

She bends to take something out of the refrigerator. A pot on the range top begins to sizzle, smells good. He says, "Before the surgery, you were thinking about remodeling the living and dining rooms so we could entertain more. Remember?"

"Of course," says Paula.

"Well, why don't we do it now?"

"Oh, I don't know. With the boys and everything—"

"Dig out some of those home decorating magazines and let's take a look."

"Are you serious?"

"Why not?" he says. "Let's be sure and get the good stuff. Our days of buying cheap furniture and hand-me-downs are over."

She gives him a long oblique look. "Okay, we'll do it after dinner. And maybe we can think about Venice again."

* * *

Saturday mornings Paula usually sleeps late but this morning she gets up with Mitchell and slips on a jacket to walk with him. On the porch is a package that came late, probably delivered Friday by UPS. They nudge it in onto the foyer floor, then close the door and head out.

The early morning cold is beautiful. As the sun breaks through trees it strikes the frost with translucent flames, fiery glass on the tips of leaves and grass blades. She inhales deeply. Everything looks brilliant and refreshed; it is cold enough to encourage them to walk and warm enough that just a windbreaker is adequate. The streets are mostly still and silent, Saturday morning sleep-ins not yet stirring, plastic bagged newspapers still lying on walkways where they have been tossed. She hears the closing of a door, some homeowner letting his dog in or out. As the morning warms, zebra stripes of melting frost streak automobiles and street signs.

A beautiful golden lab runs out to greet them, tags along for half a block, then turns back.

"I see him nearly every day," says Mitchell. "I rather enjoy his company."

"I would bet," says Paula, "that sooner or later the boys, especially Devin, will ask to get a dog."

"Yeah, probably. What would you think?"

"I don't think I'd mind, as long as they commit to take care of him."

A mud-caked maroon pickup grinds by, mufflers roaring, and they pause to watch. The windows are too fogged to see clearly, but she catches the driver's uplifted arm and waves back. A teenager or young man spoiling to find a red clay hill to climb or a mud bog to plow through. The body of the truck is so high, steps are required to climb in. For a moment, she wishes she could go along, barrel up a slippery hill, become tomboyish. She knows that a desire for freedom has little to with age or circumstances, but with attitude. By the time they turn back and stride up their driveway, the sun is up, lights are on everywhere, people stirring.

They find that Chase and Devin are also up, already in the backyard working on the storage room and walk round back to speak to them. They have both been neat, Paula thinks, and considerate of one another—one of those little personality traits their generation is not especially known for. Devin's nose is red, so are his ears, but he seems not to notice. He asks, "Where have you been, Aunt Paula, Uncle Mitchell?"

"Walking," she says. "It's such a nice day."

"I could walk with you sometime."

"Good," says Mitchell. "You'll have to get up early."

Chase brings out a box of plastic bottles, rose food, insecticides, weed-be-gone. "You think we should keep these?"

"They look pretty old. Let's dump them," Mitchell says.

He drops them into the trash bag. "There's a big box for you on the porch, Paula."

"Thank you. We brought it in."

"Devin says, "I saw your travel folders. Are we going on a trip?"

"Hush, Dev," Chase says. "I think maybe they need a little holiday away from us."

"Not necessarily," says Paula. "Maybe we'll think about going somewhere spring break."

They watch, not interfering, as the nephews work together clearing out the storage room, separating, rearranging. Patches of sun strike the trees and yard briskly. Leaves are beginning to unfurl, portending an early spring. On the patio tables and walls are chips and pieces of pinecones left by the squirrels. From way back in the room Chase pulls out some of Mitchell's old golf clubs. He takes a five iron and walks out into the grass, practices the swing.

Devin watches, taunts, "You look like a girl."

"Good," says Chase. "Nothing is prettier than a girl making a golf swing."

Mitchell says, "The turn's the thing. Shoulders, mostly, quiet hips. Don't let the shoulders drop."

She sees that Chase accepts the advice, looks better on his next stroke. "Hey, I see what you mean," he says. "Not so much hips."

"Pretend you're turning in a barrel." Mitchell indicates the turn, using his outstretched arms as a club.

Paula asks, "If we did go on a little trip where would you choose?"

She sees Chase glance at Devin, whose expression seems to ask, you really mean with us or without us? Chase says, "I think you and Mitchell should go. We'd be fine here. We can take care of things."

"I know you could." Curious, she walks over to the storage room. "Hey, look at this. You've done a great job."

"Is it okay?" asks Chase. "We've saved everything we thought was any good."

"I don't believe it's been this organized in twenty years. Well, I'm going in to make breakfast. Give me twenty minutes."

She leaves them finishing up, goes in, brings her packages from the foyer and opens them as she works on breakfast. The men come in, wash up, and they all eat together. There is definitely a lighter feel to the air. As they finish breakfast she turns to her parcels, hands one to each of the boys. "Try these on for me, will you? Let's see if they fit."

They look at each other, wondering, then sit down, slip off their sneakers, slip on the new sturdy walking shoes. "What're these for?" asks Devin.

"I thought that wherever we go we'll do a lot of walking. Always do. These have good strong ankle supports. You used to hike, didn't you? With your mother?"

"We did," says Chase. "But you wouldn't have to take us. We'd be okay here."

"Would you want to travel with us?"

"Yes!" Devin blurts.

She catches Mitchell looking at her thoughtfully. "You sure?"

"I'm sure," she says. "And look." She pulls out a colorful brochure. "We don't have to leave the country. Our Georgia mountains are beautiful in spring and fall. At Smithgall Woods you can get a cabin right on a mountain stream, hear the falls all night."

Devin takes the brochure, looks it over. "Hey, this is neat. Are there fish?"

"Mountain trout," says Mitchell. "Usually they'll have fish food in the cottage. You can feed them."

"Can you catch them?"

"Catch and release. We'll be too busy hiking to fish."

The boys stand, Paula watches critically as they walk around in the shoes, experimenting.

"How'd you know our sizes?" Chase asks.

"Oh, I checked your everyday shoes. Hiking shoes sometimes are different, though, to accommodate thick socks."

"I'd never want to change them," Devin says proudly.

"Wear them around a while, will you? Better to break them in ahead of time."

"Thanks. We will." Devin bends down, puts his arm around Paula, says huskily, "Thank you, Aunt Paula, I really like them."

"Me, too," says Chase. "We had no idea."

She smiles cheerfully. "No, you weren't supposed to."

As they run up to their rooms, Mitchell gives her a long look. "Well," he says, "what brings this about?"

"The hiking shoes?"

"You know what I mean. This decision."

"Oh, it wasn't a decision exactly," she says. "You might say it's the natural course of events."

"I see."

She smiles. "Sometimes things happen just because they happen, remember? There is no explanation."

"I see."

He gathers up the scattered wrappings, stands another moment looking at her. "Thanks."

"For what?" says Paula. "But wait. I almost forgot." She tears into another box. "I got us all some hiking staffs. We'll look just like professionals!"

Mitchell takes one, whistles. "Hey, look at that."

They are sleek telescopic black shafts with rubber grips and strong metal points.

"Wow. We've never had one of these," he says.

He slips the strap over his arm. "It's really well-balanced. This'll be a big help on the hills."

"Well, you can put them away if you like. Until the time comes."

He lifts his arms and she comes into them. "We'll have fun," he says. "But you know, I do want just the two of us to go to Venice or somewhere together..."

"We planned that a long time, didn't we?"

"I guess I've just begun to realize how much I need it."

"Well, the main thing is that you want to. That's what's important to me. But this time it'll be the four of us."

As Paula puts things away she glimpses him over her shoulder, experimenting with one of the staffs, planting it jauntily into the carpet. He lifts and swings it briskly as though the staff, his legs, his heart are light as air.

She smiles. Her pulse quickens with anticipation. They will have a good time together, she knows, just as they did with Grant and Leslie.

About the Author

Author Donald Jordan is founder of the Donald L. Jordan Award for Literary Excellence, whose mission is, "to encourage and promote writings which honor the traditional values of responsibility, gratitude, generosity, love and faith." Donald Jordan lives and works in Columbus, Georgia.

CPSIA information can be obtained
at www.ICGtesting.com
Printed in the USA
BVHW071505110220
572026BV00009B/1291